**Wei Hui** is the daughter of an army officer and spent three years of her childhood living in an army-occupied temple from which monks had been expelled during the chaos of the Cultural Revolution. She studied literature at the prestigious Fudan University in Shanghai.

First championed by the state media as a rising star of her generation, Wei Hui is now dubbed 'decadent, debauched and a slave of foreign culture.' *Shanghai Baby* was banned by the authorities in April 2000 and 40,000 copies were publicly burned, serving only to fan the flames of the author's cult status. Wei Hui calls the novel a semi-autobiographical account of her spiritual and sexual awakening. 'I grew up in a very strict family. My first year of college was spent in military training. What happened after that was natural. I rebelled. I went wild. That's what I wrote about.'

Wei Hui (*pronounced Way-Way*) is twenty-seven, has written four previous books and lives in Shanghai.

'*Shanghai Baby* possesses . . . beauty and rhythm, but it's younger and more decadent . . . a new literary personality has entered the scene, and a new kind of urban novel has been born in China. *Shanghai Baby* is beautifully written, and the young author clearly combines the qualities of natural feeling for writing with intelligence.'

Jianying Zha, author of *China Pop*

'China's most popular writer . . . one of the first in China to portray Wei Hui's generation of urban women, born in the 1970s, as they search for moral grounding in a country of shifting values . . . Wei Hui sees herself as a feminist helping her generation of women understand themselves.'

Craig S. Smith, *New York Times*

'A steamy Chinese novel in the Western style about life in contemporary China . . . condemned for exploring subjects that are completely taboo in modern Chinese literature.'

Dalya Alberge, *The Times*

'Steamy, contemporary and Western in style. It tackles the battle between love and passion in a semi-autobiographical work that looks terrific.'

Sarah Broadhurst, *The Bookseller*

# Shanghai Baby

## WEI HUI

*Translated from the Chinese*
*by Bruce Humes*

ROBINSON
London

Constable Publishers
3 The Lanchesters
162 Fulham Palace Road
London W6 9ER
www.constablerobinson.com

First published in the UK by Robinson,
an imprint of Constable and Robinson Ltd, 2001

A copy of the British Library Cataloguing in
Publication Data is available from the British Library

ISBN 1 84119 361 5

For my parents, my love,
and Fudan University

# 1

# Encounter with My Lover

'Well, there's a wide wide world of noble causes
And lovely landscapes to discover
But all I really want to do right now
Is find another lover!'
Joni Mitchell

My name is Nikki but my friends all call me Coco after Coco Chanel, a French lady who lived to be ninety. She's my idol, after Henry Miller. Every morning when I open my eyes I wonder what I can do to make myself famous. It's become my ambition, almost my *raison d'être,* to burst upon the city like a firework.

This has a lot to do with living in a place like Shanghai. A grey fog hangs over the city, mixed with continual rumours and an air of superiority, a hangover from the time of the *shili yangchang*, the foreign concessions. This air of superiority affects me: I both love it and hate it.

Anyway, I'm just twenty-five, and a year ago I published a collection of short stories which didn't make any money but got me attention (male readers sent me letters enclosing erotic photos). Three months ago I left my job as a magazine journalist and now I'm a bare-legged, mini-skirted waitress at a joint called the Green Stalk Café.

There was a tall, handsome boy, a regular at the Green Stalk, who would stay for hours drinking coffee and reading his book. I liked to watch his changes of expression, his every move. He seemed to know I was watching him, but he never said a word.

Until, that is, the day he gave me a note which said, 'I love you', along with his name and address.

Born in the Year of the Rabbit, and a year younger than me, this boy enchanted me. It's hard to put a finger on what made him so good-looking in my eyes, but it had something to do with his air of world-weariness and his thirst for love.

On the surface we're two utterly different types. I'm full of energy and ambition, and see the world as a scented fruit just waiting to be eaten. He is introspective, romantic and for him life is a cake laced with arsenic, every bite poisons him a little more. But our differences only increased our mutual attraction, like the inseparable north and south magnetic poles. We rapidly fell in love.

Not long after we met he told me a family secret. His mother was living in a small town in Spain, with a local man, running a Chinese restaurant. It seems you can make a lot of money in Spain by selling lobster and wonton.

His father had died young, suddenly, out there, less than a month after going to Spain to visit his mother. The death certificate said 'myocardial infarction', and his ashes were flown home in a McDonnell Douglas jet. Tian Tian still remembered that sunny day, and how his tiny grandmother, his father's mother, cried, tears streaming down her wrinkled face like water dripping off a wet rag.

'Grandmother was convinced it was murder. My dad didn't have any history of heart disease; she said my mother killed him. That she had another man over there, and they plotted it together.'

Staring at me with a strange look in his eyes, Tian Tian said, 'Can you believe it? I still can't work it out. Maybe Grandmother was right. But whatever, Mother sends me a lot of money every year to live on.'

He watched me in silence. His strange story grabbed me immediately, because I'm drawn to tragedy and intrigue. When I was studying Chinese at Fudan University in Shanghai, I'd wanted to become a writer of really exciting thrillers: 'evil omen', 'conspiracy', 'dagger', 'lust', 'poison', 'madness' and 'moonlight' were all words that sprang readily to mind. Looking tenderly into his fragile, beautiful face, I understood the root of Tian Tian's sadness.

'Death's shadow only fades little by little as time passes. There will never be more than a thin glass barrier between your present and the wreckage of your past,' I told him.

His eyes grew wet, and he clenched his hands tightly. 'But I've found you, and decided to put my faith in you,' he said. 'Don't stay with me just out of curiosity, but don't leave me straight away.'

I moved into Tian Tian's place, a big three-bedroomed apartment on the western outskirts of the city. He had decorated the living-room simply and comfortably, with a sectional fabric sofa from Ikea along one wall, and a Strauss piano. Above the piano hung his self-portrait, in which his head looked as if he'd just surfaced from a pool.

To be honest, I didn't much like the area. Almost all the roads were full of potholes, lined on both sides with cramped, shabby houses, peeling billboards and reeking piles of rubbish. There was a public phone box which leaked like the *Titanic* whenever it rained. Looking out of the window, I couldn't see a single green tree, smartly dressed person or a clear patch of sky. It was like not being able to see the future.

Tian Tian always said that the future is a trap set right in the middle of your brain.

For a while after his father died, Tian Tian lost the power of speech. Then he dropped out of high school in his first year. His lonely childhood had already turned him into a nihilist. His aversion to the outside world meant he spent half his life in bed: reading, watching videos, smoking, musing on the pros and cons of life versus death, the spirit versus flesh, calling premium phone lines, playing computer games and sleeping. The rest of the time he painted, walked with me, ate, shopped, browsed in book and record shops, sat in cafés or went to the bank. When he needed money, he would go to the post office and send letters in beautiful blue envelopes to his mother.

He seldom visited his grandmother. He had moved out of her house when it became a nightmare. She had sunk into a perma-nent state of delirium, fixated on that 'murder' in Spain. Her heart was broken, her face ravaged and her spirit gone, but she wouldn't die. She still lives in a western-style house in the city now, fuming with anger, cursing her destiny and her daughter-in-law.

Saturday. Clear weather. Pleasant indoor temperature. At exactly 8:30 a.m., I wake up and beside me Tian Tian opens his eyes. We look at each other for a second, and then begin to kiss silently. Our early morning kisses are tender, affectionate, smooth as little fishes wriggling in water. This is the compulsory start to our day – and the sole channel of sexual expression between us.

Tian Tian just couldn't handle sex. I'm not sure if it was related to the tragedy that had caused his mental problems, but I remember the first time I held him in bed. When I discov-ered he was impotent, I was devastated, so much so that I didn't know if I could stay with him. Ever since college I had

4

seen sex as a basic necessity (although I've since changed my mind about this).

Unable to enter me, he stared at me, speechless, his whole body in a cold sweat. It was his first time with a girl in his twenty-something years.

In the male world being able to perform sex normally is as important as life itself, any shortcoming is an unbearable pain. He cried, and so did I. For the rest of the night we kissed, touched and murmured to one another. I soon came to adore his sweet kiss and gentle touch. Kissing with the tip of the tongue is like ice-cream melting. It was he who taught me that a kiss has a soul and colours all of its own.

Kind, loving and trusting as a dolphin, it was his temperament that captured my wild heart. What he couldn't give me – sharp cries or explosive pleasure, sexual pride or orgasm – lost significance.

In *The Unbearable Lightness of Being*, Milan Kundera gives a classic definition of love:

'Making love with a woman and sleeping with a woman are two separate passions, not merely different but opposite. Love does not make itself felt in the desire for copulation (a desire that extends to an infinite number of women) but in the desire for shared sleep (a desire limited to one woman).'

At the beginning of my time with Tian Tian, I had no idea that I would experience this myself, until a series of events and the appearance of another man gave me the chance to understand it.

At nine o'clock we got up, and he got into the huge bath while I smoked my first Mild Seven cigarette. In the tiny kitchen I made corn congee, eggs and milk. With the golden sunlight outside the window, summer mornings always seemed poetic, like melted honey. I felt totally relaxed, listening to the sound of water gushing in the bathroom.

'Will you come to the Green Stalk Café with me?' I asked, taking a big glass of milk into the steam-swirled bathroom. Tian Tian's eyes were closed, and he gave a long yawn, like a fish.

'Coco, I've got an idea,' he said in a low voice.

'What idea?' I brought the milk right to him, but he didn't take it in his hand, just leaned forward and sipped a little.

'Why don't you give up your job at the café?'

'Then what would I do?'

'We've enough money not to have to work all the time. You could write your novel.'

It turned out he had been brewing this idea for some time, that he wanted me to write a novel that would take the literary world by storm. 'There's nothing worth reading in the bookshops these days, just empty stories,' he said.

'Okay,' I said, 'but not right now. I want to work a bit longer. You sometimes meet interesting people in a café.'

'Whatever,' he mumbled. This was his pet phrase, meaning he had heard and taken in the comment and had no more to say.

We ate breakfast together, then I dressed and put on my make-up and wandered round the room until I finally found my favourite leopard-spotted handbag. Sitting on the sofa, book in hand, he glanced up as I left. 'I'll call you,' he said.

This is the city at rush-hour. All sorts of vehicles and pedestrians, all their invisible desires and countless secrets, merge with the flow like rapids plunging through a deep gorge. The sun shines down on the street hemmed in on both sides by skyscrapers – the mad creations of humans – towering between sky and earth. The petty details of daily life are like dust suspended in the air. They are the monotonous theme of our materalist age.

# 2

# Modern Metropolis

'I had seen the skyscrapers fading out in a flurry of snowflakes. I saw them looming up again in that same ghostly way as when I left. I saw the lights creeping through their ribs. I saw the whole city spread out from Harlem to Battery, the streets choked with ants, the elevated rushing by, the theatres emptying. I wondered in a vague way what had ever happened to my wife.'

Henry Miller

It was three-thirty in the afternoon and the Green Stalk Café was empty. A sunbeam filtered in through the leaves of the parasol tree, and particles of dust floated in it. An odd pall hung over the magazines and the jazz music from the stereo, as if they were survivals from the 1930s.

I stood behind the bar with nothing to do. It's always boring when there's no business.

Old Yang, the head waiter, was taking a nap in the back room. He was a trusted relative of the boss and camped out there day and night, managing the money and us.

My co-worker, Spider, took advantage of the break to sneak off to the computer company on the corner in search of cheap parts. He was a problem teenager with only one thing on his mind. He wanted to be a super-hacker. You could call him a half-graduate, because despite having an IQ of 150, he hadn't completed his degree in computing at Fudan U. He was chucked out because he kept hacking into *Shanghai Online* to rip off account numbers and surf the web at their expense.

There we were, a former promising journalist and a computer hit man with a reputation, both working in a café. You can't deny that's one of life's little ironies. Wrong place, wrong roles, but united in our commitment to life's young dream. Our bodies were already tarnished, and our minds beyond help.

I began to arrange the scented white lilies in a large jar of water. So delicate, that feeling when my fingers touched those seductive white petals. My love of flowers is conventionally feminine, but I believe the day will come when I look in the mirror and compare my face to a poisonous plant. And my shocking bestselling novel will reveal the truth about mankind: violence, style, lust, joy, and then enigma, machines, power and death.

The old rotary-dial telephone rang piercingly. It was Tian Tian. Almost every day he would call about now, just as we were both getting tired of our respective surroundings. 'Same time, same place, I'll be waiting to have dinner with you,' he said urgently, as if it were important.

At dusk I took off my uniform mini-skirt and short Chinese silk jacket, and changed into a tight-fitting shirt and trousers. Clutching my handbag, I walked light-footed out of the café. The colourful street lanterns had just come on, and the fluorescent lights of the shops shimmered like shards of gold. I walked along the street, blending with the thousands of people and vehicles shuttling back and forth, like the Milky Way blazing right here on earth. The most exciting moment of the city's day had arrived.

The Cotton Club is at the corner of Huaihai and Fuxing Roads, the equivalent of New York's Fifth Avenue or the Champs Elysées in Paris. From a distance, the two-storey French building has an air of distinction. Those who come here are either *laowai* – foreigners – with a lewd look in their eyes, or slim, foxy Asian belles. Its shimmering blue sign looks just the way Henry Miller described a syphilitic sore. It's because we enjoyed this metaphor that Tian Tian and I used to go there (as well as writing *Tropic of Cancer*, Henry Miller lived to 89 and married five times, and I've always seen him as my spiritual father).

I pushed open the door, looked around, and saw Tian Tian waving to me from a corner. But what surprised me was that next to him sat a fashionable girl wearing what was obviously a wig, but a striking one, and a halter-top in shiny black. Her tiny face was dusted with gold and silver powder, as if she'd just landed from some planet incredibly far away.

'This is Madonna, we were at elementary school together,' said Tian Tian. Perhaps thinking that inadequate, he added: 'She's also been my only friend in Shanghai lately.' Then he introduced me to her. 'This is Nikki, my girlfriend,' he said, and quite unselfconsciously took my hand and held it on his lap.

We nodded and smiled, since the fact we were both friends of Tian Tian, as wholesome as a tiny butterfly, instantly disposed us to like and trust each other. But her first words startled me.

'Tian Tian has talked about you so often on the phone. He always goes on for hours. He adores you so much it makes me jealous.' She laughed, low and husky, like an actress in one of those old Hollywood movies.

I glanced at Tian Tian, who was trying to look as though he'd done no such thing. 'He likes chatting on the phone. You could buy a thirty-one-inch television with the money he spends on the monthly phone bill,' I added thoughtlessly, and immediately I realised how tacky it was to see everything in terms of money.

'I hear you're a writer,' said Madonna.

'Well, it's been a while since I wrote anything, and actually

'. . . I can't really call myself a writer.' I felt a bit ashamed: just wanting to be a writer isn't enough.

Tian Tian interrupted. 'Oh, Coco's already published a collection of stories. It's neat. She's so observant. She's going to be very successful,' he said calmly, not a hint of flattery on his face.

'I'm working as a waitress just now,' I said matter-of-factly. 'And you? You look like an actress.'

'Didn't Tian Tian tell you?' She looked briefly quizzical, as if she were trying to guess how I'd react. 'I was a *mami*, a madam, in Guangzhou, got married, then my old man snuffed it and left me a bundle of money, so now I enjoy myself.'

I nodded, outwardly calm while an exclamation mark popped up in my mind. Right in front of me was a bona fide rich widow! And now I knew where those courtesan airs came from, and those alarmingly sharp eyes, which automatically made me think of an errant heroine.

We stopped talking for a moment as the food Tian Tian had ordered arrived, one after the other – all my Shanghai favourites. 'If you'd rather have something else, just order it,' he told Madonna.

She nodded. 'Actually, I have a very small stomach,' she said, cupping her hands to make a fist-sized shape. 'The evening is the start of my day, so most people's dinner is my breakfast. I don't eat a lot. My screwed-up life has turned my body into a garbage dump.'

'I like your garbage,' said Tian Tian.

I watched her while I ate. She had the sort of face that only a woman whose life has been full of stories could have.

'Come over to my place when you have time. You'll find singing, dancing, card games, drinking and all sorts of weird people. I've just redecorated my apartment. I spent half a million Hong Kong dollars on the lighting and sound system alone. More fucking awesome than some Shanghai night-clubs,' she said, without a trace of smugness.

Her mobile phone rang. She took it out of her bag and switched to a grainy, sexy voice. 'Where? I'll bet you're at old Wu's place. One day you'll die at a mahjong table. I'm eating with friends right now. Let's talk again at midnight,' teased Madonna, eyes sparkling.

'That was my new beau' – putting down the phone – 'He's a crazy painter. I'll introduce you next time we meet. Boys today really know how to sweet-talk a girl. He just swore he'd die in my bed.' She started laughing again. 'True or not, it's enough to keep me happy.'

Tian Tian was reading the *Xinmin Evening News*, and ignored her. This paper, which he reads to remind himself that he still lives here, is the only thing that links him to the everyday side of Shanghai. And I was beginning to feel a bit inhibited in the face of the straight-talking Madonna.

'You're really cute,' Madonna said, looking straight at me. 'You're not just pretty in a delicate way, you've got an aloofness, too, that turns men on. Too bad I've washed my hands of the business, or I could make you the hottest property around.'

Before I could react, she was laughing so hard she could hardly catch her breath. 'Sorry, sorry, just kidding.' I could see her eyes darting back and forth all the time, avid with neurotic enthusiasm. She had the air of all practised flirts, past and present, Chinese and foreign, who can mix well with any company but only really get excited when new faces appear.

'Watch what you say, I'm getting jealous,' said Tian Tian, looking up amorously from his paper and slipping his arm round my waist. We always sat that way, like Siamese twins, even if it was a bit inappropriate for some places.

Smiling faintly, I looked at Madonna. 'You're very beautiful too. In a *linglei* – unconventional – sort of way; not fake *linglei*, but the real thing.'

When we parted at the door of the Cotton Club, she hugged me. 'My dear, I've stories I'd love to tell you – if you really want to write that bestseller of yours, that is.'

Madonna hugged Tian Tian close too. 'My little good-for-nothing,' she said. 'Take good care of your love. Love's the most powerful thing on earth. It can make you fly and forget everything else. A child like you would be ruined in no time without love – you've no immunity against life. I'll call you.'

She blew us a kiss, slipped into a white VW Santana 2000 at the kerb, and sped off.

I thought about what she'd said. Buried in her words were fragments of philosophy, sparkling brighter than the lights, truer than truth. And the scent of her kiss lingered in the air.

'She's a crazy woman,' said Tian Tian happily. 'But she's really something, isn't she? She used to stop me doing anything stupid when I'd been alone in my room too long, by taking me for a midnight spin on one of those raised highways. We'd drink a lot, smoke dope, and wander around on a high until sunrise.

'Then I met you. It was all pre-destined,' he went on. 'You're not really like Madonna and me. We're different types. You're ambitious and full of faith in the future. You and your drive are what give me a reason to live. Do you believe me? I never lie.'

'Idiot,' I said, pinching his bottom.

'You're a crazy woman too!' He yelped in pain.

For Tian Tian, anyone who falls outside the bounds of normality, especially anyone in a mental hospital, is to be admired. In his opinion, crazy people are only considered mad by the rest of society because their intelligence isn't understood. He thinks that beauty is only reliable when it's linked to death or hopelessness, even evil. Like the epileptic Dostoevsky, ear-slicing Van Gogh, impotent Dali, homosexual Allen Ginsberg or the movie starlet Frances Farmer, who was thrown into an asylum and lobotomised in the McCarthy witch hunts. Or the Irish singer Gavin Friday, who wore thick layers of brightly coloured make-up all his life. Or Henry Miller, who, at his poorest, would pace up and down in front of a restaurant to scrounge a scrap of steak, and wander the streets begging for a dime to take the subway. To him, these people are like wild flowers, bursting with vigour and living and dying alone.

The night colours were soft.

Pressing close together, Tian Tian and I strolled along Huaihai Road. The lights, tree shadows and gothic roof of the Paris Printemps department store, and the people in autumn garb meandering among them, all drifted peacefully among the night colours. An atmosphere unique to Shanghai, light-hearted but refined, hung over the city.

I am forever absorbing that atmosphere, as if it were a magic potion of jade or rubies that would rid me of the contempt the young have for convention and help me get deep into the guts of the city, like an insect boring into an apple.

Thoughts like that cheer me up. I grabbed Tian Tian, my lover, and whirled him into a dance on the pavement.

'You're a capricious romantic, like an attack of appendicitis,' he said softly.

'This is called "Lazy Steps To Paris", my favourite foxtrot,' I said earnestly.

As usual, we strolled slowly over to the Bund. At night, it becomes a place of heavenly quiet. We went up to the top floor of the Peace Hotel, where we'd discovered a secret passageway to the roof – through a narrow window in the women's toilet and up the fire escape. We climbed up there often and were never caught.

Standing on the roof, we looked at the silhouettes of the buildings lit up by the street lights on both sides of the Huangpu

River, especially the Oriental Pearl TV Tower, Asia's tallest. Its long, long steel column pierces the sky, proof of the city's phallus worship. The ferries, the waves, the night-dark grass, the dazzling neon lights and incredible structures – all these signs of material prosperity are aphrodisiacs the city uses to intoxicate itself. They have nothing to do with us, the people who live among them. A car accident or a disease can kill us, but the city's prosperous, invincible silhouette is like a planet, in perpetual motion, eternal.

When I thought about that, I felt as insignificant as an ant on the ground.

But the thought didn't affect our mood as we stood on top of that historic building. As the sound of the hotel's septuagenarian jazz band came and went, we surveyed the city, yet distanced ourselves from it with love talk. I liked to undress right down to my bra and pants in the moist breeze from the Huangpu. Maybe I have a complex about underwear, or I'm a narcissist or an exhibitionist or something, but I hoped this would somehow stimulate Tian Tian's desire.

'Don't do that,' said Tian Tian painfully, turning his head away.

But I kept on undressing, like a stripper. A tiny blue flower began to burn my skin, and that odd sensation made me blind to my beauty, my self, my identity. Everything I did was designed to create a strange new fairy tale, a fairy tale meant just for me and the boy I adored.

The boy sat entranced against the railing, sad but grateful, watching the girl dance in the moonlight. Her body was smooth as a swan's, yet powerful as a leopard's. Every feline crouch, leap and turn was elegant yet madly seductive.

'Please try. Come into my body like a real lover, my darling, try.'

'No, I can't,' he said, curling himself into a ball.

'Well then, I'll jump off the roof,' laughed the girl, grabbing the rail as if to climb over it. He caught her and kissed her. But broken desire couldn't find a way. Love was a miracle the flesh couldn't copy, and the ghosts defeated us . . . Dust covered us, closing my throat and my love's.

Three a.m. Curled up on the big comfortable bed, I watched Tian Tian. He was already asleep, or pretending to be, and the room was strangely silent. His self-portrait hung above the piano. Who could help loving a flawless face like his?

Lying beside my love, again and again I used my slim fingers to masturbate, making myself fly, fly into the mire of orgasm. And in my mind's eye, I saw both crime and punishment.

# 3

# I Have a Dream

'And the good girls go to Heaven,
but the bad girls go everywhere.'
Jim Steinman

'A woman who chooses the
writing profession
often does so as to give herself a rank
within male-dominated society.'
Erica Jong

What sort of person am I? To my mother and father, I'm an evil little thing devoid of conscience (by five I'd learned how to stomp out, haughtily clutching my lollipop). To my teachers or ex-boss and colleagues at the magazine, I'm smart but hard-headed, a skilled professional with an unpredictable temperament who can guess how any film or a story will end from the way it begins. To most men, I qualify as a little beauty, as pleasing as spring light on a lake's rippling surface, with a pair of oversize eyes right out of a Japanese cartoon and a long Coco Chanel neck. But in my own eyes, I'm just an ordinary girl, even if I become famous one of these days.

When my paternal great-grandmother was alive, she often said: 'A person's fate is like a kite string. One end is here on the earth, and the other is in the heavens. There's nowhere to hide

17

from fate.' Or: 'Which part of life is the part worth living for.'

This old lady with snow-white hair and a tiny frame would sit all day, like a ball of white wool, in her rocking chair. Many people believed she had second sight. She successfully predicted the 1987 Shanghai earthquake which registered 3.0 on the Richter Scale, and told her relatives of her impending death three days before it happened. Her photograph still hangs on the wall of my parents' house and they believe that she continues to protect them. In fact, it was my grandmother who predicted that I would be a writer. With a literary star shining down on me and a belly full of ink, she said I would make my mark one day.

At university I often used to write letters to boys I was secretly in love with, rich in expression and affection, almost guaranteeing conquest. At the magazine, the interviews and stories I wrote were like something out of a novel, with their twisted plots and rarefied language, so that the real seemed false, and vice versa.

When I finally realised that everything I had done until then was just a waste of my talent, I gave up my highly-paid job at the magazine. My parents despaired of me once again, since my father had had to pull a lot of strings to get me the job in the first place.

'Child, are you really my daughter? Why does your head grow horns, and your feet grow thorns?' said Mother. 'Tell me, why all these wasted efforts?' Mother is a pretty, frail woman who has spent her life ironing shirts for her husband and seeking the right road for her daughter's happiness. She can't accept the idea of sex before marriage, and absolutely cannot bear the shape of a girl's nipples when she wears a tight T-shirt and no bra.

'The day will come when you realise that a steady, down-to-earth life is the most important thing. Even Eileen Chang says that human life needs a stable foundation,' said Daddy. He knows I admire this famous author. Daddy is a slightly chubby history professor who likes cigars and heart-to-heart talks with young people. A well-mannered man, he spoiled me from the start. When I was three he trained me to appreciate operas such as *La Bohème*. He always worried that when I grew up I'd lose my body and soul to a sex maniac. I'm his most precious baby, he says, and I should treat men cautiously and never shed tears over them.

'The way we think is just too different. We're separated by a hundred generation gaps. We'd best respect one another rather than arguing our cases,' I said. 'Anyway, it's a waste of time. I'm twenty-five, and I want to be a writer. Even though the profession's totally passé, I'm going to make writing up to date again.'

When I met Tian Tian and decided to move out, there was an uproar in my family fit to upset the Pacific Ocean.

'I don't know what to do about you. We'll just have to wait and see how you'll turn out. I might as well pretend I didn't raise you,' said Mother, almost shouting. She looked as if she had been struck hard on the face.

'You've hurt your mother's feelings,' said Daddy. 'And I'm disappointed too. A girl like you is bound to be taken advantage of. You say that boy's family is odd. His father died in strange circumstances. Is he normal himself? Is he reliable?'

'Believe me, I know what I'm doing,' I said. I grabbed my toothbrush, some clothes and discs and a box of books, and left.

Amber sunlight poured over the floor in front of the sound system, like spilled Scotch. After a group of immaculately dressed Americans left, the café was peaceful again. Old Yang was in his office-cum-bedroom talking up a storm on the phone. Spider lazed against the window, snacking on a chocolate waffle left over by a customer (he was forever doing this to prove his animal-like survival instincts). Outside the window sycamore trees lined the street. The city's summer colours shone fresh and green, like the mood in a European film.

'Coco, what do you do when you're bored?' asked Spider vacantly.

'Being bored *is* when you haven't got anything to do, so what would you be doing?' I said. 'Like right now.'

'Last night I was bored, so I went online to chat. Chatting with ten people at a time is neat.' I noticed those two oblong black eyes of his, floating on his face as though imprinted there with a spoon. 'I met someone called Enchantress, and it doesn't seem like one of those guys pretending to be a girl. She said she's very pretty, and still a virgin.'

'Nowadays, virgins are after something too, didn't you know?' I teased. 'And any girl who could say that sounds shameless.'

'I think what Enchantress says is cool,' he said, without smiling. 'Our ideals are amazingly similar. We both dream of earning a pile of money in one savage swoop, and then travelling the world.'

'Sounds like that pair in *Natural Born Killers*,' I said curiously. 'So how will you make your money?'

'Open a store, rob a bank, be a whore or a gigolo. Whatever,' he said half serious. 'I've got a plan right now.' He leaned his head down and spoke a few sentences softly into my ear, which knocked me off my feet.

'No, you can't do that, you're out of your mind!' I said, shaking my head furiously.

The creep wanted me to go along with him to steal money from the café. He had noticed that Old Yang stuffed the takings into a small safe every night, and went to the bank once a month to deposit the money. Spider had a friend who specialised in safe-cracking. His plan was to hire this robber, and then, with help from us on the inside, grab the money and take off. Of course, afterwards we would have to say that an unknown thief had sneaked in and robbed the place.

The date was already set. The following Tuesday was Spider's birthday, and by chance we would both be on the night shift. He planned to use his birthday celebration as an excuse to offer Old Yang a drink. He'd get him plastered, and that would be that.

Spider's words made me nervous. I even felt a mild bout of cramps coming on. 'Stop dreaming! Forget it, think of something else. Wait a minute, this wouldn't be Enchantress's idea, would it?'

'Shhh!' Spider signalled that old Yang had finished his phone call and was approaching. I shut my mouth, terrified I might reveal a hint of Spider's plot.

The café door opened and Tian Tian came in. I felt a wave of warmth in my stomach. Wearing a grey shirt and black corduroy trousers, he had a book in his hands. His hair was a bit long and dishevelled, and his eyes a bit near-sighted and moist. Those lips of his, faintly smiling but cool too – more or less my sweet love's standard look.

'Hubby's come, and she's oh-so happy,' teased old Yang in Shanghainese, with an accent one hears in Suzhou ballads. Actually, old Yang is good and kind, if a bit simple.

Greeted like that, Tian Tian looked ill at ease. I brought him a cappuccino and squeezed his hand lightly. 'There's still forty-five minutes to go,' he said quietly, looking at his watch. 'I'll wait for you to finish.'

'Spider must have gone crazy thinking about money,' I said, disturbed. On the wall opposite the exaggerated movements of my arms made shadow plays. A candle was burning on the small round table where Tian Tian and I were playing five-in-a-row on a Chinese chessboard.

'When somebody bright gets it into their heads to commit a crime it's worse than catching rabies,' I said. 'They'll use computers to rob banks, let off bombs to destroy planes and ships, use invisible knives to kill people, even manufacture plagues and tragedies. If 1999 *is* the apocalypse, it'll be caused by weirdos like that.'

'You're going to lose, I'm about to get four in a row,' said Tian Tian, pointing to the chessboard to get my attention.

'Intelligence is a gift and madness is an instinct, but if you exploit them for material gain, that's not right.' By now, my passion for debating was beginning to kick in. 'In the end, a genius can get into a worse mess than an idiot. Lately I've felt the Green Stalk Café's too peaceful. You can almost hear yourself blink. It's because there's a murder plot or something. I've got a worrying premonition.'

'Then leave the place and come home and write,' said Tian Tian simply.

When he said 'home' it always sounded so natural. This residence of three bedrooms plus a living-room, filled with the scent of fermenting fruits, cigarette butts, French perfume and alcohol, filled with books and music and limitless space for fantasising, was tightly wrapped around our bodies like a bank of clouds from enchanted forests. You could wave them away, but they stayed put. Actually, our apartment was a block of space that felt more predestined, and more genuine, than a home.

Let's go home. Now must be the time to cut to the heart of things. Start writing; set off on this journey of writing using your dreams and your love. Use flawless prose to complete beautiful novels, one after the other. Use wit and passion to handle the story's opening, suspense, climax and conclusion, like the world's most fantastic singer standing on Everest, singing at the top of her lungs.

A hand grabbed this idea and wrote it in my mind. Tian Tian wanted me to promise him that I'd call old Yang tomorrow and leave my job.

'Okay,' I said. Quit a job, leave someone, throw something away. To a girl like me, abandoning something was almost instinctive, as easy as the flip of a hand. Drift from one goal to another, push oneself to the limit, and keep moving.

'From the moment I first saw you at the Green Stalk, I just felt you were cut out to be a writer,' Tian Tian went on to flatter my vanity more. 'Your eyes are deep and your voice carries real emotion. You never stop watching your customers. And I've even heard you discussing existentialism and voodoo with Spider.'

I hugged him gently. His words were a caress that brought me a joy no other man had ever got near. Often, hearing his voice and looking at his eyes and lips, my sex would suddenly feel like a warm torrent and be soaked through in an instant. 'What else? Go on. I like hearing this,' I begged him, kissing his earlobe.

'Plus . . . you never let people see through you. Maybe born writers all have split personalities. I mean, they're a bit unreliable.'

'What are you worrying about?' I asked, confused, moving my lips away from his ear.

Tian Tian shook his head. 'I love you,' he said. He put his hands lightly around my waist, and rested his head on my shoulder. I could feel his eyelashes quivering against my neck, triggering a burst of velvet tenderness in my heart. One pair of hands reached my tummy, while another pair made contact with his buttocks. We stood face to face, and saw ourselves in the mirror – our reflection in the water.

Later, he had fallen asleep in an S-shape on the bed, and I held him from behind, in a daze. Indeed, all along his stubbornness and his fragility were a mystery to me. For no good reason, I felt responsible for him – and also a sense of remorse.

In fact, nothing happened at the Green Stalk Café on Spider's birthday: no professional thief appeared, no safe disappeared and there was no plot – not even a fly disturbed things. As usual, old Yang was comfortable and worry-free, counting his money, supervising the staff, working the phone and napping. When she got down to work, the new waitress was no worse than me, and soon afterwards Spider left with his wicked schemes, evaporating without a trace like a bubble.

My attention turned to writing. I had no time to spare for anything else. My priority was to set up a hotline to my soul, and await the stealthy arrival of plot and characters amidst a madhouse-like silence. Tian Tian watched over me like a slave driver, pushing me to use my magical power to write a genuine book of enchantment. This became the core of his life.

He discovered a passion for shopping in supermarkets. Like our parents' generation, we pushed our shopping trolley in Tops Supermarket, conscientiously buying food and daily necessities. Health experts say, 'Don't get hooked on foods like chocolate and popcorn,' but those were just the things we liked.

At home, I spread out my snow-white manuscript-to-be and occasionally looked at my reflection in a small mirror, to check whether my face now had the wisdom and rarefied air of a writer. Tian Tian trod softly in the apartment, poured Suntory soda for me, prepared fruit salad with Mother's Choice salad dressing for me, gave me Dove chocolate bars for inspiration, chose discs which were stimulating but not distracting, and adjusted the level of the air conditioning. On the huge desk stood dozens of cartons of Mild Seven cigarettes stacked neatly like a brick wall, books and a thick ream of manuscript paper. I didn't know how to use a computer and didn't plan to learn.

I had already thought up a long string of book titles. My

ideal literary work would have profound intellectual content and a bestselling, sexy cover.

My instinct told me that I should write about turn-of-the-century Shanghai. This fun-loving city: the bubbles of happiness which rise from it, the new generation it has nurtured, and the vulgar, sentimental and mysterious atmosphere to be found in its back streets and alleys. This is a unique Asian city. Since the 1930s it has preserved a culture where China and the West met intimately and evolved together, and now it has entered its second wave of westernisation. Tian Tian once used the English term 'post-colonial' to describe it. The customers in the Green Stalk Café speaking all sorts of languages reminded me of the days when old-fashioned salons with their florid talk were in vogue; but time and place had altered, and now it was just like international travel.

When I had written what I thought was a good passage, I would read it out to Tian Tian, full of feeling.

'My darling Coco, you've got what it takes. You can use your pen to create a separate reality, more real than the one we live in. Here . . .' He grabbed my hand and put it on the left side of his chest. I could feel the rhythm of his heart. 'I guarantee this will bring you unlimited inspiration,' he said.

He would buy totally unexpected gifts, as if spending money on beautiful but useless knick-knacks were his sole pleasure.

But I'd rather have had him. How could I wait until the day when he would give me his body?

The deeper the love, the sharper the flesh aches.

Late one night, I had an erotic dream. In it, I became entangled, naked, with a man wearing dark glasses. Both sets of four limbs entangled like an octopus, embracing and dancing, the man's golden body hair glistening so provocatively that my body itched all over. When my favourite acid jazz music ended, I woke up.

I felt a twinge of guilt about this dream, but then a question occurred to me: just what was it that was preoccupying Tian Tian? He was more focused on my writing than I was, to the point of being almost fixated; perhaps writing really could function as an aphrodisiac, cultivating the inexplicable, but imperfect love between us? Did it come with a mission, and with divine blessing? Or, just the opposite . . . who knows?

I thought and thought and then turned and hugged Tian Tian. He woke immediately. His face could sense the moisture on mine, and without asking or saying a word, his hand gently caressed my body. No one had taught him how, but he had the gift of making me fly. Don't cry, don't speak of separation. I just want to fly to the other side of the night.

Our lives are short and bitter and romantic dreams leave no trace.

# 4

# The Seducer

'From Berlin I hail, and your love is mine.
When the night nears, hold me, my love, and we shall soar.'
Boris Bracht

Madonna invited us to a retro theme party called *Return to Avenue Joffre* on the top floor of the high-rise at the corner of Huaihai and Yandang Roads. Avenue Joffre in the 1930s, Huaihai Road today, has long symbolised Shanghai's old dreams. In today's fin-de-siècle, post-colonial mindset, this boulevard – and the bygone era of the revealing traditional dress, the *qipao*, calendar-girl posters, rickshaws and jazz bands – is fashionable again, like a bow knotted over Shanghai's nostalgic heart.

Tian Tian wasn't in a good mood, but he still came with me. As I said, we're often inseparable, shadowing each other like Siamese twins.

In my tailored *qipao* and Tian Tian's traditional *changshan*, we walked into the lift. 'Please wait a minute,' said a voice from somewhere. Tian Tian pressed his hand between the closing doors, and a tall Western man strode in, bringing with him the scent of CK cologne.

A pale, purplish light shone on our heads. With men to my left and right, and the indicator lights flashing the floor numbers in order as we climbed, I lost my sense of gravity for a moment. Then I caught a glimpse of the tall foreigner's expression; absent-minded yet sensual, the hallmark of a confirmed playboy.

When the lift door opened, a wave of noise mixed with the smells of tobacco and bodies assailed me, and the tall man smiled to indicate that I should go first. Tian Tian and I walked past a polystyrene Avenue Joffre street sign, and lifted back the heavy velvet curtain. A sea of faces dancing to yesterday's decadent music appeared before us.

Madonna's effervescent face looked like a phosphorescent deep-sea creature as she walked towards us, radiating a 1,000-watt glow.

'My dears, you're here at last. Oh, God, Mark, how are you?' She struck a sexy pose for the benefit of the tall man behind us. 'Come on over. Let me introduce you. This is Mark from Berlin, and this is Tian Tian and Coco, my good friends. Coco's an author, no less.'

Mark politely extended his hand. 'Hello.' His hand, warm and dry, was comfortable to the touch. Tian Tian had wandered off on his own and was sitting on a soft sofa smoking, his eyes fixed on the distance.

Madonna admired my black satin *qipao* (custom-made at a Suzhou silk factory, with a lovely but rather imposing peony embroidered on the bosom). And she praised as *ku*, cool, the antique western-style suit Mark was wearing, with a tight-fitting collar and three buttonholes. He said he'd bought it for a high price from the heir of a Shanghainese capitalist, and while it had faded a bit, it still had an aristocratic air.

Some other guests walked our way. 'This is my boyfriend Ah Dick. Here are Number Five and Cissy,' introduced Madonna.

The long-haired guy named Ah Dick didn't even look eighteen, but he's actually fairly well-known in Shanghai as an avant-garde painter. The cartoon characters he draws aren't bad, and it was his gift of a pile of cartoons that had first touched Madonna, with their hodge-podge of talent, off-colour language and childishness that aroused her maternal instinct.

Number Five is a go-kart ace. He and his cross-dressing girlfriend Cissy, in suit and tie, looked cut out for one another – a pair of odd-looking bunnies.

Mark's eyes scanned in my direction, and after an instant's hesitation he walked over. 'Would you like to dance?'

I glanced at the sofa in the corner. Head down, Tian Tian was rolling a joint. In his hand was a plastic bag containing several ounces of marijuana. He always smoked lots of marijuana in the build-up to one of his reclusive periods.

I sighed. 'Let's,' I said.

A crackling vinyl record on the turntable reproduced the golden voice of Zhou Xuan singing 'Four Seasons'. Despite the crackling and distortion, the singing surprisingly made one's heart flutter. Mark seemed to be enjoying himself, his eyes half-closed. I saw Tian Tian close his eyes too, curled up on that roomy sofa. Drinking red wine and smoking dope always makes you drowsy, and I was sure that he had already fallen asleep. He often found it easier to go to sleep amid noisy voices and phantom shadows.

'Your mind's elsewhere,' said Mark suddenly, in English with a thick German accent.

'Oh, really?' I looked vacantly at him. His eyes were shining in the darkness, like those of an animal lurking in the shrubbery. I was surprised by the feeling those eyes gave me. His clothing was crisply ironed and neat from top to bottom, and he'd applied lots of hair gel too, so he looked like a brand new, furled umbrella. Those eyes of his seemed like the epicentre of his body, and all his energy emanated from there. A white man's eyes.

'I'm looking at my boyfriend,' I said.

'Looks like he's fallen sleep,' he smiled slightly.

His smile aroused my curiosity. 'Do you find that droll?' I asked, using the French word.

'Are you a perfectionist?' he asked, changing the subject.

'I don't know. I don't understand myself all the time. Why do you ask?'

'I get that feeling from the way you dance,' he said. He seemed a sensitive, confident type. A smile with a slight sneer to it edged across my face.

The music switched to jazz, and we began to do the foxtrot. All around me was a neo-classical, hazy universe woven from velvet, silk, calico and indigo cloth. Gradually, it spun itself into a light-headed happiness.

When the music ended and people drifted away, I discovered that the sofa was empty. Tian Tian wasn't anywhere to be seen, nor was Madonna. I asked Number Five, who said Madonna and Ah Dick had just left but Tian Tian had been on the sofa a moment ago.

Then Mark came out of the men's room to report, let's say, not entirely bad news: Tian Tian was slumped down next to the urinal, but he hadn't thrown up or cut himself. He must have fallen asleep suddenly in the washroom. Mark helped me get him downstairs and out to the street, and hailed a taxi.

'I'll go with you,' said Mark. 'You can't do this by yourself.' I glanced at Tian Tian, who was out cold. He might be thin, but once he had passed out, he was as heavy as a baby elephant.

The taxi sped along the street at two o'clock in the morning. Outside the window were skyscrapers, shop windows, neon lights, advertising billboards, and one or two people stumbling along. In this city, which never sleeps, there is always something happening secretly.

The smell of alcohol came and went in bursts, and a subtle but persistent scent of CK cologne floated now and then deep into my lungs. My mind was vacant. One of the men next to me was out cold, the other silent. In the silence, I could sense the shadows stuck to the pavement and a strange man's surreptitious gaze upon me in the dark.

The car soon arrived at our place, and Mark and I carried Tian Tian up the stairs into the apartment. We laid him on the bed, and I covered him with a blanket.

Mark pointed at the desk. 'Is this where you work?'

I nodded. 'I don't know how to use a PC. Anyway, some people say it causes skin disease, and others say it makes you pessimistic, obsessive-compulsive, unwilling to leave your house. Anyway . . .' I suddenly realised that Mark was coming towards me, with that distant but extremely sensual smile of his.

'Very pleased to meet you. I hope I may see you again.' He kissed me lightly on both cheeks in the French style, said good-night and left.

Left in my hand was his business card. On it were the address and phone number of his firm, a German-owned multinational investment consultancy on Huashan Road.

# 5

# Unreliable Man

'Whatever else can be said about sex,
it cannot be called a dignified performance.'
Helen Lawrenson

My admiration for tall men is partly due to vanity, but mostly because of loathing for a pint-sized ex-boyfriend of mine.

He was less than five-and-a-half feet tall, had a plain face, wore a pair of cheap glasses, and was a fake Christian convert (later events proved he was really a believer in something like Manichaeism or Zoroastrianism).

I don't quite remember why I fell for him. Perhaps it was his erudition or his ability to recite famous Shakespearean works in Oxford English. Or when he sat with me behind Mao's statue on the lawn, right in the middle of Fudan U., going on for three days without stopping about the instant of Jesus Christ's birth in a stable and how it signified truth.

The grass was like a furred tongue licking my thighs through my skirt, tickling me. A light wind brushed against our faces. He went on and on, as if under a spell, and I, mesmerized by the same spell, couldn't stop listening to him. It seemed we could have sat there for seven days and seven nights until we reached glorious nirvana.

And so I turned a blind eye to his disappointing shortness and threw myself into the arms of his learned, eloquent soul (maybe all the men I ever become infatuated with will, first and foremost, be widely learned, highly talented, and passionately eloquent, with crenellated brains. I can't imagine myself falling for a man who can't cite ten proverbs, five philosophical allusions, and the names of three composers). Naturally, I very soon realised that I had thrown myself into a slimy-green pond instead.

He wasn't just a religious fanatic, he was also a sex maniac and enjoyed using my body to try out all sorts of positions from porn videos. He fantasised about sitting in the dark corner of a sofa, voyeur to my rape by a crude carpenter or plumber. Even when we took a bus to visit his parents, he wouldn't miss the opportunity to open his fly, grab my hand and put it inside. That thing of his, dripping like a candle and hidden behind a big newspaper, could hardly contain its excitement. It all made me feel sad and utterly hopeless, like the terrifying sounds out of *Boogie Nights*.

When I discovered he was a congenital liar (even going to a kiosk for a newspaper became meeting a friend for tea) and a money-grubbing clown (he plagiarised large sections of articles by other writers, wrote them up in a massive work and had it published in Shenzhen), my patience ran out – especially since the source of all of this nasty behaviour was a plain man less than five-and-a-half feet tall. I felt deceived; my eyes had been befuddled by my imagination. Humiliated, I left him.

'You can't leave just like that!' he blurted out at my back from the door of his dormitory.

'You disgust me,' I retorted. Mothers always warn their daughters, as they leave on their first date, not to trust men. But, in the girl's ears her words are just so much hot air. Only when a woman looks at men and their half of the world with truly mature eyes can she clearly see her own position in it, and realise the order of things.

He called my dormitory, and the voice of the old lady from Ningbo in the porter's office came over the loudspeaker again and again, 'Nikki, phone call for you, phone call for you, Nikki.' Later on, every weekend I spent at my parents' place became another part of the nightmare. He would call me there relentlessly, unwilling to admit defeat before he located me. It got to the point where the phone would ring like a prank call at three o'clock in the morning, until the phone number was changed. During that phase Mother totally lost faith in me and didn't want to see me. She saw the fact that I had attracted such scum as entirely my fault. I had chosen unwisely, failed to distinguish between a flower and a weed. And erring in one's choice of boyfriend is a woman's greatest humiliation.

My ex-boyfriend's craziest behaviour was to stalk me at school, on the road and in the subway, and then unexpectedly call out my name in the midst of a crowd. Wearing a pair of tacky sunglasses, his bulging face quivering, he would hurriedly duck behind a nearby tree or into a shop just as I whipped my head around, like a stunt actor in a cheap action movie.

During that stage, I longed for a man in a police uniform to walk down the street with his arm wrapped around my waist. My heartbeat was like an S.O.S. call. Not long after I began working at the magazine I used my contacts to find a friend in the Administrative Affairs Office of the city government and then, via a local police station, finally delivered a warning to my ex. Since he wasn't crazy enough to seek confrontation with a government department, he gave up chasing me.

Afterwards I went to visit a friend, David Wu, who was a psychologist at the Youth Centre. 'From now on, I'll never go for a short boyfriend again,' I said, sitting in a chair that seemed to have a hypnotic effect. 'Guys like that shouldn't even think of coming through the door. I've had enough. I'm a bad girl, through and through, at least in the eyes of my mother. She gets provoked so easily. I've never done anything for her but hurt her feelings.'

He told me that the clash between my natures as a female and as a writer doomed me to chaos. Artists have a decided tendency towards weakness, dependence, contradiction, naivete, masochism, narcissism, Oedipus complex and so forth. My ex just happened to cater to several of those split dispositions, from dependence to masochism to narcissism, and my need to atone to my mother for my sins would be an emotional theme throughout my life.

'As to a person's height,' said David, clearing his throat, 'I do believe that it can have a certain impact on their adult behaviour, particularly for a man. Shorter men often express themselves more intensely than those of normal height. For instance, they study harder, make greater efforts to earn money, have a stronger desire to defeat their competitors, and further, prefer to pursue beautiful women as some sort of proof of their manhood.

'Sean Penn is rather short, isn't he? But he's one of Hollywood's great actors, and was once loved by Madonna, even if he was always tying the world's sexiest starlet to a chair like a turkey and torturing her. One can cite many men like that. They are extremely memorable.'

He sat in this soft-lit room immersed in myriad thoughts. Because he often played a role as though he were God's spokesman to his patients, his face didn't look all that real. His body shifted back and forth in the leather chair, occasionally emitting a muffled fart. Despite the room's stale air, a few potted *pao-ferro* trees and tortoiseshell bamboo grew luxuriantly green all year round.

'Okay,' I said. 'Of course a person's ability to love can't be judged by his height, but anyway, I want to forget it all. A lot of life can be consigned to oblivion, and as far as I'm concerned, the more unpleasant one's experiences, the faster they're forgotten.'

'That's why you'll be a good writer. A writer buries the past with her words,' said David kindly.

# 6

# Perfumed Night

'Night is everything in motion.'
Dylan Thomas

The weather grew cooler, and the city seemed to turn into a huge block of clear glass. Autumn in the south is clean and bright and conducive to romance.

One uneventful afternoon I got a call from Mark. When a German-accented greeting sounded in my ear, my first reaction was: 'Here comes a tall Western man!'

We exchanged our *ni hao, ni hao*, commenting on the marvellously comfortable weather, and how Berlin was even cooler than Shanghai at this season, though summer had been good too . . .

Both of us were a bit distracted. I knew Tian Tian was on the bed listening to me with his eyes closed, and I also knew why the German on the other end of the line was calling. This sort of delicate situation is like a hash brownie; a taste is no big thing, and even a bit more is no big thing, but when you take that third bite something unpleasant yet liberating takes place. And maybe I'm the kind of girl who, deep down, is itching for that to happen.

'Next Friday there's a show of avant-garde German art at the Shanghai Exhibition Centre,' said Mark in closing. 'If you and your boyfriend want to come, I'll send you invitations.'

'That would be great. Thank you.'

'Okay, see you next week.'

Tian Tian's eyes were closed, seemingly in sleep. I turned the TV down – it's on twenty hours a day. Recently we'd taken to watching TV and videos in bed, caressing one another against the scarlet backdrop of Quentin Tarantino's violent films, and falling asleep in concert with Uma Thurman's moaning and John Travolta's gunfire.

I lit a cigarette, sat down on the sofa and thought about the phone conversation, about that man with his tall, tall body steeped in fragrance from head to toe, and his wicked smile. I thought and thought and suddenly felt very irritated. He was flagrantly attempting to seduce a girl who already had a boyfriend, knowing she wouldn't leave that boyfriend. And all this might lead to nothing more than a purely sexual diversion.

I went over to my desk and, as I did daily, put down on paper the latest chapter in my emerging novel. I wrote about the randomness of Mark's appearance on the scene, and the inevitability of certain events in my life. Various premonitions of mine were lying in wait within my novel, and one by one, were realised and resolved with every step forward.

That night Madonna and Ah Dick showed up uninvited. I could hear Madonna's voice in the stairwell a few floors down. Shining a torch, they were calling as they came up the stairs – they'd forgotten which floor we lived on. Both of them were wearing tiny sunglasses in the darkness, and feeling their way clumsily.

'God, no wonder I kept feeling there wasn't enough light. I almost hit somebody's bike when I was driving a minute ago,' laughed Madonna as she took hers off. 'How could I have forgotten I had these on?'

Looking pale but attractive in an Esprit black wool sweater, Ah Dick had a few cans of Coke and beer in his hands. Their entrance shattered the room's tranquillity, and Tian Tian had no choice but to put down his English magazine, famous for its countless brain-twisters. (His favourites were maths and crossword puzzles.)

'We were just going for a drive, but we ended up driving past here, so we came up. I've got a video in my bag, but no guarantee it's a good movie.' She scanned the room. 'Want to play mahjong? Four people makes a full table.'

'We don't have any mahjong tiles,' said Tian Tian quickly.

'But I do, in my car,' said Madonna, narrowing her eyes and smiling at Ah Dick. 'Ah Dick could go and get them.'

'Forget it, let's just hang out,' said Ah Dick, looking a touch irritable as he stretched his slender fingers and ran them through his hair. 'We wouldn't be interfering with your writing, would we?' he asked, looking at me.

'No problem.' I put a record on, and a sultry woman's voice gradually emerged from a background sound like the music of a vintage French movie. The sofa was quite comfy, the lighting pleasant, and red wine and sausage were laid out in the kitchen. Little by little everyone took to this atmosphere, and the conversation zigzagged between well-founded and baseless rumours and ambiguous opinions.

'This city is so claustrophobic. Just a handful of people are on the circuit,' said Madonna. The circuit she meant is composed of artists, real and phony, foreigners, vagabonds, greater and lesser performers, private entrepreneurs of industries that are currently fashionable, true and fake *linglei* and Generation Y types. Members of this circle move in and out of the public eye, now visible, then hidden, but ultimately dominating most of the city's trend-setting scene. They are like beautiful insects whose bellies give off a blue light, existing secretly and subsisting on desire.

'Once, I ran into the same faces in different places three nights in a row, but I never did get their names,' I said.

'Yesterday I came across Mark at Paulaner's Brauhaus. He said next week there's going to be a German painting exhibition,' Madonna butted in. I looked at her out of the corner of my eye and then glanced at Tian Tian. 'He already phoned,' I said matter-of-factly, 'and said he'd send us invitations.'

'Same old M.O., same old faces,' said Ah Dick. 'They're all party animals.' His face grew paler the more he drank.

'I'm not into that,' said Tian Tian, putting hash into a pipe. 'Those people are flashy and superficial. In the end, some of them just disappear like bubbles.'

'That's not true,' said Madonna.

'Shanghai is a city obsessed with pleasure,' I said.

'Is that the theme of your novel?' asked Ah Dick.

'Coco, go ahead and read from your writing,' said Tian Tian, his eyes sparkling as he gazed at me. This was the moment when he felt doubly reassured and content. Once my writing had become part of our shared life, it was no longer purely an act of writing. It became associated with our passion and fidelity, and with our unbearable lightness of being too.

Everybody looked merry as a hash-filled pipe, a few bottles of wine and a stack of manuscript paper passed from one hand to another.

*'The ferries, the waves, the night-dark grass, the dazzling neon lights and incredible structures – all these signs of material prosperity are aphrodisiacs the city uses to intoxicate itself. They have nothing to do with us, the people who live among them. A car accident or a disease can kill us, but the city's prosperous, invincible silhouette is like a planet in perpetual motion.*

*'When I thought about that, I felt as insignificant as an ant on the ground . . .*

*'A tiny blue flower began to burn my skin, and that odd sensation*

*made me blind to my beauty, my self, my identity. Everything I did was designed to create a strange new fairy tale, a fairy tale meant just for me and the boy I adored.*

*'The boy sat entranced against the railing, sad but grateful, watching the girl dance in the moonlight. Her body was smooth as a swan's, yet powerful as a leopard's. Every feline crouch, leap and turn was elegant, yet madly seductive . . .'*

We longed for those carnival-like poetry happenings of the 1960s in the West. Allen Ginsberg won fame by taking part in more than forty consecutive poetry salons where words and pot were shared. Our impromptu get-together that night unwittingly brought me a kind of lyrical joy brought on by alcohol, innocence and love. I basked in the influence of their gaze and associated it all with God: with Vivaldi's *Four Seasons* playing in the background, water and meadows stretched out endlessly. We were like lambs lying in a big book – not the Bible, but my naive and presumptuous novel every sentence of which was tattooed on my pale skin.

The wall clock struck midnight. Everyone was hungry, but when I brought out a platter of sausage, Madonna asked: 'Don't you have anything else?'

'We've eaten everything.' I shook my head apologetically.

'We could order a takeaway,' said Tian Tian. 'Little Sichuan stays open very late. Give them a call and they'll deliver, no problem.'

'Darling, you're so clever,' said Madonna happily as she put her arm around Ah Dick's slim, muscular waist, and gave Tian Tian a peck too. She's one of those women who are easily excited, and once excited she becomes sexy and flirtatious.

A restaurant employee delivered four cartons of food and rice. I thanked him and gave him a small tip. At first he wouldn't take it, but eventually he accepted the 10 RMB, red-faced. His shyness made me curious. When I asked, he said his family name was Ding, that he had just come from the country and he had only been working in the restaurant for a few days. I nodded, knowing that newcomers are often sent here and there on small errands.

We finished the food off and then started drinking, and didn't give up until we were ready to fall asleep. Madonna and Ah Dick spent the night in the spare room. Furnished with a bed and air con, we had originally set it aside just in case one day Tian Tian and I had an argument and needed to be apart. But up until then, we never had.

It must have been around two or three in the morning. Something hazy and soft was there in the black night. Then I saw it clearly – a thread of moonlight glancing in through a chink in the blinds which hadn't been pulled quite shut. I stared at this thread of light for a good half-hour. It looked feeble and frigid, like a small snake hibernating in a crevice. I stretched the tip of my foot straight out, pointing my toes as if I were ballet dancing, slowly moving it under the ray of light, slowly wiggling it along the path of the light. I could hear the faint breathing of the boy next to my body and the muffled sound of the pair of lovers thumping against the mattress in the guest room next door.

I heard my own heartbeat, the sound of blood in motion, a northern European man's sensual moaning and the tick-tock of the electric clock. Fingers furtively rubbed the swollen spot between my legs. Orgasm came suddenly and rippled from my lower abdomen throughout my entire body. Drenched, the fingers withdrew from the spasming crotch and slid, fatigued, into my mouth. My tongue tasted a sweet yet raw and melancholic flavour, the true flavour of my flesh.

The moonlight on the sheet had disappeared and that little snake had vanished in a puff of smoke.

# 7

# A Day in Our Life

'Found my coat and grabbed my hat
Made the bus in seconds flat
Found my way upstairs and had a smoke,
Somebody spoke and I went into a dream.'
The Beatles

There was only sunlight, no leaves on the trees. We stayed in our room all day, not giving more than a glance out of the window, or a yawn. The washing machine in the bathroom was stuffed with stiff socks and dirty sheets. Tian Tian was against hiring a daily or a maid to do the housework, because he didn't want a stranger in his personal space, touching his underwear, ashtrays or slippers. But we were getting lazier and lazier. Ideally, we would even do without three meals a day.

'All we have to do is take in 2,790 calories, 1,214 IUs of vitamin A and 1,094 milligrams of calcium each day,' said Tian Tian, waving several bottles of green, white and pale-yellow pills in his hands. He reckoned these provided the required nourishment for the human body. 'To make them more palatable, you can dissolve them in fruit juice, yoghurt and so on, and take them that way,' he said earnestly.

I believed every word he said, but you would probably eat

45

your way to neurosis and depression like that. I'd rather get a take-away from Little Sichuan every day.

Tian Tian, like an overseer, urged me on with my writing. Meanwhile, he was in the other room painting without pause, doing little leopards, contorted faces, goldfish bowls. He bought a lot of Yi Er Shuang underwear from the supermarket, and painted directly on them with acrylics. After our meal, we each displayed our works of art for the other's benefit. I read out an excerpt from my novel, and a section which I later deleted made him burst out laughing. It was a 'Dialogue between Female Patient and Male Psychologist':

*'My husband disgusts me. He's a pig.'*

*'In bed or out of it?'*

*'He's got no brain. He just likes to screw. He wouldn't pass up the chance to do it with a goat. Some day I'm going to lose it and castrate him, just like Lorena Bobbit in that case in Virginia seven years ago.'*

*'Are you really considering that?'*

*'God, men all think they're in the right! What are women in your eyes? Pretty, passive playthings? It looks like even an analyst can't solve this problem. I'm wasting my money on a blithering idiot.'*

*'What do you mean?'*

*'Can you provide any genuine insight? I can't bear to be manipulated any more!'*

*'If you don't have faith in me, then you're free to leave! And please close the door on your way out.'*

*'Oh, I can't take any more. You're all pigs!' she screamed as she ran out.*

'That's so vulgar, like something out of a farce,' chuckled Tian Tian. 'But it's funny.'

I tried on one of the white T-shirts that Tian Tian had painted with a large cartoonish cat face. It looked great. Much of the underwear featured line-drawings of the moon, lips, eyes, the sun and beautiful women. The sofa was piled high with several dozen hand-painted pieces. 'We could find a place to sell these,' I said.

'Do you think people will like them?'

'Let's give it a try. Anyway, it'll be interesting, and if we can't sell them, we can give them to friends.'

Fearing embarrassment, Tian Tian was unwilling to hawk his wares on the street so we chose the nearby campus of East China Normal University, which has a nice feel to it, refreshing, very green, well kept. It always gives one a sense of being cut off from the outside world.

Of course that's a misconception; even ivory towers have a window open to the world.

Next to the sports grounds, on the side of a road lined with little shops selling sundries, we selected a spot to set up shop. It was dinner time, and students were carrying their empty mess tins to the caféteria. They looked curiously at us as they passed by, and some of them knelt down, gave our goods the once-over, and asked about the prices. I handled everything. Tian Tian kept silent throughout.

'T-shirts are sixty RMB, pants forty.'

'Too much!' they said, and proceeded to haggle mercilessly. I stood my ground, because too low a price meant a lack of respect for Tian Tian's artistic labours. The sky grew dark, students rode their bikes to night-time study halls, and there was no one left playing ball on the pitch.

'I'm starving,' said Tian Tian quietly. 'How about we call it a day and go home?'

'Wait a bit.' I took a piece of chocolate out of my pocket for him and lit up a cigarette. 'Let's give it another ten minutes.'

Just then a handsome, dark-skinned man walked over, with

his arm around the waist of a white girl with glasses. 'Hello there,' I greeted him in English. 'Hand-painted underwear on the cheap.' With someone as shy as Tian Tian next to me, I had to be bold and confident, even though when I was little just going to the bakery to buy bread for my mother would make me so nervous my little hand would sweat as it held the money.

'Did you paint these yourselves?' inquired the white girl, smiling as she eyed our goods. 'They're really cute.' Her mellow voice was pleasing, and there was something smart in those eyes.

'They were painted by my boyfriend,' I said, pointing at Tian Tian.

'He paints very well. Looks a bit like Modigliani, or perhaps Matisse,' she added.

Tian Tian looked at her happily. 'Thank you,' he said, and then whispered to me: 'Sell her some stuff at a discount. This *laowai* woman's nice.' I pretended I hadn't heard, and smiled sweetly at the black-and-white student lovers.

'Moya, what do you think? I'd like to buy them all,' said the girl, beginning to reach for her wallet. The dark-skinned man named Moya had the dignified air of a chieftain, and might have been from somewhere in Africa. He hugged the girl thoughtfully. 'Let me,' he said, pulling out a wad of 100 RMB notes too. But the white girl insisted on paying herself. 'Thank you. Looking forward to seeing you again,' she said, smiling, as they left.

We had just earned nearly 1,000 RMB. Tian Tian jumped about, hugged me and gave me a kiss. 'I can earn my own money after all! I never knew that,' he said, surprised but pleased.

'That's right. You're a remarkable person. As long as you want to, you can be a success at lots of things,' I encouraged him.

We ate dinner at a nearby restaurant. Our appetites were

unusually good, and we even sang British love songs in a private karaoke lounge with a miserable sound system. 'My dear, if you lose your way, I'll be there by your side. My dear, if you're hurt or afraid, I'll be there by your side . . .' went the old Scottish folk song.

# 8

# My Divorced Cousin

'There's nineteen men livin' in my neighborhood.
Eighteen of them are fools,
and the one ain't no
doggone good.'
Bessie Smith

My parents both rang me. They had surrendered. Chinese parents give up easily to keep in with their children. Over the phone, they tried very hard to come across as warm while standing by their principles. They asked how I was doing and if I'd been having any problems. When they learned that there was no one to do the housework, Mother even offered to come over and help out.

'Take better care of yourselves. You should get out more,' I urged them. I wished they could be more selfish and worry less about me.

Mother also broke a piece of news to me. My cousin Zhu Sha had got divorced. Having moved out of her old place and temporarily unable to find a suitable new one, she was staying with them, since my bed was empty. On top of that she wasn't happy with her job, so her mood wasn't too good lately. If I had time, I should hang out and chat with her.

I was slightly taken aback. Zhu Sha divorced?

Zhu Sha was a lady-like young woman, four years older than me. She married a classmate after graduating with a degree in

German from the Foreign Languages Institute, and currently worked in a German-run trading firm. She always disliked the way people called her a 'white-collar beauty'. In some ways, I liked her independent attitude, and her, despite the fact that our temperaments and ambitions differed.

When I was small, my parents were forever encouraging me to be like Zhu Sha. Even when very young she cut a brilliant figure: a class leader's triple stripes on her sleeve, the top exam results in the entire school, and talented at singing *and* dancing *and* reciting. A photo capturing her innocent smile was even blown up huge and mounted in the display window of Shanghai Photo Studio on Nanjing Road, and many of her friends and classmates went to take a look.

Back then I really envied her. Once, during the June 1st International Children's Festival celebrations, I secretly dripped ink from my blue fountain pen on to her white georgette skirt. As a result, she made an utter fool of herself performing *Five Little Flowers* in the school auditorium and burst into tears as soon as she got off stage. No one realised it was my doing. At first I wanted to laugh when I saw how upset she was, but afterwards I began to feel bad about it, because in fact she was normally kind to me, taught me arithmetic, shared her lollipops with me, and always took me by the hand when crossing the street.

As we grew up, we met less and less frequently. I was still at Fudan U when she married. At first it was a bright, sunny day, but when the videotaping of the newly-weds began on the lawn at Dingxiang Lilac Gardens, heavy rain suddenly bucketed down. The sight of Zhu Sha in her drenched wedding veil is etched on my memory. The shrouded smile on her face, her wet black curled hair, and her white gauze gown soaked to the point of indecency – it all had an odd, fragile beauty which is hard to put into words.

Her husband Li Ming-Wei had been chairman of the department's Student Council. Large, tall, fair-skinned and wearing a pair of silver-rimmed glasses, he served briefly as a translator at the German Consulate, and by the time they married he was editor of a financial newsletter for the German Chamber of Commerce. He wasn't a good communicator, but he was quite a gentleman and he always sported a calm, cool smile. I once thought that while a man with a smile like that might not be suitable as a lover, he would be a very suitable husband.

I never imagined that she would divorce.

I got through to Zhu Sha on her mobile. Her voice was clearly depressed, and since the connection wasn't very good, it sounded as if cold rain was pitter-pattering in the background. I asked where she was. In a taxi, she said. In a minute she would arrive at the Windsor Castle, a popular women's health club.

'Would you like to come?' she asked me. 'We could exercise together.'

I gave it some thought. 'No, I don't work out. But we could chat.'

I crossed a walkway and found a room full of older women wearing leotards, performing an amateur version of *Swan Lake* under the instruction of a Russian coach. In another room I found my cousin amid a mass of equipment, sweating heavily as she jogged on the treadmill.

Her figure had always been very good, but now she was verging on skinny. 'Hi', she waved at me.

'Come here every day?' I asked.

'Yeah, especially lately,' she said, running as she spoke.

'Be careful not to over-exercise. Your whole body'll become rock-hard. That's worse than divorce,' I joked.

She said nothing, running quickly, her face wet.

'Take a break,' I said. 'Stop bouncing back and forth. I'm getting dizzy just watching you.'

She gave me a bottle of water and opened one for herself. Sitting on the stairs, she gave me the once-over. 'You're getting prettier and prettier. All ugly girls grow up to be pretty,' she said, trying to be witty.

'Girls in love are the good-looking ones,' I said. 'What happened between you and Li Ming-Wei, anyway?'

She grew silent, as if she didn't want to dredge up the past. But then she briefly told me what had happened.

For a long time after they got married, their life seemed harmonious and trouble-free. They mixed in a social circle of similar professional couples, where parties and *shalong*, salons, were regularly held. The couples travelled, holidayed, chatted, dined, went to plays together, and generally complemented one another. She and her husband both liked athletic activities like tennis and swimming, and enjoyed the same operas and books. It was an uneventful life, leisurely yet not boring, with an adequate but not enormous income.

Behind the glossy facade of this life, however, lay a problem. She and her husband had had virtually no sex life since their wedding night, when she had screamed in agony during her first sexual experience. They were both still virgins, each the first and last object of the other's love. As a result, their marriage became slightly monotonous.

They didn't attach a lot of importance to sex, however, and gradually began to sleep in separate rooms. But early every morning her husband would knock on her door carrying breakfast, kiss her and call her his princess. Whenever she coughed, he would prepare cough syrup for her, and with the monthly arrival of her period, he would break out in an anxious sweat. He went with her to the traditional Chinese herbal doctor, and browsed with her in department stores. She spoke, and he listened attentively. In a word, they were a model couple in their modern white-collar circle, sex aside.

At the time, the film *Titanic* was all the rage. They went to see it hand in hand. I don't know what there was about it got to Zhu Sha. Perhaps the heroine's final choice, her refusal of a doting yet tiresome fiancé in favour of a short-lived romance with a passionate man. She used up a whole pack of tissues wiping her tears, and suddenly realised that she herself had never loved. And a woman nearing thirty who has never loved is a pathetic thing.

That night her husband wanted to spend the night with her. He asked if she wanted a child. She said no. Her mind was in chaos and she needed some time to sort out her thoughts. Adding a child to a loveless marriage would be an utter mess. Her husband was angry. She was angry too, and told him that when she said she didn't want a child, she meant it.

A rift opened between them. Her husband began to suspect she was having an affair. One evening he asked her why she had reversed her stockings; it turned out that in the morning he had noticed a trace of red nail polish on her left leg which was now on her right. Another time a friend called very late at night, and when she picked up the phone she heard the click of the extension being picked up too.

The loving breakfasts delivered to the door had long ago ceased, and once when she forgot her key he let her knock at the door for an hour . . . without opening it.

'It's horrifying when you really think of it. It's like the whole world has been turned upside down when the man you thought you knew so well can treat you like that. You've lived together five years, and suddenly you drop down to earth. In the blink of an eye he becomes a stranger – or even more horrible than a stranger, because he understands you and knows the most unbearable ways to torture you . . . That's men for you.' Zhu Sha spoke softly, her eyes red, shuddering at the painful memory.

'It's frightening.' I nodded. A gentle, cultivated, thoughtful and good man becomes a woman-torturing master of evil overnight. Truly frightening.

'Why is it that when a woman wants to leave a man, he assumes it must be because she's having an affair? Can't a woman make that choice based just on her own feelings? Do they actually believe that a woman can't exist without them?' asked Zhu Sha emphatically.

'They're just a bunch of self-deceiving idiots!' I consoled her as if I were president of the Association for Women's Rights.

# 9

# Who's Knocking at
# the Door?

'Don't come and bother me.
Don't knock at the door,
and don't write.'
William Burroughs

Someone was knocking at the door. The stereo was playing
Tchaikovsky's *Sleeping Beauty* at high volume, but I could
still hear the knocking. Tian Tian looked at me. 'Who is it?'
'Wouldn't be Madonna, would it?' I said. We didn't have many
friends. This was both our weakness and our charm.

I walked to the door and looked through the peephole. It was
a stranger. I opened the door a crack and asked who he was
looking for. 'If you're interested and have a moment, I'd like to
introduce our firm's newly developed vacuum cleaner.' His face
filled with a warm smile while his hand adjusted the tie beneath
his Adam's apple. It seemed all I had to say was 'Yes,' and he
would instantly launch into a speech.

'Well . . .' I didn't know how to handle this. You probably
have to be thick-skinned to dismiss a man rudely who is neither
unattractive nor threatening. The fact that he could wear a
cheap Western-style suit as neatly as he did conveyed his whole-
someness. One shouldn't deflate that kind of self-esteem.
Anyway, I had nothing to do.

Tian Tian watched in disbelief as I led the stranger inside. He took out a business card and presented it graciously to Tian Tian, then proceeded to open the large bag he was carrying and take out a shiny vacuum cleaner.

'What's he going to do?' whispered Tian Tian.

'Let him do his demo. I was too embarrassed to refuse him,' I whispered back.

'If he demonstrates it and you don't buy it, you'll be even more embarrassed.'

'But he's already started,' I said half-heartedly.

This was the first time I'd come across this sort of thing since moving into the apartment. The early nineties brought a *tsunami* of door-to-door sales to the city, a new phenomenon of the market-oriented economy, which has since gradually subsided. Today was a strictly random event.

Back bent, vacuum cleaner in hand, the stranger vigorously and repeatedly swept the carpet. The vacuum cleaner emitted a good deal of noise. Tian Tian hid in the other room.

'This machine features particularly strong suction. It can even vacuum up mites from your carpet,' the man said loudly.

I was taken aback. 'Mites?'

When he had finished vacuuming, he poured a pile of dirty stuff on to a newspaper. I was unwilling to look closely, afraid I'd see insects wriggling about. 'How much?' I enquired.

'Three and a half thousand RMB,' he said.

That seemed very expensive to me, though I admit I'm ignorant about the prices of things.

'But it represents good value. Wait until you have children, then its handiness will be even more obvious. It helps maintain a sanitary household environment.'

My face dropped when he mentioned 'children'. 'Sorry, I don't want to buy one.'

'I can give you twenty per cent off,' he continued, unfazed. 'Guaranteed for one year. We're a large, reputable firm.'

'Thanks. I've wasted your time.' I opened the door. Without batting an eyelid he put all his things away and left calmly. 'You have my card,' he said, turning round. 'If you change your mind, feel free to contact me.'

'Coco, you like to experiment with everything. You're always making trouble for yourself,' said Tian Tian.

'What trouble? At least he swept the carpet.' I sighed and sat down at the table. I really didn't know what Tian Tian was getting at with 'you like to experiment with everything'.

The sound of knocking came again, and I grabbed the door and opened it. This time it was the fat woman from next door. In her hand was a pile of water, electricity, gas and phone bills which had piled up in the postbox downstairs, plus two letters. I remembered it had been ages since we had checked the postbox. I thanked her, and she left chuckling.

Everyone in that district shares a warm-heartedness unique to the older Shanghainese. Almost none of them have any money to speak of. These laid-off housewives arrange their daily lives meticulously. Small, air-dried fish and pickled turnips hang from kitchen windows, and smoke from a coal stove drifts over from time to time. Kids in green school uniforms and red bandannas play ever-popular war games. Old people gather in a corner of the small park playing Big Ghost (a card game played between two teams of three), the wind occasionally ruffling their snowy beards.

To the majority of older Shanghainese, this kind of neighbourhood is what they know best, and it has a nostalgic air. To the new generation, it's a place that's been rejected and will eventually be replaced; a lowly corner devoid of hope. But when you've lived here for a while, you can appreciate its simplicity and vigour.

One of the letters was from Spain. 'It's from your mother.' Just then, he was lying on the bed. I tossed the letter into his hand. He tore it open and read a few lines. 'She's getting married . . . and she mentions you.'

Curious, I moved closer. 'May I read it?' He nodded and I jumped on to the bed. He hugged me from behind, and held the letter up with both hands for me to see.

'My son, how have you been lately? In your last letter you mentioned that you're living with a girl now, but you didn't describe her in detail (your letters are always so disappointingly brief). I am guessing that you really love her. I understand you. You don't easily get close to someone. That's very nice. At last you have someone to be your partner.

'The first of next month I will be getting married, to Juan, of course. We've been living together for a long time now, and I'm confident we can be happy together long-term. Our Chinese restaurant here is still going well. We are considering opening a restaurant in Shanghai in the near future. It will be an authentic Spanish restaurant. I long for the day when I'll see you again. I've never understood why you wouldn't come to Spain – it seems you have never trusted me, as if something bad has kept us apart – but time has passed so quickly, ten years have gone by and you have already grown up. But no matter what, you are my most beloved son.'

'If that's so, you and your mother can see one another.' I put the letter down. 'For ten years she never came to Shanghai to see you, and you never went there to see her. Pretty weird.' I looked at Tian Tian, who didn't look pleased. 'So I can't imagine what it will be like when mother and son reunite.'

'I don't want her to come to Shanghai,' said Tian Tian, his body leaning backwards and falling into his thick, fluffy pillow. He opened his eyes wide and looked up at the ceiling. The term 'Mother' had taken on a bizarre, unfathomable aspect in the tale

Tian Tian had told me. Clearly, it still carried with it the shadow of his father's death.

'My mother looked like a fairy with her long, long hair. She spoke very delicately and always wore perfume,' Tian Tian told the ceiling. 'Her hands were very soft, very white, and she could knit all sorts of pretty sweaters . . . That's how she was when I saw her ten years ago. She sent me some photos later, but I threw them all away.'

'What does she look like now?' I was filled with curiosity about this woman in Spain.

'I don't know the woman in the picture.' He rolled over, turning his back to me, annoyed. He was willing to send letters or postcards to keep in touch, but he couldn't imagine that one day she would stand before him in the flesh. That wouldn't do. If that happened, his defences would crumble. There are many mothers and sons in the world, but few like Tian Tian and his mother. A barrier of suspicion lay between them, and neither tenderness nor instinctive, blood-based affinity could overcome it. Their battle of love and hate will last to the end of this story.

The other letter was from Mark to me. Inside were two invitations and a brief note. 'You left a deep impression on me at that party. Hoping to see you again.'

I waved the invitations at Tian Tian. 'Let's go to the painting exhibition. That German guy Mark actually kept his word.'

'I'm not going. You go by yourself.' Tian Tian closed his eyes, looking unhappy.

'Hey, you always like exhibitions,' I said in disbelief. It was true. Camera on his shoulder, he would often go to all sorts of art, painting, film, book, sculpture, furniture, calligraphy, flower and car shows, even exhibitions of industrial machinery, lingering contentedly amid a mass of mind-boggling products. He was an out-and-out exhibition freak. They were a window through which he could secretly view the true face of the world.

According to my psychoanalyst David Wu, reclusive people are often also dedicated peeping Toms.

'I don't want to go.' Suddenly looking into my eyes, Tian Tian said, 'Is that German guy always so attentive to other people's girlfriends?'

'Oh, is that what you think?' I shot back. This sort of situation was very rare. When Tian Tian's eyes became suspicious, they turned cold as snails. It made me uncomfortable. But perhaps the reason I hit back so crudely was my own psychological weakness, as if sensitive Tian Tian had scratched open a hidden wound inside me.

Tian Tian clammed up and walked mutely into the other room. His back seemed to be telling me: 'Don't take me for an idiot. You danced the night away with him cheek-to-cheek, and then he came with us into our room here.' I closed my mouth too, speechless.

# 10

# Take Me to Your Place

'A healthy sex life. Best thing
in the world for a woman's voice.'
Leontyne Price

'Every woman adores a Fascist,
The boot in the face, the brute
Brute heart of a brute like you.'
Sylvia Plath, 'Daddy'

I went to the exhibition by myself. Liu Haisu Art Museum was a sea of heads, every sort of human effluvium thriving under the lights. You could smell that there were rich and poor people here, sick and healthy, artists and wannabes, Chinese and foreigners.

In front of a painting entitled *U-Shaped Transformation* I saw Mark with his golden crown towering in front of me. 'Hi, Coco!' He put one hand on my back, gave me a French-style kiss on both cheeks and an Italian-style hug. He looked happy. 'Your boyfriend didn't make it?'

I smiled, shaking my head, and pretended to concentrate on the paintings.

He stood constantly by my side, shadowing me as I moved through the gallery, his whole body diffusing a scent from another land. There was something disquieting in his casualness, almost like the restraint of a hunter confronting his longed-for prey. Most of my attention was focused on him, the paintings before me becoming a mass of chaotic colours and random lines.

The crowd wriggled forward slowly, and as we were crushed together, at some point his hand fastened on to my waist.

Two familiar faces suddenly jumped into my line of vision. Just over there, standing out from the crowd gathered in front of the third painting to my left were Madonna and Ah Dick, dressed to kill. They both wore trendy thin-framed glasses, and heads of painstakingly dishevelled hair. Startled, I hastily worked my way back into the crowd and moved in another direction. Mark and his questionable intentions stuck close to me, his hand on my waist like a pair of tongs, searing and dangerous.

The appearance of that sexy couple gave me a sudden urge to behave badly. Perhaps I'd been prepared to do the unthinkable from the very beginning. 'I just saw Madonna and her boyfriend,' said Mark, with his dubious but enchanting smile.

'I see them too, so let's get out of here,' I said, acknowledging what was on our minds. No sooner had the words escaped me than Mark seized me like a bank robber, allowing no argument, and dragged me out of the gallery in a flash, depositing me in his BMW. Basking in masochistic joy, my mind went kaput.

At that instant, all I needed was an ounce of self-control. I should have walked away from him right then, and none of what followed would ever have happened. But I wasn't the least bit cautious, and didn't want to be; I was twenty-five and had never longed for security. 'A person can do anything, including those things that should be done, and those that ought not.' Dali put it something like that.

When I opened my eyes wide and saw him lowering his body towards me, I noticed that the huge room was bottle-green, spacious and silent, and filled with the smell of a stranger and a stranger's furniture.

He kissed my lips, and suddenly lifted his head and laughed. 'Want a drink?'

I nodded vigorously, like a child. My body was cold and my lips icy. Maybe a drink would do me good. With a drink, I'd become a hot woman.

I watched his naked body get out of bed and walk towards the glittering bartop. He took out a bottle of rum and poured two glasses.

Next to the bar was a sound system, and he slid a disc into it. Surprisingly, the music was a ballad in the Suzhou dialect. An unfamiliar woman's voice sang out something, *yee yee ah ah*. I couldn't clearly hear the soothing Suzhou lyrics, but the effect was unique.

He walked over. 'Do you like Suzhou *pingtan*?' I asked, to make conversation.

'It's the best music to make love to,' said Mark. I drank some rum and coughed a bit. With a faint smile, he patted me on the back.

Yet another kiss, long and leisurely. This was the first time that I realised kissing before lovemaking could be so comfortable, steady, unhurried, enhancing my desire. His golden body hairs were like fine rays of sunlight, zealously and intimately nibbling at my body. The tip of his rum-soaked tongue teased my nipples, and then moved slowly downwards. He penetrated my protective labia with deadly accuracy, and located my budding clitoris. The cool taste of the rum mingled with his warm tongue, and made me feel faint. I could feel a rush of liquid flow out of my uterus, and then he went inside. His huge organ made me feel swollen. 'No,' I began to cry out. 'No way!'

But he showed no pity, never stopping for a second. The pain burst into a kind of apoplexy. I opened my eyes wide and looked at him, half in love, half in hate. I was aroused by his naked white body, only faintly coloured from the sun.

I imagined what he would be like in high boots and a leather coat, and what kind of cruelty would show in those Nordic blue eyes. These thoughts increased my excitement. 'Every woman adores a Fascist/The boot in the face, the brute/Brute heart of a brute like you . . .' wrote Sylvia Plath. I closed my eyes and listened to him moan a sentence or two in indistinct German, sounds from my dreams that struck the most sensitive part of my womb. I thought I could die and he would keep right on going, but then I climaxed with a sharp cry.

He lay at my side, his head cushioning a few strands of my hair. We wrapped our naked bodies in the bedsheet and smoked. Just in time, smoke clouds filled the void before our eyes, and we didn't need to speak. Sometimes one doesn't want to utter a sound; instead, you slip into a silent film, your mind at rest.

'How do you feel?' His voice seemed to rise above the mist, faint and light. He held me from behind, his big hands on my breasts, and we lay stacked against one another on our sides, two silver spoons shining a cool, metallic light.

'I'm going back,' I said listlessly. He kissed me behind the ear. 'Okay. I'll take you.'

'No need, I'll go by myself.' My tone was weak but definite.

When I sat up to get dressed, I was draped in depression. The passion and orgasm had passed. When the film is over and the filmgoers leave *en masse*, all you hear is the bang of seats returning to their upright positions, the sound of footsteps, throats clearing: the characters, the story and the music have all gone. But Tian Tian's face just wouldn't stop moving back and forth in my brain.

I dressed quickly, not even glancing at the man at my side. All men are uglier when they dress than when they undress; no doubt many women are too.

'This was the first and last time,' I told myself disingenuously.

The thought was temporarily effective, and I pulled myself together and marched out of that lovely apartment. I got into a taxi and Mark mimed he'd call me. I smiled vaguely. 'Who knows?' The car pulled away, as if escaping from him.

I didn't have a mirror in my bag, so I could only look at myself in the window. All I could see was a blurred phantom. I tried to think what my first words should be when I met Tian Tian. 'The exhibition wasn't bad. I ran into several people I knew, and of course, Mark was there . . .' Women are born liars, especially when they traffic between men. The more complex the situation, the more resourceful they are. From the moment they can speak, they know how to lie. Once, when I was young, I broke a priceless antique vase, and said the family cat had done it.

But I wasn't used to lying to Tian Tian and his eyes, where black was so distinct from white. But how could I avoid it?

As I walked into the dark hallway, I smelt spring onions, oil and fried meat: our neighbours were cooking dinner. I opened our door and switched the light on. But Tian Tian wasn't in his room, and there wasn't even a note on the desk.

I sat on the sofa for a moment, looking at the black leggings wrapped around my thin legs. A very short golden hair was stuck to my left knee. Mark's. Under the lamplight, it shone pale. I recalled the way Mark's head had moved downwards from my chest . . . I burnt that strand of hair until it frizzed to nothing. Then an uncontrollable fatigue engulfed me. I lay flat on the sofa, placed my hands on my chest like a corpse at peace, and quickly fell asleep.

# 11

# I Want to Succeed

'I don't pretend to be an ordinary housewife.'
Elizabeth Taylor

'Everywhere I go, I am asked if I think universities stifle writers.
My opinion is that they don't stifle enough of them.'
Flannery O'Connor

Novelists who long for the past always write something like, 'I want to sleep for ever and never wake up.' Psychoanalysts are endlessly digging up dreams from under pillows. When I was little my mother would wake me up every morning, make my breakfast, hand me my satchel and my head would be filled with the bubble-like remains of my dreams. I was a dream-loving child even when I was little. What makes me feel most liberated about my life now is that I can sleep just as long as I please. Occasionally, the sound of neighbours arguing, a noisy TV, or the shrill of a phone wake me up, but I can still bury my head in the covers and return to my interrupted dream. Sometimes, of course I can't get back to it. When I can't resume my romance with that unknown man I feel so frustrated I could cry.

My life with Tian Tian was a bit like a dream right from the start. I like that kind of dream – pure colours, intuitive and unburdened by loneliness.

Mark was perhaps one of the things that, like the sound of arguing or a phone ringing, could interrupt my dream. Of course, even if I hadn't met Mark I might have met someone else who would have seduced me. My life with Tian Tian had too many fine cracks that we couldn't mend on our own, so there was always the threat that an external force would make its way inside.

I woke in the middle of the night and realised that Tian Tian was back. He was sitting on the arm of the sofa, looking intently at my face and cradling a black-and-white cat. The cat was staring at me too. I saw myself in its liquid green eyes. Startled, I jolted upright and the cat jumped down from Tian Tian's arms, darting across the wooden floor and out of the room.

'Where have you been?' I asked, taking the initiative.

'I went to see my grandmother. She kept me for dinner,' said Tian Tian softly. 'It's been a long time since I went. Her cat had a new litter and she gave me a kitten. She's called Fur Ball.' His face was tender as he caressed my hair, my cheeks, my jaw and my slender neck. His hand was a little cold, but gentle.

My eyes widened at a sudden fear that he meant to strangle me, but the idea fled as fast as it came. A feeling of extraordinary remorse made me open my mouth, and I wanted to tell him everything that had happened. But Tian Tian plugged my mouth with a kiss. His tongue tasted bitter, and a scent like rain-soaked leaves spread through the room as we kissed. His hands were cascading over every inch of my skin and I felt sure that he knew everything; that his fingers could detect a stranger's secretions and particles on my skin. Tian Tian was so sensitive that one touch would set him off, almost like a madman.

'Maybe I should go to a doctor,' he said, after a moment of silence.

'What?' I looked at him sadly. Everything that had happened and was about to happen wasn't my wish. At that instant, we were utterly alone, and neither he nor I could leave.

'I love you.' I held him and closed my eyes. It sounded too much like a line out of a film. Even when you're sad it still makes you feel awkward to talk like that. My mind was filled with flickering shadows, like those made by a candle. Then a shower of sparks glittered before my eyes. My novel – my novel would explode like a firework and give meaning to our existence.

Deng, the editor of my short-story collection, phoned me. She's a middle-aged woman who lives alone with her middle-school-aged daughter, while her husband studies in Japan. She has all the characteristics of a middle-aged Shanghainese woman: the pale complexion of a neurotic, her hair always up in a bun, wearing leather pumps and narrow, midi-length poly-cotton skirts. She has a passion for ice cream and gossip of all sorts.

With her help I had published *Shriek of the Butterfly*, which provoked such curious reactions. Everyone was whispering about this risqué book, and rumour had it that I was a bisexual with a predilection for violence. Students were caught stealing my book from bookstores.

I got letters, with erotic photos enclosed, from men via my editor, wanting to know what my relationship was with the heroine of the book. They hoped for a dinner date with me at Saigon Restaurant on Hengshan Road, dressed up as one of my romantic characters. Alternatively, they offered to take me for a ride in a white VW Santana 2000 GSi, and make love to me in the car when we got to Yangpu Bridge. It was all like something out of a tabloid.

But to get to the point, I didn't earn much money from it, because after the first printing of a few thousand had sold out, there was no second printing. When I asked Deng why, she said the publishing company had recently had some management problems, and I should bring the matter up a bit later. I'd been waiting ever since.

My boyfriend at the time, Ye Qian, said what I wrote wasn't suitable for young readers; I'd gone too far, and that was it for that book. And once the book had run its course, so had my brief relationship with him.

He was a bit of a lad with a devil-may-care attitude who worked for a big advertising house. I met him when I was interviewing the firm's English boss. He looked intelligent, sharp and pretty laid-back. I don't know what it was that made him hit on me, because at the time I was still suffering from a bout of male phobia, thanks to that pint-sized ex-boyfriend of mine, and preferred to find friends among women.

But he very patiently chatted me up, and having listened to my story of failed romance, stood up and announced: 'See how tall I am? And I haven't any bad intentions. I just want to get to know you better, that's all.'

That very night he successfully improved his knowledge of me, from my breasts down to my toes, from heavy breathing to loud cries. He was tall and handsome, and his balls warm and clean. When I held them in my mouth, I got that sense of unquestioning trust that the act of sex bestows upon one's partner. His penis moved like a corkscrew. His straightforward lovemaking healed my grey memories, and restored my healthy attitude to sex. He patiently taught me how to distinguish between clitoral and vaginal orgasms, and often made me climax both ways at once.

In the end, he made me believe that I'm luckier than many women. The statistics say some seventy per cent of Chinese women have some sort of problem with sex, and ten per cent have never had an orgasm.

My relationship with Ye Qian lasted several months, and happened just as my book was being published. My impulsive state at that time brought him, and the sex he brought with him, into my life. When *Shriek of the Butterfly* had sold out, and I couldn't hear the sound of money jingling in my pocket, we parted without argument or ill will, rationally and harmlessly.

Tian Tian is from a different species to my earlier men. He was a foetus soaking in formaldehyde who owed his life to unadulterated love, and his death was inextricably linked to that love. He couldn't give me a complete sexual experience, and I couldn't keep my body unsullied for him like a piece of jade. Everything was unfathomable. Perhaps my love grew from how greatly I was needed; however much he needed, that was how much I provided. Tian Tian needed my existence like he needed oxygen and water, and our love was a bizarre crystal formed by the oppressive atmosphere which surrounded us.

It was early autumn, and the air had the dry, cool smell of tobacco or petrol. My editor phoned to ask, 'How are things going with your novel?'

'Okay,' I said. 'I might be needing an agent.'

'What kind of an agent?' she asked.

'Someone who could help me realise my dream and avoid the problems I had with my last book,' I explained.

'Tell me more.'

'My dream is one that any smart young woman would have, and that's the kind of person I'm writing for. There should be a road show with parties throughout China to promote the book. I'd wear a backless black dress and a grotesque mask. The floor would be littered with confetti made from my book, and everyone would be dancing madly on it.'

'My God,' she laughed. 'You're crazy.'

'But it's do-able,' I said, taking exception to her laugh. 'All we need to make it happen is the cash and the brains.'

'All right,' said Deng. 'There are a few authors holding a literary event in Shanghai. One of them's a young woman a bit older than you. Ever since she married a famous critic, she's been dying to find inspiration from every hair that falls from his head. You should meet them. It might be useful.' She named a restaurant on Xinle Road and said she would be there too.

I asked Tian Tian if he'd like to go with me, but he pretended not to hear. He had a low opinion of most other authors.

I agonised for a long time over what to wear. My wardrobe is divided into two distinct styles: one is androgynous, loose-fitting with quiet colours, and makes me look like something out of a medieval painting, the other tight-fitting, foxy clothing, like some cat-lady. I tossed a coin and went for the latter. The 1960s retro look from the West – purple lipstick and eyeshadow, and my leopard-look handbag – very chic in Shanghai just then.

The taxi made me dizzy racing around in circles. The cabby was new, on the job for just a few days, and without realising it he brought us back to our starting point. I've no sense of direction to speak of and just kept yelling at him, so we ended up driving one another mad. I saw the meter ticking away and threatened, 'I'm going to make a formal complaint.' He said nothing. 'Because you're not acting in the best interests of your customer,' I added for effect.

'Okay, okay. What's the big deal? I won't charge you.'

'Hey. Just stop here,' I said, seeing a familiar light and large glass window with lots of blond heads moving about behind it. 'That's right, I want to get out here.' I had changed my mind and decided to forget about meeting up with Deng's authors. Why not look for a bit of fun here at YY's Bar, run by Kenny?

YY's has two floors. The lower one, down a long staircase, houses the dance floor. The atmosphere in the room was joyous, full of alcohol, perfume, money, saliva and hormones.

I saw my favourite DJ on the stand, Christophe Lee from Hong Kong. When he noticed I was there, he made a face at me. They were playing House and Hip-Hop, both totally cool, like a raging blind fire. The more you danced, the happier and more unfettered you felt, until you were vaporized out of existence and your right and left lobes were both quaking – then you knew you'd reached the peak.

There were plenty of fair-haired foreigners, and lots of Chinese women, their tiny waistlines and silky black hair their selling points. They all had a sluttish, self-promoting expression on their faces, but in fact a good many of them worked for multinationals. Most were college graduates from good families, some had studied abroad and owned their own cars. They are the *crème de la crème* of Shanghai's eight million women, but when they were dancing they looked tarty. God knows what was going on in their minds.

Of course, some were prostitutes who specialised in the international market. They often wear their hair incredibly long (the better for the foreign devil to admire his Asian woman's magical hair when she's pressed close beneath him and he's in sexual ecstasy). Most can speak basic English ('A hundred for a hand job, two for a blow job, three for a quickie, five for an all-nighter') and like to focus on their targets, licking their lips sensually in slow motion. You could shoot a film called *Chinese Lips* just describing the amorous adventures of foreigners at hundreds of bars in Shanghai. It would begin with lip-licking, all sorts of lips: generous and thin ones, black lips, silver lips, red lips, purple lips, lips with cheap lipstick, lips with Lancôme or Christian Dior lipstick. The movie *Chinese Lips*, starring all the seductive women of Shanghai, would be more successful than the Hollywood blockbuster *China Box*.

When I dance, my mind fills with fantasies and inspiration gushes forth, the result of feeling uninhibited. I should have a laptop-toting secretary glued to my every move, especially when I'm dancing to techno music, to take down all my hallucinations. That'd be a thousand times better than anything I write at my desk.

I'd already forgotten where I was. A smell of marijuana (or cigar?) found a nerve centre in my right nostril. I figured I'd already attracted the eyes of plenty of men with my dancing – like a princess in a Middle Eastern harem, and a bewitching Medusa, too. Men are often desperate to mate a bewitching female who will eat them alive, like a black widow spider.

I looked down at my silver navel ring, shimmering madly under the lights, like a poisonous flower on my body. A hand from behind hugged my naked waist. I didn't know who it was and didn't much care, but when I turned round, smiling, I saw it was Mark. He lowered his face towards mine, exhaling hot breath smelling of a James Bond Martini. His voice was low, but I could still hear him saying he wanted me, here and now. Muddle-headed, I asked: 'Here? Now?'

We were pressed up against each other in the grubby women's lavatory on the second floor. The music seemed far away. I was getting cold and I could hardly keep my eyes open, but I kept Mark's hands at bay. 'What are we doing here?' I asked.

'Making love,' he said, using the glib phrase without insincerity. On the contrary, his blue eyes were anything but cold. Waves of tenderness radiated from them. No one could ever understand how pure desire could cause the seamless intimacy that we achieved in that smelly toilet!

'I feel totally disgusting, like a criminal – and even more like I'm being tortured . . .' I murmured.

'The police will never find us here. Trust me. Everything's perfect.' He put on a film-gangster voice. He propped me up against the purple wall, lifted my skirt, nimbly slipped off my CK underpants, balled them up and stuck them in his hip pocket. Then he forcefully lifted me up and, without another word, rammed accurately inside me. Sitting on his big red cock felt like sitting on a fire hose.

'You bastard!' I screamed, unable to control my language. 'Put me down right now. This won't do. I feel like a specimen nailed to a wall!'

He gazed at me, full of passion. We changed positions. With him sitting on the toilet, I sat on him. That way I could direct his movements to suit my sensitivity.

Someone was knocking at the door, but the perverted couple inside the toilet weren't done yet.

Orgasm approached amid feelings of dread and awkwardness, yet once again it was perfect, despite the uncomfortable position and the smell. He pushed me aside, pulled the cord attached to the suspended tank, and his semen disappeared with the swirling water.

I began to cry. This was all so inexplicable. I was increasingly losing my self-confidence, and suddenly felt even cheaper than the prostitutes dancing downstairs. At least they had profession-alism and a certain coolness, while I was awkward and horribly torn between two personalities. I couldn't stand the face I saw reflected in the grimy mirror. Something in my body had been lost, leaving a gaping hole.

Mark hugged me. He kept apologising, 'Sorry, sorry,' holding me as tight as a dead baby, which only made me feel worse.

I pushed him away and pulled my pants out of his pocket, put them on and straightened my skirt. 'You didn't rape me,' I said, low but harsh. 'No one could. Don't keep saying "Sorry, sorry". It's so rude. I'm crying because I look ugly. If I cry I'll feel a bit better, you know?' I said.

'No, you're not ugly,' said Mark, in that stern way of his.

I smiled. 'No, I mean the day will come when I'll die ugly. Because I'm not a good girl, and God doesn't like girls like me. Though I do like myself,' I said, beginning to cry again.

'No, no, baby. You don't know how much I care for you. Really, Coco.' His eyes were utterly tender, and in the washroom light that tenderness became sorrow.

Someone was knocking at the door again, no doubt a woman who had come to the end of her patience. I was scared to death, but he signalled me not to speak and calmly kissed me. As the sound of footsteps receded, I pushed him gently away. 'We can't see each other again.'

'But we'll run into one another. Shanghai's very small.'

We left the washroom quickly. 'I'm going,' I said as I walked out of YY's. He wanted to drive me home, I insisted I didn't want him to.

'All right,' he said, waving for a taxi. He took a note from his wallet and put it in the cabby's hand. I didn't stop him. I sat down inside. 'I still don't feel good. I feel ashamed.' He leaned over and kissed me. Neither of us mentioned Tian Tian.

The taxi radio was tuned to 'With You Till Dawn,' and the DJ was listening to a housewife pour out her heart. Her husband was having an affair, but she didn't want to divorce him; she just hoped the other woman would disappear, but didn't know how to win back her husband's heart. The cabby and I were silent. City dwellers are used to listening absent-mindedly to the intimate details of others' lives. But we don't sympathise, and we can't help.

As the cab drove up on to the flyover, I saw a sea of lights, magnificent and astonishing. I imagined all the stories that were happening in every corner of Shanghai, at the source of each of those lights; so much noise, unrest and fighting – and so much emptiness, indulgence, joy and love, too.

Tian Tian was still up. He was lying on the sofa with his cat Fur Ball, holding a notepad and writing a long letter to his mother in far-off Spain. I sat down beside him and Fur Ball ran away. He turned abruptly and looked at me, and my heart jumped, afraid that once again he had sensed the smell of an unfamiliar male. I have to say that Mark had a slight body odour, an animal smell which I always enjoyed.

But Tian Tian's eyes were as cold as ice and I couldn't stand it. I nervously got up and walked towards the bathroom. He lowered his head and kept writing.

Hot water poured out of the tap and steam condensed on the mirror until I couldn't see my face. I breathed a sigh of relief, lowered myself into the hot water and relaxed. Whenever trouble looms, I hide away in a hot bath. The water is so hot. The mass of my black hair floats about like a water lily. All the memories I recall then are happy and lovely.

Whenever I remember my childhood, I see myself sneaking off to Grandma's attic. There's a broken old leather chair on wheels, and a big red sandalwood chest covered in dust, with copper-plated corners. When I open the chest, there are blue ceramic tiles with 'Salt' on them, scraps of fabric used to make a *qipao*, and other arcane objects. I used to sit all by myself on that broken leather chair, playing with those things as the sky darkened through the dormer window, bit by bit.

'Nikki,' Grandma called me, but I pretended I hadn't heard. Once again: 'Nikki, I know where you are.' Then her plump silhouette climbed the stairs. I rushed to close the chest, but my hands and clothing were already dirty. 'Don't keep climbing about up here,' said Grandma, annoyed. 'If you like these things so much, I'll give them to you as your dowry.' But later, when the Shanghai city government built the subway, the old French-built block was condemned, and in the hustle and bustle of moving those treasures of my youth were lost.

With my feet poking out of the water, I thought how childhood events always seem so far away, as if they happened in a previous life. Except for that feeling of tenderness one relives so vividly, everything seems fake.

Just then the bathroom door opened and Tian Tian came in. His eyes were red, and he knelt down by the bath.

'Finished writing?' I asked softly.

'Yes,' Tian Tian said, focusing silently on my eyes. 'I told Mother to forget about coming to Shanghai to open a restaurant. When I went to Grandma's I mentioned it to her and Grandma said she'd be coming back just in time, because she still wants to square accounts with her . . . I don't want Mother to come either. It's better to get by on my own until I die . . .' His voice sounded dismal, and he started crying.

'Coco, no matter what, don't ever lie to me.' He fixed his eyes on mine, and an invisible chisel slashed my heart. A dense, terrifying silence seeped out like blood. The more hopelessly in love you are, the more you get caught up in deceptions and murky nightmares.

'I love you,' I said. I hugged him tight and closed my eyes. Our tears ran into the bath and the water grew hotter and hotter, darker and darker, and finally turned into boiling plasma, devouring our sobs and our fears. From that night on, I swore to myself that I wouldn't reveal anything about Mark or our affair to Tian Tian. Not one bit of it.

# 12

# Dejeuner sur l'Herbe

'Oppose monotony, support diversity,
oppose inhibitions, support wild passion,
oppose unanimity, support hierarchy,
oppose spinach, support snails in their shells.'
Salvador Dali

It was afternoon. The autumn sun illuminated the street and the crowds, casting a faint brush-stroked shadow. The trees sprouted hints of autumn, yellowing leaves dangling from branches like ageing insect specimens. Wind blew on your face, bringing a burst of coolness.

Things happen in quick succession in daily life, making one forget the changing seasons and how easily time passes.

Tian Tian actually went to the Reproductive Health Care Centre, and the first day I went with him.

The atmosphere of the building was unpleasant. There was something stifling in the air. The hallway, posters and doctors' faces were too sanitised. The examining doctor wore a large pair of glasses, his eyes expressionless. He put the relevant questions to Tian Tian, writing forceful notes on the medical history form.

'When was your first nocturnal emission? Do you sometimes wake up to an erection in the morning? When you read *those* sorts of books or watch *those* sorts of movies, do you normally have a reaction? Never had a successful instance of intercourse –

by which I mean, were you able to insert yourself and maintain an erection for more than three minutes? Does your body typically have any other irregular reactions?'

Tian Tian grew increasingly pale, his forehead covered in tiny beads of sweat, and he could barely speak in complete sentences. I sensed that, had I taken his hand and pulled him up just then, he would have darted out of the room at lightning speed. I sat in the corridor while he was led into a treatment room next door. He looked awful, as if he might faint at any moment. As he got to the door, he glanced at me with sheer terror in his eyes.

I covered half my face with my hand. For Tian Tian, this was just too cruel.

A long wait. The treatment room door opened, and out came the doctor followed by Tian Tian, his head down, not looking at me. The doctor scribbled away on the diagnosis form. 'Your reproductive system is quite normal,' he said to Tian Tian. 'The key lies in your mind.' He recommended that Tian Tian join a psychiatric therapy group at the centre, and take some medicine as a supplementary treatment.

And so a new routine was introduced into Tian Tian's life. He went once a week to the Reproductive Health Care Centre, staying a few hours each time. It probably wasn't the treatment itself that got him hooked, but rather the group of victims who shared their similar secrets with him. Everyone formed a circle and took turns speaking out, sharing their pain and tensions with a sympathetic audience. Suffering within a group helps dispel an individual's internal anxieties, according to David Wu.

Tian Tian soon tired of the centre and its therapy group, but he befriended one fellow-sufferer, a young man called Li Le, and occasionally invited him to join in our circle of friends.

Autumn is made for outdoor activities, so we held a picnic

on the lawn at the Xingguo Guest House. That afternoon the sun shone lazily on us, and our noses were tickled by the smell of Lysol carried by the wind from a nearby clinic. The view was lovely, the many layers of greenery and buildings contrasting with one another in the warm colours of an autumn day.

A checked blanket was spread out on the lawn, with some enticing dishes arranged on it. Our friends were scattered about like chess pieces, seated or prone, like Manet's famous painting *Dejeuner sur l'Herbe*. That scene, overflowing with mid-nineteenth century bourgeois atmosphere, is something I've always yearned after.

Anyway, living too much indoors is oppressive; reflection, writing, silence, dreams and imagination can bring one to the brink of madness. Scientists have proved, through totally inhumane experiments, that locking a human alone in a closed room for four days is enough to make him shoot out through a window like a stone from a catapult. It's easy for a person to go mad.

On the postcard my father sent me (he and Mother were travelling in Hangzhou), he wrote: 'My daughter, try to walk outdoors more often. Grass and fresh air are the most precious gifts life can give you.' In those days he used maxims and aphorisms to communicate with me.

Li Le came, wearing grubby-looking but trendy clothes. He was scrawny with big eyes and a shaven head: my first impression of him was that he swore a lot. He also pinched the tip of his nose all the time, until it was red and pointy. I didn't like him. The word was that at the age of ten he began chasing older women and at eleven was seduced and lost his virginity to the mother of a classmate.

After that he went to bed with more than fifty women of both his mother's and his elder sister's generation. A year before, he'd been caught in bed with someone's wife. The husband gave him a nasty beating and cut off the long hair he had been so proud of, and he became impotent after that.

The son of displaced intellectuals, both sent away from Shanghai, he had no one to watch over or care for him. He was working as a salesman for one of the Adidas stores on Nanjing Road. He often practised the drums in a basement, and organised an informal rock band of his own. Rock music became a temporary substitute for sex, soothing his youthful body and soul. What impressed Tian Tian about Li Le was not just his strange attitude to life (uninhibited, unassertive, naive, marching to his own beat), but also because he loved to read and to ponder life's mysteries.

Zhu Sha also accepted my invitation to our lawn party, and she brought a present for me – a bottle of Shiseido skin toner. She said she'd brought it back from a business trip to Hong Kong, where it sells for a hundred RMB less than in Shanghai. It had been a while since I'd seen her, but her lady-like air remained unchanged. It looked as if she'd got out from under the shadow of her divorce.

'I heard from Auntie that you've started to write a novel?' she asked, smiling at me as she sipped a carton of fruit juice through a straw. Sunlight shone faintly on her, and she smelt sweetly of young grass. 'Oh, by the way,' she said, pulling out a name card for me, 'this is the company I'm working for now.'

I looked at the card and went dumb for an instant. Wasn't that the investment consultancy where Mark was?

'Right, I'm writing a novel. I hope it'll be a bestseller so I'll have enough money to go travelling in Europe,' I said.

'And your boyfriend? Are you still stuck in the same room all the time? I can't imagine a life like that. Doesn't at least one of you want to get a job outside? It's not good for you. It could make you ill,' said Zhu Sha delicately.

'We often go out for a walk, or sometimes to a bar for a

drink, or go dancing,' I said. I was thinking that if I were to travel to Europe, Tian Tian would certainly be willing to come along. Travelling doesn't just give you a change of time and place, but to some extent it can also influence one's mental and physical well-being. I fantasised about making love with Tian Tian in some hotel in a small French town (he'd be okay there), and later in a German motel, an abandoned small church in Vienna, the Roman Coliseum, a motorboat in the Mediterranean . . . The story would unfold little by little – as long as there was love and desire, freedom and love would encircle the forests, lakes and sky.

I walked over to Tian Tian, sat down and kissed him. He stopped his conversation with Li Le and smiled back at me. 'Let's play Frisbee,' I said.

'Okay.' He stood up. Under the sun, he looked terribly young, like a schoolboy, with his close-cropped black hair, striped black cotton shirt and limpid eyes.

Our eyes met for a few seconds. A fresh passion aroused my body, and I could feel my heart thumping. He laughed again. The Frisbee flew back and forth like a tiny UFO, until it landed at Zhu Sha's feet. Zhu Sha smiled and passed it to Tian Tian. She was chatting with Ah Dick, and seemed to be enjoying her conversation.

When Madonna had finished discussing something with friends from the Xingguo Guest House, she came over and joined in playing Frisbee. Go-kart ace Number Five and his girlfriend Cissy were sunbathing, their bare backs to the sun, playing a board game called Airplane. They were both wearing dark glasses, and with their pale backs exposed in broad daylight, were unquestionably a couple made for each other.

Suddenly an older woman, a severe-looking foreigner, appeared before us. Madonna and I walked over to her, while the others kept playing. 'Excuse me. I'd like to request you all to leave,' she said in American-accented English, with a heavy twang.

'Why?' I asked in English.

'Well,' she shrugged, 'my husband and I live in the building right across from here,' she said, pointing. On the far side of the lawn I could see a lovely three-storey, French-style building beyond the low enclosing wall. A beautiful but useless chimney towered over it, and there were stained-glass windows and two balconies, surrounded by ivy-clad balustrades sculpted with flowers. 'We always enjoy the view of this stretch of grass from our balcony.'

'So what?' My English was rather rude. But I didn't want to be particularly polite. What on earth did this old American lady want, anyway?

'But you-all have spoiled the serenity of the lawn here. You're too noisy and too disruptive,' she said authoritatively. There was something frosty about her blue eyes that conveyed she would not be defied. She had a head of silver hair like my grandmother, and the same lines on her face, but there was nothing grandmotherly about her at all.

Speaking in a low voice in Chinese, I told Madonna what the old woman wanted. 'What? She actually wants to chase us out?' Madonna got all pumped up at the old lady's ridiculous request. She's the kind of person who refuses to be meek in the face of aggression. She likes a fight.

'You tell her that this lawn doesn't belong to her, so she has no right to ask such a thing.'

I relayed Madonna's meaning to the old woman.

She began to laugh, as if to say 'You vulgar Chinese woman.'

Madonna lit a cigarette. 'We won't be leaving, so perhaps our esteemed old lady should go home and take a rest,' she said.

The old lady seemed to understand, but continued in a

measured tone. 'My husband is the President of Meiling Bank. We decided to rent that house precisely because we took a fancy to this stretch of lawn. We are both old, and we require good air and a clean environment. Finding a decent lawn in Shanghai isn't easy.'

I nodded in agreement. 'It's not, and that's why we've come here to relax, too.'

The old lady smiled. 'Do you rent, too?'

I nodded.

'And how much is your rent?'

'That's my business, not yours.' I smiled.

'Our rent is twenty-five thousand US dollars a month,' she said, one syllable at a time. 'That price is related to this lawn. You Chinese know that a good neighbourhood commands a high price. So I'm asking you to leave at your earliest convenience.' She was smiling, but her tone was harsh.

Frankly that price surprised us. There was no way of knowing how powerful she and her President husband really were, or whether they had a special relationship with the guesthouse management. Madonna, to prove her street-savvy, feigned a smile, but got her English wrong. 'OK,' she said. 'We'll be leaving. See you late.'

On our way back we all talked about that sign in Shanghai's former French Concession: 'Chinese and Dogs Keep Out.' Now that the multinational corporations and financial giants were staging a comeback, their economic clout would undoubtedly give them a sense of the foreigner's superiority. For the first time, we Chinese 'Generation X'ers' felt a direct threat to our own self-esteem.

Mark called that evening when Tian Tian was in the bath.

'Don't call me again. It's not right,' I said in a low voice.

He agreed. 'But how will I find you?'

'I don't know. Perhaps I'll call you.'

'You could get an e-mail address,' he suggested in all seriousness.

'Fine,' I said. But then I couldn't resist telling him what had happened that afternoon. 'If you were living in that building, would you chase us out?' I asked severely. It was virtually a diplomatic test, one that involved national self-esteem.

'Of course not,' he replied. 'Or how could I keep on ogling you out there?'

# 13

# Departure

'I saw his huge face over the plains with the mad, bony purpose and the gleaming eyes; I saw his wings; I saw his old jalopy chariot with thousands of sparking flames shooting out from it; I saw the path it burned over the road; it even made its own road and went over the corn, through cities, destroying bridges, drying rivers.'

Jack Kerouac

December, a cruel season. No lilacs blossom in the century-old, secluded courtyards. No beauties dance naked on the stone steps of the garden or through the gaily-decorated arcade at Takashi's Le Garcon Chinois restaurant on Hengshan Road. No pigeons, no joyful outbursts, no blue shadows of jazz music.

Winter drizzle floats dismally, and leaves a bitter taste on the tip of one's tongue. The dampness in the air makes you rot, rot right into your brain. The Shanghai winter is wet and disgusting, like a woman's period.

Tian Tian decided to travel. Every year at this season he would leave Shanghai for a time. He couldn't bear the cold, damp weather; even the occasional sunshine is grey and gives you goosebumps when it shines on you.

'I want to get away for a while,' he said.

'Where to?'

'To the south, some place where there's more sunshine and bluer sky, like Haikou.'

'Want to go alone?'

He nodded.

'Okay. But take care of yourself. You've got an IC phone card, so you can call whenever you like. I'll be here in the apartment writing my novel.'

The thought that I'd never be able to finish this novel frightened me. But with Tian Tian gone I'd have more time to myself, and a sense of physical space. I don't know if Tian Tian knew whether or not his trip was a temporary escape from the threat posed by our daily contact. He was a hundred times more sensitive than a normal person. At times, our affection bound us too closely together, and when we could no longer breathe freely and our creativity was at a low ebb, then perhaps it was time to travel.

Besides, Mark had begun to embed himself in the weakest link of our love, like a tumour. The tumour existed because of a virus spreading in a certain place in my body – and that virus was sex.

Many people think love and sex shouldn't be lumped together. For many liberated women, finding a man she adores and who adores her, and who can give her an orgasm, is the ideal arrangement for her personal life. These women would say, 'Separating love and sex needn't conflict with a healthy attitude to life.' Women's intuition and aspirations are shaped by the daily grind, and they look for a lifestyle that gives them a sense of security. They put the key that can unlock life's secrets under their pillows. They have more freedom than women of fifty years ago, better looks than those of thirty years ago, and a greater variety of orgasms than women of ten years ago.

The Dazhong taxi ordered by phone was parked downstairs. I made a final check of Tian Tian's luggage: a carton of Ted

Lapidus cigarettes (you can only get them at specialist outlets in Shanghai), Gillette razors, mouthwash, five pairs of white underpants and seven pairs of black socks, a Discman, Dylan Thomas's selected poems, Salvador Dali's diary, a filmography of Alfred Hitchcock and a framed picture of us. In another bag was the kitten, Fur Ball, whom Tian Tian insisted on taking. Then we grabbed an umbrella and got into the cab. Since he was taking the cat he couldn't go by plane and was taking the sleeper to Haikou instead.

Raindrops struck the taxi windscreen. The streets were shrouded in grey, and shops and pedestrians were like running colours with distorted lines. Tian Tian was finger-painting in the condensation on the window, making weird symbols. The radio was playing a sugar-sweet pop song, 'Girl Over There, Look Over Here', by Richie Ren.

As our taxi approached the station, Tian Tian grabbed my hand and placed it on his lap. I began to feel indescribably uneasy. We were going to be separated for two months. We would suddenly discover the other wasn't next to one's pillow. No one would bang on the bathroom door wanting to shower together. There would be no need to cook for two, or to wash two people's clothes. No worrying about the other's misgivings or tears. No hearing each other talking in our sleep.

There were still a lot of migrant workers milling around in the rainy square in front of the station. I reminded Tian Tian to put his ID, credit card, IC phone card and train ticket somewhere safe. We went up the escalator to the second floor where tickets were already being checked, and then Tian Tian, holding the bag with Fur Ball on his right and suitcase on his left, waved to me and followed the flow of people surging towards the platform.

Outside, the rain had stopped. I took the bus, and when it got to the Maison Mode department store, I jumped off. This section of Huaihai Road has a foreign air that has been adapted to popular Chinese tastes, and clusters of the fashionable young hang out there. Huating Road is where young people go to catch up on the latest trends. Small it may be, but it embodies the innate ability of the Shanghainese to exploit every inch of space. Everywhere you look are enticing, inexpensive clothes, as well as handbags, shoes, hats, handicrafts and toys. This street, which features in all the guidebooks to Shanghai for overseas visitors, follows international fashion closely, and prices are much cheaper than anywhere else. Once I saw a beaded silk handbag priced at 250 RMB in the Hong Kong Commodity Fair at the Shanghai Exhibition Centre, but that afternoon on Huating Road I bargained the same model down to 150 RMB.

Whenever I'm feeling down, like other girls I go to Huating Road, stroll from one end to the other, and buy up a storm. But when I take home the heap of things I've bought – beautiful enough to float away in – I usually only wear them once or twice, because I bought them in a bad mood. There isn't a single style that isn't exaggerated or X-rated. They're only suitable for dressing up like Marilyn Monroe and viewing oneself narcissistically in the mirror at home.

On Huating Road there were plenty of Chinese and foreign teenagers dressed as street toughs. A team of Japanese boys on roller skates looked like mounted butterflies as they showed off their techniques, their dyed hair like feather dusters. A Shanghainese girl with black lips strolled next to her silver-lipped companion, licking Fruit Treasure lollipops. There were concerns that girls like that would ingest too much cheap lipgloss and die of poisoning, but to date there's been no official report of it happening.

Among the crowd came a group of smartly-dressed businessmen, one of whom raised his hand and greeted me warmly. I thought he must be waving at someone behind me and walked on without acknowledging him. But he kept waving, and called out my name. I stared at him, surprised.

'Hey, I'm Spider!'

I wondered if today were April Fool's Day. The Spider I knew was a youth between school and job, with criminal impulses and a frighteningly high IQ. I'd assumed that by now he was either a hacker busy robbing banks or still working half-heartedly at some day job and spending his nights in front of a computer, infatuated with cyberspace.

But the young man in front of me was wearing a pair of those frameless glasses so popular with white-collar men, bright white teeth and a healthy smile. 'Oh my God! You don't even recognise me.'

'Oh my God' was Spider's mantra.

I laughed. 'You're looking *piaoliang,* cute,' I said.

'So are you,' he said, without satire. His every gesture was measured.

The street-side Manabe Café. We sat down facing one another. The fragrance of coffee is so aromatic it can poison you over time, and a lot of people become addicted, sitting in cafés all afternoon. Even if they while away one-fifth of their lives in a café, as long as they have the illusion that they've distanced themselves from the heavy burden of their work, that's good enough for them. And there's the music, never disturbing, and the staff who look like male dancers.

Our conversation touched on the Green Stalk Café. 'That's a neat place,' said Spider. 'Too bad that when I was working there I was only thinking of earning a buck.'

'And how to pry open the safe,' I teased.

'Oh my God! Don't mention that again. I've reformed.' He laughed. He handed me his business card with *Golden Apple Computer Company* on it, and said it was a little company he had started up with a few college classmates, specialising in software development, network installation and computer sales. Things were just beginning to look up. 'I reckon we'll be coining it by the year's end.' He was still swollen with the desire to make money, but he was more rational about it now.

'What about Enchantress? Still in touch?' I recalled his former girlfriend on the web.

'We often meet for coffee, to see a film or play tennis.'

'Thank heavens. The premonition I had about her must have been wrong. It seems you and Enchantress really hit it off. Will you marry her?'

'No way. Enchantress is a girl on the net, but in real life she's a guy,' he quickly corrected me. Seeing my surprise, he went on: 'Of course, we're just friends, period.' He laughed, not caring if I believed him or not.

'If he pretended to be a girl on the web to attract boys, he must have some sort of complex,' I said.

'Yeah, he's been thinking of having a sex-change operation for a long time. I hang out with him because he's kind and smart. He knows I'm not gay, but we can be friends, right?'

'I'd really like to meet this Enchantress. He sounds special.'

# 14

# My Lover's Eyes

'The warm bodies
shine together
in the darkness,
the hand moves to the
center of the flesh,
the skin trembles in happiness
and the soul comes joyful to the eye.'
Allen Ginsberg

That night I couldn't write a word. There was a haze in my brain, and I felt like a fly searching endlessly for a bit of food to drop on. But my hunt didn't yield any inspiration. The novel had brought me a new worry. I didn't know how to disguise myself effectively to my readers. In other words, I didn't want to mix my novel up with my real life, and to be honest, I was even more worried that, as the plot developed, it could have an impact on my future.

I've always believed that writing is like sorcery. Like me, my heroine did not want to lead an ordinary life. She is ambitious, has two men, and lives on an emotional rollercoaster. She believes in these words: suck dry the juice of life like a leech, including its secret happiness and hurt, spontaneous passion and eternal longing. Like me, she was afraid that when she went to hell there would be no films to watch, no comfortable pyjamas to wear, no heavenly sounds of records to be heard; just suffocating boredom.

I smoked a cigarette, paced about, turned up the volume on the stereo and even went through Tian Tian's drawers to see if he hadn't left a few scraps of paper as a nice surprise for me. Finally I turned to Mark's phone number in my address book. Should I call him? Tian Tian had just left, and there I was thinking about calling another man. I frowned at the thought.

But then two excuses occurred to me. First, I don't love the man, so he can't take Tian Tian's place in my heart: his face has nothing but lust on it. Second, his mobile phone might be turned off anyway.

So I dialled a string of digits and heard the long ringing tone on the other end. I exhaled smoke, distractedly examining the fingernails on my left hand. My well-manicured nails accented my tapered fingers. For an instant I envisioned my two hands climbing along Mark's athletic lower back, like spiders, teasing and pressing lightly, and the hissing sound of pheromones being released and their scent swirling about in the air.

A woman's voice suddenly came from the other end of the phone, interrupting my reveries. 'Hello!' she said.

Spooked, I instinctively said, 'Hello.' Then I asked: 'Is Mark there?'

'He's in the bathroom. Would you like to leave a message?' She spoke English with a thick German accent.

I politely said no; I would contact him later. Depression hit me. So the German had a lover – or it could be his wife, of course. He'd never talked about his personal life, and I'd never asked. So far, our relationship had been limited to a fuck here, a fuck there.

I lay depressed in the bath, surrounded by rose bath bubbles, a bottle of red wine within reach of my right hand. This was my most vulnerable but also my most narcissistic moment. I fantasised that a man would push open the bathroom door, walk over to me, skim the bubbles and rose petals off the water, and scoop out ecstasy from the most secret part of my body. Look how I quiver like a flower petal being shredded in the hollow of his rough hands. Look how my eyes moisten with shame under the light. My mouth opens and closes as the tide swooshes back and forth, and my legs beat like wings, opening and shutting in harmony with the sensation of pleasure.

I remembered how Tian Tian had so often used his incomparable poetic fingers to perform an act of sexual hypnosis on me, somehow more than simple carnal pleasure. Yes, a kind of hypnosis in which layer upon layer of mist was peeled away, piercing the very centre of love. My eyes closed, I drank red wine and caressed the spot between my legs. This torment made me understand why in the film *Burnt by the Sun* Aleksandr chooses to die in a bath.

The telephone rang. 'Tian Tian,' I cried out in my heart, opening my eyes wide, as I grabbed the handset mounted on the wall to the right of the bath.

'Hello, it's Mark.'

I took a breath. 'Oh!'

'You just called me, didn't you?' he asked.

'No I didn't!' I said. 'I didn't fucking call you. I've been bathing, by myself and happy . . .' I hiccuped drunkenly, then chuckled.

'My wife told me that a girl with a Chinese accent called when I was in the shower – I guessed it must be you,' he said, as if he held the winning lottery ticket, dead certain I must be pining for him.

'So you have a wife.'

'She just arrived from Berlin to spend Christmas in Shanghai. She'll be going back in a month,' he said in an oddly consoling tone, as if this news would upset me.

'She must be quite busy, eh? Oh, did you change the sheets? I'm sure you did – or she'd smell the scent of a Chinese woman.'

I laughed light-heartedly, realising I was a little drunk. Feeling tipsy is marvellous. You can see the positive side of everything, like when a fog lifts.

At twenty-five, my resilience was very strong. Even if he said he wanted to break up, or go to Mars for that matter, it wouldn't drive me to despair. I could handle our relationship in a clear-headed manner.

He laughed too. Christmas was just around the corner, his firm would be closed for a good long vacation, and he hoped we could get together. He spoke in Chinese, so I guessed his wife must be there, unable to decipher a word. Men will pursue the object of their desire even in front of another woman. They will say, 'Loving you and being faithful to you are two different things.' Most men can't adapt to monogamy. They have fantasies about three thousand concubines hidden away in an imperial harem.

Mark said that in a few days a journalist friend of his would be arriving from Germany and he'd like to introduce us, as this friend wanted to interview some unusual young Shanghainese women.

Having dinner with a lover and a journalist is no bad thing. Before I went out, I dressed carefully. I love that narcissistic feeling when I pencil my eyebrows, apply blusher and roll on my lipstick; for this alone I'd choose to be reborn as a woman. A careful understated toilette, a reserved elegance nonetheless capable of stunning onlookers – Shanghainese women are innately calculating, as is apparent in the subtlest details.

My horoscope says black is a lucky colour for my sign. I wore a tight-fitting, high-collared black shirt, and a pair of boots with frighteningly high heels. My hair, which I put up, was held in place with an ivory hairpin, and on my wrist was a silver bracelet Tian Tian had given me. Dressed like this I felt safe, knowing that I was pretty.

M on the Bund, known for its pricey but not very tasty cuisine, is a restaurant run by a pair of Australian sisters. Business isn't bad, and *laowai*, who work in the newly developed Pudong district to the east, meet up and cross the harbour to dine there. With its two-metre-high lighting fixtures and ornate balustrade, the décor is grand but soulless, although perhaps it appeals to the severe aesthetic of Mark and his race. The main attraction is the huge balcony outside the restaurant, where you can lean on the balustrade and view both sides of the city on the Huangpu River.

Mark's journalist friend, with black eyes and black hair, was called Ruanda, and his grandparents had emigrated from Turkey to Germany. At first we chatted about football and philosophy. Talking to a German about football can make one feel a bit inadequate, but when it comes to philosophy, China's no slouch. Ruanda worshipped Confucius and Lao Tzu, the former encouraging him to wander the world in search of eternal human truths, the latter consoling him when he was in pain or lonely, a bit like morphine.

At his suggestion, I began to talk about my life, including my collection of short stories and the bizarre reactions to them, my views on the generation gap, and my various boyfriends. When I mentioned Tian Tian, I looked at Mark, but he pretended not to have heard, cutting a slice of roast lamb in a vegetable sauce.

I was very forthright. Tian Tian was my only love, a gift from God. Even though I'd always felt that our love was doomed, I didn't want, couldn't, change anything about it. I would never regret it, to the day I died. As for dying, I wasn't afraid of that, only of a boring life, so I wrote. My spoken English wasn't all that good, and some of what I said to Ruanda had to be interpreted by Mark.

Mark kept pretending that we were just friends, but he couldn't help fixing his eyes on me. Then he told some funny stories, like the time when he had just begun learning Chinese and kept confusing the word for 'wallet' with 'foreskin'. One day he had invited a Chinese colleague to dinner and when they were halfway to the restaurant he felt his pocket, and said awkwardly: 'Excuse me, I haven't got my foreskin with me.'

I burst out laughing. He talked a lot of business, and his jokes were all off-colour. His hand searched for my leg under the table. That's risky behaviour, as I wrote in one of my stories: in one scene the hand finds the wrong leg. But he found my knee without error, tickling me. I couldn't help laughing. Ruanda said: 'Keep smiling just like that, and I'll take a few pictures.'

In Chinese, I asked Mark: 'This kind of interview isn't up to much, is it? Won't it just feed the desire for novelty, writing about a vast and mysterious oriental country, and a young, rebellious female author?'

'No, not at all. I like your stories a lot, and I'm sure you'll be widely respected,' said Mark. 'One day your books will be translated into German.'

After dinner, we went to the Goya Pub on Xinhua Road, well known for its forty-plus recipes for a Martini, its sofas, candelabra, sensuous draperies, and absolutely hypnotic music. I like the owners, an attractive couple returned from the USA. The woman, Song Jie, is a not bad painter, and the whiteness of her face is the most mysterious I've seen, the kind that can't be imitated, no matter how much powder one applies.

We ordered our drinks, and I asked the bartender to change the music. I knew Goya had *Dummy* by Portishead, and only that kind of music complements this kind of drink.

Tian Tian and I used to come here often. It's like an old ship at the bottom of the sea. From time to time, drowsiness presses down from the ceiling, weighing on your brain, putting you in a trance. The more you drink, the deeper you sink into the sofa. Occasionally someone drinks and drinks until his head tilts crookedly in sleep on the back of the sofa, then comes to, takes another sip, and dozes off again until startled back to consciousness by the distant laugh of a pretty girl. In fact it's an extraordinarily dangerous world of gentleness, and when someone wants to lose himself for a bit, he hops in a cab and comes here. I often run into well-known painters, musicians and paparazzi here, but even if we know one another from elsewhere, here we just nod and say, *ni hao ma*.

Mark was sitting next to me saying something in German to Ruanda, and the language separated me from their world. I amused myself drinking. Leaning back and drinking is marvellous, and I recalled a swan from a dream of mine. I lost myself in romantic fantasies. Mark's hand stealthily came to greet my waist.

Suddenly my cousin Zhu Sha and a familiar man's face appeared in my field of vision. I opened my eyes wide. Their hands intimately linked, she and Ah Dick came in and almost immediately noticed me. Their reactions betrayed nothing out of the ordinary, and they quickly came over to us.

Mark recognised Zhu Sha and greeted her by her English name. 'Hi, Judy.'

So Zhu Sha *was* working for Mark's company!

Hearing me introduce her as my cousin, Mark looked puzzled. 'You don't resemble one another at all. But you're both enchanting and clever,' he added in clumsy flattery. Perhaps unexpectedly running into one of his firm's junior staff here – and one who happened to be the cousin of his secret lover – put him off balance. I could imagine a different Mark at work, prudent, thorough, rigorously demanding, a man who means what he says to his staff, and who always does things by the book. A well-oiled, high-precision machine, like the German clock on our apartment wall which is never a second out.

Zhu Sha seemingly guessed my relationship with Mark,

smiled and winked at me. I noticed she was wearing a G2000 coat with an hourglass silhouette. Standing tall and straight, she looked like a model on a poster for the *Paris Printemps* department store.

But what intrigued me was something else: Ah Dick was with my cousin, hand in hand, obviously not just friends, looking like a couple madly in love. And where was Madonna?

The music and alcohol made me drowsy, and I dozed. When I woke, Zhu Sha and Ah Dick had left, and Ruanda wanted to return to the Galaxy Hotel where he was staying. 'I'll take you back to your hotel,' Mark said, then turned to me, 'then I'll drive you home.'

Maybe I'd had too much to drink. I leaned my head against Mark's shoulder, and smelled both a flowery fragrance and a hint of body odour from the vast lands of Northern Europe. The exotic scents of his body were perhaps the most moving thing about him.

The car stopped at the Galaxy Hotel, where Ruanda got out, and drove on towards my apartment. I nestled obediently in Mark's silent embrace. Outside the window, slabs of city blocks and street lights sped by, and I realised that I still didn't know what I meant to him. But it didn't matter; he wouldn't divorce or go broke for me, and I hadn't dedicated all my light and passion to him. Life's like that. Days and years are idled away in releasing our libido and shifting the balance of power between men and women.

We arrived at my place. I admit I was feeling a bit emotional: one tends to after drinking. Mark got out of the car and came up with me, and I didn't say 'No'.

Just as he began to undress me, the phone rang. I picked up the receiver and heard Tian Tian's voice.

His voice was distant but clear, though I could hear the intermittent crackle of static and a cat's miaow. He said he was staying at a hotel near the beach and, thanks to the East Asian financial crisis, rent and food were both very cheap, no more than 200 RMB a day. When he went to the herbal sauna room, he was the only guest. He sounded very happy, and said Fur Ball was too. He planned to go swimming at the beach the next day.

I couldn't think of anything to say to him. Mark picked me up and placed me on the desk next to the phone. I was holding the handset in one hand while my other hand clutched his shoulder. His head was arched over my stomach as he licked at my private parts through my underwear, giving me an incredible prickling sensation and making me feel weak all over. I tried to sound natural, asking Tian Tian how hot it was there, what kind of skirts the girls were wearing, and if he had been to the coconut groves. No one was targeting him, were they? People might look indifferent, but that didn't mean they were – he should look after his money and possessions.

Tian Tian laughed, and said I was an even more hard-core sceptic than he was, not trusting in anything, always looking on the bad side, and deep down, holding a negative view of life.

His words floated like feathers into my ears, then disintegrated: nothing was getting through. His laughter made me feel that he was able to adapt to an unfamiliar environment better than I'd expected. His voice became music, like Beethoven's *Moonlight Sonata*, taming the confusion inside me. I only felt a surge of joy coursing upwards from the soles of my feet, and this joy that relaxed my muscles and bones was white, one hundred per cent pure milk with a mellow aroma. Tian Tian wished me a good night, and gave me several very noisy kisses over the phone.

When I put the phone down, Mark unloaded his semen on to my skirt; so white, so much, like one hundred per cent pure milk.

'Forbidden fruit is sweeter', goes the saying. At Tian Tian's funeral, when I began to remember many earlier things, I recalled that phone call, and it took on a sort of symbolic significance. It was as if it wasn't someone else, but rather Tian Tian, inside me, via a telephone wire traversing ten thousand *li*. His low voice was right there in my ear, the sound of his breathing and his laughter present in the most sensitive place in my heart. My eyes closed, and for the first time I felt the incomparably real and perverse carnal sensation Tian Tian gave me; a lissom, putrid, swishing air flow, a baptism where our souls communed. I've always been fascinated by the idea of souls communing, and this was also the first time I felt the uncanny sensation when body and heart mesh, an almost religious experience. But the most important thing was the vague but maddening thought that sooner or later I would bear a child. A light wind lifted a golden flower in the foggy darkness, and a winged infant took flight in the darkness. It was this man's, or that one's. It was this time, or that.

When Mark had gone I found his wallet on the floor, the object he had repeatedly misnamed his *baopi*, foreskin, when he had first arrived in China. Inside were his Visa and Master cards, Grand Club VIP card, and a family photo. Only then did I learn that he not only had an elegant wife with a winning smile, but also a three- or four-year-old son with curly gold hair and blue eyes like Mark's.

I opened my eyes wide and shook my head. They looked so happy it was enough to make one envious. I kissed Mark's handsome face and then, without even giving it a thought, removed a few bills from the fat stack of RMB notes in the wallet, and slipped them inside a book. He wouldn't notice he was missing a few small bills. When you've dealt with *laowai* for a while, you realise that most of the time they're as simple-minded and direct as children. They like what they like, and when they don't, they tell you right out. And they aren't petty, unlike Chinese men who sometimes fuss over the smallest details.

Afterwards I wondered what was behind my petty thievery. I decided it was possibly caused by envy of the happy family mood in that photo. And there was also a subtle desire to punish my German lover in it, making him lose some RMB without knowing it, and then long for me passionately as always.

I had no expectations to speak of for our relationship and felt no responsibility for it. Sex was just that, and I could use money and betrayal to defend myself against the threat of it metamorphosing into love. From the start, I had feared truly falling for Mark, and being incapable of leaving this red-hot, titillating, utterly satiating secret affair.

Half an hour later Mark knocked at my door, gasping for breath. I handed the Yves Saint Laurent wallet over to him, and he gave me a kiss, stuffed the wallet in his pocket, smiled, then turned and ran down the stairs.

I watched him slip back into his BMW, which disappeared quickly down the empty street.

# 15

# Cold Christmas

'I wasn't doing anything.
I just kept waiting for Edmondson to call.'
Jean-Philippe Toussaint

David Wu sat in his leather swivel chair, blowing his nose repeatedly. The evening newspaper reported that Type A3 influenza was hitting the city, and residents should pay attention to hygiene and ensure that they were getting enough sleep, nutritious food and good ventilation to avoid falling ill. I opened the window, sat next to it in the fresh air, and tried to get comfortable.

'I often dream of a room where there's a potted sunflower. The blossom wilts, its seeds drift away and grow into more sunflowers. It's terrifying. There's also a cat that wants to eat the flowers. When he jumps up, he falls out the window, and disappears. Suddenly I'm outside the room watching all this, my heart racing. And there's another dream about a box. When I open the box I find a smaller one inside it, and when I open that one, there's an even smaller one inside, until the very last box, which disappears leaving me with a book in my hand, quite heavy, and then I want to send this book to someone, but I've forgotten the name and address.'

David Wu looked benignly at me. 'You have a deep-seated fear that your body will undergo some sort of change and that your writing will be blocked. An anxiety about becoming pregnant, for instance, or the prospects for your book. You long for your dreams to come true, but there's always something standing in your way. Do you know what I mean? All of this comes from a cell you've created for yourself in your imagination. As Thomas Morton said: "The only true pleasure in life is to escape from the prison of one's own making." Let's talk about your love life.'

'It's not that bad, but it's not complete.'

'What are you worried about?'

'A feeling of emptiness which I can never dispel, and at the same time, my heart is swollen with a love of sorts, but I can't release it. The boy I love can't give me sexual satisfaction, and worse, he can't give me a sense of security. He smokes drugs, and he's disengaged from the world. Now he's carried his kitten off to the south, and it seems as if he could leave me at any time. I mean, for ever. Meanwhile, a married man is giving me physical satisfaction, but has no impact on my emotions. We use our bodies to interact, and rely on them to sense each other's existence, but they're also a protective layer between us, keeping us from connecting mentally.'

'Fear of loneliness is what teaches us to love,' said David.

'I think too much, and 99.9 per cent of men don't want to get involved with a woman who thinks too much. I can even remember my dreams and write them down.'

'That's why we say life isn't simple. It's not everyone who can value her every thought and action. You already know what to do. Use your mind to overcome your despair. You won't accept mediocrity, and you're naturally very attractive.' His words were soothing, but I didn't know if that was just how he always consoled female patients. Ever since I had chosen him as my psychoanalyst, I rarely asked him out to eat, play tennis or go dancing any more, for fear of having my every move analysed.

The sunlight poured in as dust danced about, like fragments of thought. I sat on the sofa, my hand cradling my head, asking myself if I really understood myself as a woman. Was I really attractive? Wasn't I a bit hypocritical, snobbish and fuzzy-minded too? The problems of my life stacked up one on another, and it would take an entire lifetime just to overcome them.

Christmas. No one called me all day. At dusk the sky was grey, but it wouldn't snow. For a long time now in Shanghai it hasn't snowed when it should. I watched videos all day and smoked a pack and a half of Mild Seven cigarettes. Suffocated by boredom, I called Tian Tian, but no one answered. Halfway through dialling Mark's number I dropped the idea. Tonight I wanted a man I could just talk to.

Agitated, I circled the room. At last, I decided I had to leave the apartment, for where I didn't know, but I had money in my handbag and my face was made up. I believed that whatever should happen that night would happen.

I hailed a taxi. 'Where to, miss?' he asked.

'Just cruise around for a while.'

Outside the window, the streets were full of people in holiday mood. Christmas isn't part of Chinese culture, but it gives the young, trendy crowd an excuse to revel to their hearts' content. A stream of lovers entered and left restaurants and department stores in pairs, their hands grasping shopping bags full of sale bargains. Yet another night filled with foaming joy.

The cabby kept trying to make conversation but I didn't pay much attention. The radio was playing a guitar solo, and then the disc jockey buzzed in, talking about a band which had broken through the clutter of the so-called 'new voices of Beijing'. Then, oddly enough, I heard a familiar name: Pu Yong.

A few years ago, when I was still working for the magazine, I'd gone to Beijing to interview him and his band. We'd ended up walking hand in hand across Tiananmen Square. He stood on the overpass and said he wanted to stage a piece of performance art for me, ripped open his fly and pissed up into the air. Then he held my face in his hands and kissed my lips. He intrigued me, but I was worried that if we made love he would demand to pee on my body, or something else kinky. We'd never been more than friends and saw each other rarely.

Pu Yong's voice came on the air. He answered some lame questions from the DJ about writing music, and then he began to take listeners' calls. 'Does China have any rock'n'roll it can call its own?' asked one girl. Another boy asked Pu Yong what kind of musical inspiration he got from girls. He cleared his throat a few times, and unloaded a bunch of bullshit on these kids in a deep, sexy voice.

'Wait for me here a few minutes,' I told the cabby.

I got out of the taxi, walked over to a phone booth at the kerb and inserted my IC card. I got through easily.

'Pu Yong, *ni hao*,' I said gaily. 'This is Nikki.' Next I heard the sound of an exaggerated and exciting greeting: 'Hi, Merry Christmas!' He didn't call me *baobei*, baby, bearing in mind that he was on a radio show. 'Why not come to Beijing tonight?' he said in a carefree tone. 'We're doing a gig at the Busy Bee Bar, and then we're having an all-night party.'

'OK. On Christmas night I'll fly to Beijing to hear your music.'

I hung up and paced a bit around the phone booth, and then resolutely dived back into the taxi. 'To the airport, the faster the better,' I told the cabby.

There was a Beijing-bound flight just after five. I bought a ticket and then had a coffee in the café next to the departure lounge. I didn't feel happy as such, just no longer cross or at a loss; at least at that instant I had a goal, something to do – to fly to Beijing for a lively rock'n'roll show and get through a Christmas without lover or inspiration.

The plane took off and landed on schedule. Every time I take a plane, I'm afraid it will fall out of the sky, because big, bulky metallic things do so. But I still love flying.

I went off for a good supper on my own, not having touched a bite on the plane. Beijing restaurants are a bit pricier than those in Shanghai, but the food's okay. I was repeatedly eyed up by the northern men at a nearby table. That typical northern look can thoroughly reassure a single Shanghainese girl in Beijing for Christmas. At least it tells her she's attractive.

The Busy Bee Bar, where rockers congregate, hosts countless long- and short-haired musicians, their faces sickly but their buttocks taut in tight-fitting pants. They compete over who can play the fastest guitar, and argue about the best tricks for picking up girls. All the *guroupi* here have huge busts like Hollywood starlets. This is one of the essentials (including money, power, talent, looks, and so forth) for attracting the bad apples of the music circle.

The music was raucous, and the smell of tobacco, booze and perfume was overpowering. Across a hallway as dark as a blackout, I saw Pu Yong. He was smoking and stringing silver beads together.

I walked over and tapped him on the shoulder. He looked up, smiled broadly and then put the things in his hands into those of the girl sitting next to him and gave me a fierce hug.

'So you really came? Crazy Shanghai woman. How are you?' Pu Yong examined my face carefully. 'Seems you're a lot thinner. Who's mistreating you? Tell me and I'll put him in his place. Mistreating a pretty woman isn't just wrong, it's a sin.' It's said that Beijing men can utter one truckload after another of impassioned bullshit, but they forget it as soon as they've finished saying it, and no one brings it up again. But I still enjoy this way of consoling, hot as a flame and cool as ice cream.

We kissed one another loudly, and he gestured to the girl at his side and introduced her: 'My friend Lucy, a photographer,' and to

Lucy, 'This is Coco from Shanghai. She's a Fudan grad and writing a novel.' We shook hands.

She had already finished stringing the silver beads, and Pu Yong took the bracelet and put it on his wrist. 'I broke it when I was eating,' he murmured. He brushed his hair back and signalled the waiter. 'How about a beer?'

'Thanks,' I nodded.

There were people fixing the wiring on the stage, and it looked as if the performance would soon begin. 'I went to your place, but you weren't in. Oh, right, can I stay the night?' I asked Pu Yong.

'Hey, don't sleep, party all night. I'll introduce you to some cool studs.'

'I'm not interested,' I grimaced. His girlfriend pretended she didn't hear us talking. Her expressionless gaze emerged from low-hanging hair on both sides, focusing on something in the distance. She had a pretty nose, long, shiny hair and full breasts, and wore a long, yellowish-green linen skirt made of flax shot through with exotic colours like the Nile.

A divine man walked in. He was so handsome that it made your heart ache, and made you afraid that you might fall for him – only to be rejected. He had smooth skin, a towering body and glistening hair that stood vertically on his head like wild grass. His eyes were mist and poetry, and he squinted like a fox when he looked at someone. His features were aquiline, with a Bohemian air. A rounded goatee on his chin, added a brutish, *linglei* element to his otherwise clean, good looks.

He obviously knew Pu Yong and Lucy, and came over to say hello. Pu Yong introduced us. His name is Flying Apple, and he's a stylist famous in Beijing and throughout China. With his US green card, he flies around the world to hunt for the latest trends and inspirations for beauty. Every woman in show business in China counts herself lucky if she can get him to be her fashion consultant.

We began to chat and he kept smiling, his eyes glistening like peach blossoms. I couldn't help feeling uncomfortable. I didn't dare look his way too often, for fear of ogling. I certainly wasn't planning on a romantic encounter that night. Women whose lives are littered with ex-lovers are a dime a dozen. When they pass thirty, their faces reveal their lack of inhibitions. I sometimes wish men would treat me as a writer and not as a woman, I thought to myself disingenuously.

The band came on the stage. The electronic guitar roared like a beast in the jungle, and the crowd was instantly alive. Their bodies rocked back and forth as if they'd been electrified, their heads flipping about like they might fall off at any moment. I moved into the crowd and swayed in unison, happy because I wasn't thinking; I had relinquished control to the hell-fire music.

Faces shone blue, ankles stiffened and strangers flirted in the red-hot atmosphere. A fly couldn't have flown unscathed through this catastrophe of high-decibel, fast-moving particles.

'I'm soooo happy,' sang the man on the stage hysterically.

Flying Apple stood next to me, and smiled as he touched my bottom. I couldn't stand this beautiful man, this bisexual whose smiling face bore the tell-tale signs of make-up. Powder had been applied to his eyebrows, sideburns and cheeks. He courted men and women, and said his girlfriends were all jealous of his boyfriends. He was forever trapped in romantic complications and unsure of his direction. I said: 'There are eight billion peasants in our country still trying to scrape a living, so you're a very lucky guy.'

He said he found me intelligent, and intriguing, with my tranquil face and securely-fastened buttons like a proper young lady. I said 'fuck' several times. I didn't respond to him, but I secretly thought that he was attractive enough to drive me crazy. I never liked to swear.

'You've got a cute ass,' he shouted in my ear. The music was too loud.

At 2:30 a.m., there was no moon in the sky, but there was chilly frost on the rooftops. The taxi drove through Beijing, the city vast as a medieval forest.

At 3:00 a.m., we came to the home of another member of the rock'n'roll brotherhood. The room was huge. The hostess was a *laomei*, an American, once a well-known *guroupi* who had seen the error of her ways and married a drummer, also a *big-nose*. The drummer had fenced off a small greenhouse, in which, it was said, he grew marijuana. A group of people drank, sang, played mahjong and computer games, danced a bit and spoke words of love.

At 4:00 a.m., there were people making love in the Jacuzzi; some had already fallen asleep, others were on the sofa groping one another, and the rest of us left to go to a Xinjiang restaurant to eat hand-pulled noodles. I held on to Pu Yong's sleeve, afraid of getting lost in Beijing at night. Being alone at that hour would not just be no fun, it would be terrifying, because the winter night air cut like a knife.

Flying Apple had disappeared; he wasn't among those eating Xinjiang noodles with us. I came up with five possibilities, one being that he had gone off with someone, another that he had taken someone off. Who knows? He was the ever-beautiful hunter or hunted. Fortunately, I hadn't given him my phone number, or I would have felt upset, as if I'd been abandoned. Coco at Christmas is me at my most bored and pathetic.

At 5:30 a.m., I took some pills and lay down on the sofa at Pu Yong's house. The sound system played some serene pieces by Schubert. Everything was peaceful, but for the occasional truck on the road outside. I couldn't get to sleep. Sleep was like a shadow with little wings that flew far away from me, leaving behind a wide-awake consciousness and a weak shell of a body. The deep grey darkness soaked through me, and I felt swollen, very light, yet very heavy. This illusion of being transported to another universe isn't particularly unpleasant; caught between a dream and reality, unclear whether one is dead or alive, except that your eyes can still open wide and see the ceiling and the darkness everywhere.

I finally picked up the phone, leaned against the sofa and called Tian Tian. He still wasn't properly awake. 'Who am I?' I asked him.

'You're Coco . . . I called you, but you weren't at home,' he said softly, with no hint of reproach, as if he were confident I would have arranged everything just right.

'I'm in Beijing,' I said, as my heart was seized by a sharp wave of tired tenderness. I didn't even know why I was in Beijing at this moment. I was so agitated, a heart that never knew where it belonged, floating here and there, never resting, so tired, so useless. I had nothing, just taking a plane from here to there, just sleeplessness night after night. Neither music nor drink nor sex could save me. I just lay there in the heart of darkness like one of the living dead, unable to sleep. I thought to myself, God will marry me to a kind blind man, because all I see is darkness. I began to sob over the phone.

'Don't cry, Coco. It makes me feel very bad. What's the matter?' asked Tian Tian, bewildered. He still hadn't come out of the deep, heavy sleep induced by the sleeping pills he took every night (as I did).

'Nothing really, my friend's gig went just fine, I'm feeling quite excited . . . But I can't get to sleep. I feel like I'll die with my eyes open . . . I don't have the energy to go back to Shanghai, and you're not in Shanghai. I miss you . . . When will I see you again?'

'Come down south, things are great here . . . How's your novel going?' he asked.

As soon as he mentioned my novel, I fell silent. I knew then I'd go back to Shanghai and go on writing. That was how Tian Tian liked me, and I knew it was my only possible choice, or I would lose the love of too many people, including myself.

# 16

# Magnificent Madonna

'Don't accept rides from strange men –
and remember that all men are strange as hell.'
Robin Morgan

'Give a girl the right shoes
and she can conquer the world.'
Marilyn Monroe

I went back to Shanghai. Life went on its chaotic yet predestinate groove.

I felt like I was getting thinner. My body fluids were becoming black ink, oozing out of me into my pen, trickling into each word and phrase I wrote.

Takeaways from Little Sichuan Restaurant arrived regularly, delivered by Little Ding. When I was in a good mood, I lent him some books to read. Once he brought a short piece that he'd written for 'Voice from the Heart', a column for migrant workers published in Shanghai's the *Xinmin Evening News*. I read it and was surprised to find his style wasn't bad at all, and his thinking quite original. He shyly told me that his dream was to write a book. Kundera says that in the twenty-first century any of us can become an author. All we need do is pick up a pen and tell our own stories. The desire to pour one's heart out to others is a spiritual need common to every human being.

Dressed in my pyjamas, hair dishevelled, I would write through the night. In the early mornings, when I awoke and lifted my head from the desk, there would be purple ink marks on my forehead. The room would be empty and quiet. Tian Tian wouldn't be there, nor would the phone have rung (but then, I kept disconnecting the phone and forgetting to plug it back in). Then I would go to my bed, lie down and sleep some more.

One night around ten o'clock I was suddenly jolted awake by a knock at the door. I was grateful, because it came just in time to save me from a nightmare. I'd been dreaming that Tian Tian was aboard an old-fashioned steam train packed with strangers. I looked on helplessly as the train started to move, brushing close by my face. A man wearing military uniform and a steel helmet leapt aboard, but I hesitated for just a second and the train roared past me. I cried in utter despair, hating myself for having misread my watch or mistaken the departure. In that last second, maybe I simply lacked the nerve to jump on the train. To me, the dream suggested that Tian Tian and I were passing in the night.

I opened the door to find Madonna, dressed in black, a cigarette dangling from her lips. She looked particularly slender and long-legged in black.

My mind was still clouded by my dream, so I didn't notice anything unusual about her at first. She did seem to have been drinking, and she was wearing too much Opium perfume as well. Her hair was bundled on top of her head like a woman from the old days, and her eyes shone like glass. Something about her made me feel uncomfortable.

'God, have you been banged up here all this time? Still writing without a break?' She took a few steps into the room.

'I was just having a nightmare.' As I spoke, I suddenly realised I hadn't eaten anything all day. 'Have you had dinner yet?' I asked.

'Okay, let's go out and have a decent meal. My treat.' Madonna stubbed out her cigarette butt, tossed me her overcoat, sat down on the sofa and waited for me to get ready.

Her white VW Santana 2000 was parked outside. She opened the car door and started up the engine. I sat down beside her, buckled up, and the Santana took off with a screech. The car windows were all open. I find smoking in the wind a real pleasure, creating the illusion that all your worries are being blown away. Madonna drove up on to a flyover. Ever since these began appearing around Shanghai, a band of speed demons has also emerged. The stereoplayer played a love song by the Taiwanese pop star Jeff Chang: 'Have you got another guy?/Don't worry about hurting me./Just come out and say it.'

It was then that it dawned on me that Madonna wasn't quite herself. Suddenly I recalled running into Ah Dick and my cousin Zhu Sha at the Goya Pub, and then I got the picture.

Madonna is someone people just can't read. Her lifestyle is just too impromptu, carefree and intense. I've never been able to guess with any accuracy just what kind of past, present and future belong to her. And I couldn't tell if she was serious about Ah Dick, because the way she talked, she'd had plenty of lovers like him. On that basis, one shouldn't expect him to be the last dessert on her menu.

'What would you like? Chinese? Western? Or Japanese?'

'Whatever,' I replied.

'Now that's a cop-out. I hate it when people say "Whatever, whatever." Give it some thought and make a choice.'

'Let's go Japanese,' I said. The city has a strong preference for things Japanese. Songs by Anmuro Namie, books by Murakami Haruki, TV shows by Kimura Takuya, countless Japanese-style comics and Japanese-made electrical appliances have won the hearts of the Shanghainese. And I love Japanese cuisine and cosmetics, which I find refreshing and refined.

Madonna stopped the car outside the Edo Restaurant on Donghu Road. Light poured on to the floor tiles like liquid amber as the neat waiters, dressed in puppet outfits, moved purposefully about the restaurant. One by one, orders of chawan mushi, tuna sushi, pickled cucumbers, and dried shrimp and seaweed soup were served.

'Did you know that I split up with Ah Dick?' she asked, looking gloomy.

'Really? Why?' I really didn't know the ins and outs of it, but I didn't want to admit that I'd seen Zhu Sha with Ah Dick at the Goya Pub. Zhu Sha is my cousin, and Madonna is my friend, so I had to try to be impartial.

'Have you still got your head buried in the sand? Your cousin Zhu Sha stole my man,' she snorted, and downed her glass of sake.

'Is there any chance Ah Dick made the first move?' I asked calmly. Zhu Sha is a lady through and through. In the morning she takes an air-conditioned bus or taxi to the office, wearing impeccably applied make-up. At noon, she orders an 'Executive Set Lunch' in a western-style café or restaurant. And in the evening, when the colourful lights have just begun to glow, you'll find Zhu Sha among the women parading past the windows of Maison Modes department store on Huaihai Road, where the latest world-class brands are displayed in quiet glory, then on to the Changshu Road escalator down to the subway, their recently refreshed faces showing a hint of satisfied fatigue.

It's because Shanghai is home to so many women like Zhu Sha that it's become a city whose vibrancy is tempered by feminine elegance. The aimless ennui of Eileen Chang's unmarried women and the refined melancholy of Chen Dan-Yan's writing are rooted here. Some people call Shanghai 'The Women's City', but that's probably in comparison to the macho cities of northern China.

'I thought I had Ah Dick figured, could guess his every thought, but somehow I didn't guess that he'd lose interest in me so quickly. I've got a lot of money, but I'm ugly, aren't I?' said Madonna, smiling as she touched my hand and turned her face a bit towards the light.

What I saw was a face which couldn't be called pretty, but one also not easily forgotten: pointed features, oblique eyebrows, pale skin with slightly enlarged pores, and expensive lipstick that threatened to drip off her lips. Once beautiful, but now a dream in which willow branches have withered, clouds have scattered and drifting petals have fallen to the ground. A face that has been corroded by pleasure, impetuosity and dreams, each of which has left scars on it, leaving it sharp yet worn, capable of hurting, yet vulnerable as well.

She smiled, her eyes damp. She was a walking woman's history book, a specimen, a vehicle for the attitudes, values and instincts of all women. 'Do you really care about Ah Dick?' I asked.

'I'm not sure . . . I guess deep down I can't accept it. After all, *he* dumped *me*. I feel burnt out, and I don't want to look for another man. There probably aren't any young men interested in me.' She was drinking sake like water and her face was flushing deep red, like a Van Gogh sunflower under the sun. I was caught totally off guard when she threw her cup to the floor where it shattered like white jade.

A waiter came running over. 'Excuse us, it was an accident,' I rushed to explain.

'Really, you're awfully lucky. You have Tian Tian, and you have Mark. Right? You've got it all. For a woman, isn't that happiness?' She kept a hold of my hand, and my palm broke out in a cold sweat.

'What *about* Mark?' I tried hard to keep calm. A waiter who looked like a schoolboy was watching us. Two young women discussing their private lives are bound to attract attention.

'Don't try to fool me, Coco. Nothing gets past these sharp eyes of mine. And I've got my intuition. I didn't work as a *mami* down south for nothing, you know.'

'It's okay, I'm not going to tell Tian Tian.' She smiled. 'That would be the end of him. He's too naive, too weak. And you haven't done anything wrong. I understand you.'

I put both my hands on my head as the deceptively harmless-tasting sake began to take effect. My head was spinning and I felt as if I was floating. 'I'm drunk,' I said.

'Let's go for a facial next door.' Madonna paid the bill, took me by the hand and led me out of the restaurant and into the beauty salon next door.

The salon wasn't big. All four walls were covered with paintings, originals and copies. The owner has an artistic background, and occasionally men walk in – not to view the women, but to buy a bona fide painting by the likes of Lin Feng-Mian.

Light music. Delicate scent of fruit. Soft faces of young women.

I lay on a bed next to Madonna's, two cool slices of cucumber covering my eyes. A young woman's delicate fingers moved nimbly over my face. Music can lull one to sleep, and Madonna said she often falls asleep during a facial. The atmosphere lends itself to a subtle feeling of intimacy and mutual sympathy between women. Having one's face stroked by a girl's jade fingers is much nicer than being stroked by a man.

A faintly lesbian air permeated the salon. Someone was having her eyebrows tattooed, and I could hear the barely audible buzz as metal met flesh. It made my hair stand on end. But then I relaxed, and fell asleep delighted at the thought of waking up looking like the young Elizabeth Taylor.

The white Santana flew like the wind along the empty road. We listened to the radio, smoked and enjoyed a moment of tranquillity. 'I don't want to go back to my place. It's too big and too quiet. Without a man, it's like a tomb. Can we go to yours?' asked Madonna.

I nodded my consent.

She was in the bathroom for a long time. I got through to Tian

Tian at his hotel, but his voice sounded sleepy (as it always did on the phone). His familiar breathing travelled over the telephone wires and into my ears. 'Were you already asleep? I'll call back later,' I said.

'Mm, no, it's all right . . . I feel very comfortable. I must have been dreaming, dreaming of you. And there were birds singing. I want to eat a bowl of your Russian borscht . . . Is Shanghai cold?' He sniffled. He must have caught a cold.

'Not too cold. Madonna's going to stay over here tonight. She's feeling down. Ah Dick and Zhu Sha are dating . . . Are you and Fur Ball both feeling okay?'

'Fur Ball had diarrhoea so I took her to the vet. They gave her a shot and some medicine. I've had a cold ever since I came back from a swim in the ocean, but it's no big deal. I saw a Hitchcock film. His style reminded me a bit of those martial arts novels by Gu Long.

'Oh, by the way, I want to tell you something I saw with my own eyes. Yesterday when I was taking a bus a young punk got on. He couldn't have been more than fourteen or fifteen,' said Tian Tian. 'Right in front of everybody, he ripped a gold necklace off the neck of a middle-aged woman. Nobody did anything to stop him, and he just got off the bus and disappeared.'

'That's horrible,' I said. 'You've got to be careful. I miss you very much.'

'I miss you too. It's good to have someone to miss.'

'When are you coming back to Shanghai?' I asked.

'When I've finished reading a few books and done a few more sketches. People here are different from in Shanghai. It's got a Southeast Asian feel to it.'

'Okay. Here's a kiss for you.' There was a smacking of lips, and then after counting one, two, three, we hung up simultaneously.

Madonna called from the bathroom. 'Darling, give me a bathrobe.' I opened the wardrobe and took out one of Tian Tian's padded-cotton robes. She had already opened the door, and was drying herself in clouds of steam.

I tossed her the robe and she struck a flirtatious Marilyn Monroe poster pose. 'What do you think of my figure? Still attractive?'

I folded my arms, gave her the once-over and told her to give me a back view. She obediently turned halfway about, and then did a full circle.

'Well?' She stared at me enthusiastically.

'Want the truth?' I asked.

'Of course.'

'Your body bears the marks of many men, at least a hundred.'

'What do you mean?' She still hadn't put the bathrobe on.

'Your breasts aren't bad. They're not big enough, but they'd fit nicely in one's palm. Your legs are slim. Your neck is your best point. Only blue-blooded Western women have necks like that. But your body's too tired. It's burdened with the memories of too many men.'

She kept pinching her breasts, pitying herself but treating them as little treasures at the same time. As I spoke she caressed her legs, and then moved her hands up to touch that fine neck. 'I adore myself. The older and tireder I get the more I adore myself. You don't find me attractive?' she queried.

I passed by her and walked out of the bathroom. I simply couldn't bear the way she caressed herself. Man or woman, one couldn't help being aroused by it. 'Your place is even more comfortable than mine!' she said loudly behind me.

She wanted to chat, so we shared a bed, leg against leg, covered by my down duvet. The light was turned right down, and I could see my wardrobe and window on the other side of her nose. When I was at Fudan, female roommates often shared a bed. It was probably the best place to share secrets, pleasures, desires, humiliations and dreams, such as odd friendships, intuitive trust, and subconscious anxieties that no man would understand. She told me stories from her past, and in return I offered my own – which were less colourful than hers, of course.

Her life was like a burst of wild, flowing Chinese calligraphy, written under the influence of alcohol. Mine was a more uniform, rounded script; pain, anxiety, happiness and pressure had not made me an outcast. I was still a cute, soft-skinned girl . . . at least in the eyes of some.

Madonna grew up in the shanty area of Shanghai's Zhabei District, and wanted to be an artist from an early age (and later took artists as lovers). But at sixteen she dropped out. Her father and an older brother were drunks, and used her for target practice when they were boozing. Gradually their violence took on sexual overtones, and they would kick her or throw burning cigarettes at her chest. Her mother was a weak-willed woman who couldn't protect her daughter.

One day she boarded a train bound for Guangzhou. She didn't have much choice. She began working as a bargirl, sitting with guests while they drank. (Cities in the south at that time were enjoying a boom: there were lots of wealthy people, some of them so rich it left you speechless.) Even her smallest movements expressed a refinement that women from other provinces didn't have. The clients liked her, flattered her and were willing to do things for her. Her standing rose quickly, and in no time she had begun to recruit girls and run her own business.

They called her 'foreign doll', a pet name Shanghainese give to girls who are fair-skinned and pretty. She wore long black dresses with spaghetti straps, and diamond rings from her admirers. With her black hair lying against her white face, she looked like a queen who lived in the secluded, innermost palace, behind layers of thick curtains. She wielded considerable power through an intricate network of shady relationships.

'When I remember scenes from that time in my life, it really seems like a previous incarnation. A simple title captures it: "Beauty and the Beasts". And I did master the principles of how to domesticate a man. Maybe when I get old I'll write a book just for women, teaching them how to interpret a man's mind and understand his worst habits. To kill a snake, you have to strike it below the head but above the belly. Men also have pressure points where they're vulnerable. Young women nowadays may mature earlier, and they're tougher and braver than we were, but women still get the short end of the stick in many ways.'

She adjusted her pillow, looked over and said: 'Don't you agree?'

'When you get down to it, the social system still devalues the needs of women and doesn't like their efforts to recognize their self-worth,' I said. 'Girls who are street-smart are put down as "crude" and those who are gentler are treated like "empty-headed" flower vessels.'

'Anyway, girls need to improve their minds. Being a bit smarter doesn't hurt.' Madonna paused, and asked if I agreed. I said I did. I wouldn't set myself up as a women's lib warrior, but what she said rang true, and helped me discover the hidden place in her mind, which housed her deeper and more mature thoughts.

'So how come you married . . . your late husband?' I asked.

'Something happened which taught me that in that world, no matter how much influence I might wield through my connections, I was really just a pretty flower who could easily shrivel. At the time I particularly liked a girl from Chengdu. She'd studied management at Sichuan University, read widely, and could talk about things like art with me (okay, I know, I can be quite vulgar, but since I was a child I've always been attracted to the art world. Back then one of my boyfriends was a graduate of Guangzhou Art Institute who painted surrealist paintings, like Ah Dick).

'The girl didn't have anywhere to live, so I took her in to share my flat. One evening three fierce-looking guys came looking for her. It turned out they were from her hometown in Sichuan, and they'd pooled cash and given it to her so she could come to Guangzhou and invest in futures. But literally overnight she lost all the money, a hundred thousand RMB. She was penniless and had no choice but to work as a bargirl. But she avoided contact with the other Sichuanese, and didn't tell the investors about her failure. In the end, these guys came looking for her with knives.

'I was taking a shower when they came, and when they discovered me, they took me along too. It was terrifying. My room was turned upside down, and my jewellery and thirty thousand RMB stolen. I explained that all this had nothing to do with me, and they should let me go. They just shoved a gag into my mouth. I thought they planned to sell us to slave traders in Thailand or Malaysia.

'We were locked in a dark room. My brain was empty, hopeless. The atmosphere was ominous, as if something could happen at any minute. Just think, a few hours before I'd been leading a life of luxury and now I was reduced to a slab of meat awaiting slaughter. What miserable kind of fate was that? Then they came and beat the girl up badly and said she was only fit to be a whore. When they pulled the cloth out of my mouth I decided to do whatever I had to do to save my skin, come hell or high water. I recited a long list of important people on both sides of the law, from the police chief down to the gangsters who controlled each street. They hesitated for a moment and went outside for a talk. That lasted a good, long time; they seemed to be arguing. Then the slightly taller of the two men came back in and said, 'It turns out that you're the celebrated "Foreign Doll". This has all been a misunderstanding. We'll send you back immediately.'

Her cold, clammy hands clung to mine. As she told her story, her fingers trembled. 'So you chose to get married?' I asked.

'Yeah, to get out of the business,' said Madonna. 'At the time there was an old codger – a multimillionaire in real estate – who wanted to marry me. I overcame my repugnance at the thought of sleeping with a wrinkled mummy and agreed. I guessed he wouldn't live long, and I was proved right. Now I have money and freedom, and I'm luckier than most women. Even though I'm bored silly, I'm still better off than your typical laid-off seamstress.'

'The mother next door to us has been laid off, but things aren't too grim. She still cooks a dinner of rice and vegetables for dinner, and waits for her old man and kid to come home,' I said. 'The three of them gather around the dinner table and eat together happily. God's fair. He gives you something but takes away something else. So sometimes I can see my neighbour as fortunate.'

'Okay. Let's say you've got a point. Time to sleep,' said Madonna. With her hands on my shoulders and her breathing growing increasingly louder, she fell into a deep sleep.

I couldn't sleep. She and her story were like a lamp shimmering in my mind. Her body was pressed tight up against mine, and I could feel her warmth, her grief and her dreams. She existed in the no-man's land between trust and distrust. Her body was frighteningly sensual (as a woman I sensed this even more clearly), and a dreadful air of danger surrounded her. She'd had experiences most normal people hadn't: I felt she could lose control at any time and be as deadly as a knife.

I tried to loosen her grip on me, because I couldn't sleep unless we were further apart. But she hugged me even tighter. She moaned as she dreamed, and then began to kiss my face passionately, her lips moist and threatening. But I wasn't Ah Dick or some other man in her life. I tried frantically to push her away, but she didn't wake up. She was like ivy wrapping herself tightly about my body. I felt hot all over and panicked.

She awoke suddenly, eyes wide open and her eyelashes moist. 'Why are you holding me?' she scolded. But I could see she was quite happy.

'It was you who held me,' I retorted, in a whisper.

'Oh, I must have been dreaming,' Madonna sighed. 'I saw Ah Dick . . . maybe I really have fallen for him. I'm just so lonely.' She got out of bed, put on Tian Tian's robe and tidied her hair. 'I'd better sleep in the other room.' As she walked out she suddenly smiled, and her expression was quite extraordinary. Turning, she asked: 'Did you like it when I held you like that?'

'God!' I grimaced at the ceiling.

'I think I really do like you. No kidding. We could be even closer. Maybe it's because our signs are compatible.' She made a gesture to forestall my protest. 'I mean, perhaps I could be the agent for that wonderful novel of yours.'

# 17

# Mother and Daughter

'I am reluctant to let my young daughter appear in public
and face the cruelty of life. She should remain
in our living room as much as possible.'
Sigmund Freud

I sat upstairs on the double-decker bus rocking back and forth the whole way, moving along these streets past high-rises and trees I know so well, and got off at Hongkou. The twenty-two-storey building is striking in sunlight, though the pale yellow of the façade has been stained by pollution. My parents live on the top floor. From the window of their apartment, streets, crowds and buildings look small, and the bird's-eye view of the city is microcosmic, rich and colourful. But the place is so high that some of my parents' friends who have vertigo no longer visit regularly.

I, on the other hand, really enjoy the feeling that the building could collapse at any moment. Unlike many cities in Japan, Shanghai is not on a fault line, and has suffered just a few minor quakes. I remember one on an autumn evening, while I was having dinner with my magazine colleagues on Xinle Road. At the first tremor I threw down the hairy crab in my hands, fled, and was first down the stairs. When my workmates had all come down we chatted quietly at the door of the restaurant, and when the swaying stopped, we went back up. Newly aware of the value of life, I quickly finished off the fat crab on my plate.

An old guy in an old military uniform was the regular liftman. I always imagined that for every floor the elevator climbed, a tiny, tiny fissure would crack open in the city's frail surface. As the elevator ascended and descended, Shanghai would be sinking by 0.0001 of a millimetre per second towards the bottom of the Pacific.

The door opened, and Mother looked pleased to see me, but she controlled herself. 'You said you'd be here by ten thirty; you're late again,' she said coolly. She'd had a meticulous hot-oil hair treatment and styling, probably done at the small salon downstairs.

Daddy heard us and came out. Chubby, wearing a brand new Lacoste T-shirt and with a Crown Imperial cigar in his hand, my father is still – to my delighted surprise – a good-looking, amiable old chap, even after all these years.

I gave him a big hug. 'Happy birthday, Professor Ni.' He smiled sweetly, the lines on his face smoothing out. Today was a day of double blessings for him. It was his fifty-third birthday, and it was also the day when he finally achieved the rank of full professor. His hair had turned grey waiting for that. 'Professor Ni' has a much better ring to it than 'Associate Professor Ni'.

Zhu Sha came out of my bedroom. She was still staying here while her new three-bedroomed apartment was decorated. My parents firmly refused to accept any rent from her. Several times she had secretly stuffed money in their handbags or drawers, but was told off each time. They objected: 'Our own kin! What kind of people would we be to be so money-grabbing? Even in a market economy one must respect family ties and uphold certain principles, right?'

So Zhu Sha often gave them little gifts of things like fruit. For this birthday, she'd bought a big box of cigars. Daddy only smokes China-made Crown Imperial cigars, and it tickles him that a few visiting scholars from Europe have, on his recommendation, taken to these too.

I brought a pair of socks for my old daddy, partly because I believe they're the best gift for a man (I also gave socks as birthday presents to all my boyfriends), and partly because my savings had just about dried up, and it would be a long while yet before my new book would bring in any money, so I had to be careful.

Among the guests were several of Daddy's graduate students. As usual, Mother was cooking up a storm in the kitchen with the help of a part-time maid. From Daddy's room came the sound of earnest debate, the men discussing some lofty topic of no practical importance. Daddy had once suggested introducing one of his protégés to me as a potential boyfriend, but I didn't agree, because the boy's studious airs turned me off. A learned man should also understand romance: he should know what the beauty of a woman is, what a good woman is, and what a woman's sorrow is. At the very least, he should be capable of flirting. Love first enters by way of the ear, and only then reaches the heart.

I sat talking to Zhu Sha in her small room. She had cut her hair in a style from the latest issue of *Elle*. The saying that love brings a new look to an old face is absolutely true. Her skin looked fresh and clean (I was willing to assume that this glow stemmed from romance rather than from her Shiseido face cream), and her eyes moist. Sitting sideways in the carved wooden chair, she was like a beautiful woman in a traditional Chinese painting.

'You're forever wearing black,' said Zhu Sha.

I looked at my wool sweater and narrow-legged pants. 'What's wrong with that?' I asked. 'Black's my lucky colour, and it makes me look pretty and elegant.'

She laughed. 'But there are other pretty colours, aren't there? Actually I was thinking of giving you some of my clothes.' She stood up and began flipping through the wardrobe.

I looked at her back, and it occurred to me that although she was always generous and kind-hearted, perhaps this time she was trying to get into my good books. Her thing with Ah Dick was on my account – it was through me they'd met, and Madonna was my friend.

She brought out a few garments that looked perfectly new, and spread them out before me. 'You'd best keep them,' I said. 'I don't have a lot of occasion to wear fashionable things. I'm always holed up at home in pyjamas, writing.'

'But you'll have to meet publishers, journalists and so on, and do book signings. Believe me, you'll be a celebrity,' she smiled, flattering me.

'Tell me about Ah Dick,' I said suddenly, perhaps without the necessary preamble. She went dumb for a second, and then laughed. 'Great. We get on really well.'

They had swapped addresses and phone numbers at the picnic. In fact, it was Ah Dick who took the initiative; he called her to ask her out on a date. Before she kept the rendezvous, Zhu Sha wore herself out dithering. Did she want to keep a date with a man eight years younger, and worse still, one who had been involved with a formidable woman, a former *mami*? But in the end, she went.

Why? Perhaps she had grown tired of caution. She no longer wanted to be seen as virtuous but soulless, a proper young lady. Nice girls can also feel the urge to step into a different world. Hence the phrase 'nuns can go crazy too'.

They sat facing one another in a forgettable restaurant. She made a point of not putting on make-up, and she'd dressed down. But she still found a flame burning in his eyes, just like the scene in *Titanic* when Rose discovers the light in Jack's eyes that sets her heart thumping.

That evening she went to Ah Dick's place, and they made love to the sound of Ella Fitzgerald's jazz arias. It was like the pitter-patter of spring rain. She had never had such a marvellous and tender sensation, as if her love could reach deep into her lover, melt into water and flow through his body, tracing every line and shadow, expressing itself in music. She was giddy.

'Am I a bad woman?' she asked her young, passionate lover. Right then he hadn't a stitch on, and leaning against the head-board he looked at her and smiled.

'Absolutely. Because you made me fall for you,' he replied. 'A good woman in the outside world, a wicked woman in bed. Where can you find a woman like that?' He buried his head in her bosom. 'I guess I'm a lucky guy.'

She wasn't sure how dependable he was, but she didn't care any more. Don't worry about the future, what will be will be. She wasn't looking for someone to lean on. She had a good job and a good brain, typical of Shanghai's new generation of well-educated, self-sufficient women.

'Will you . . . get married?' I asked curiously. 'I'm just concerned about you,' I added. Prying into another's privacy is an occupational hazard in my profession. Zhu Sha was only recently divorced and she hadn't known Ah Dick for long, but I felt she was the kind of woman born to marry and raise a family. She's maternal and has a sense of responsibility.

'I don't know, but we do have an uncanny affinity.' I thought to myself that affinity should be comprehensive, including what goes on in bed. 'We like to eat the same food, listen to the same music, and watch the same movies. When we were small both of us were lefties, forced by adults to use our right hands.' She looked at me and laughed. 'I don't feel at all as if he's eight years younger than me.'

'The handsome Go master Chang Hao also married a girl eight years older than him.' I began to laugh too. 'Affinity is such a difficult thing to explain . . . I've never really understood Ah Dick. He's actually quite introverted. Are you sure you can handle him? Young artists can bring out the maternal instinct in a slightly older woman. Artists are unreliable; they're in flux, and their quest is for art, not a particular woman,' I said. (A few months later the newspapers were all wildly exaggerating the divorce of Beijing rock star Dou Wei and Faye Wang in Hong Kong. Dou Wei's reason: he loves himself and his music most, and it's irrelevant to him that his wife is the Empress of Asia's music scene.)

'You're an artist too, don't forget,' she said, smiling faintly, her face dignified, like a dew-covered jade statue in a garden at dawn. She stood up, walked over to the window and looked into the distance. 'Okay.' She turned and smiled. 'Let's hear all about your novel, and your Tian Tian.' Her smile made me wonder if I had underestimated her ability to decipher life, and her innate feminine intuition.

'How's Mark been recently?' I asked. We hadn't been in touch for some time now, and I imagined he must be enjoying time with his family.

'The Christmas vacation is over, and the company's very busy at the moment. A lot of business has to be done to tight deadlines. But Mark's a perfect boss. He has good judgement, a good head and the ability to organise – only sometimes he's too serious.' She patted me on the knee, a naughty smile on her face. 'I would never have imagined you two being an item.'

'I fell for his firm butt and Western frame. And him – maybe he's attracted to my Asian body, its smooth golden colour and silk-smooth mystery. Oh yes, and I have a boyfriend who can't have sex, and I'm a novelist. Those are all the reasons we're attracted to each other.'

'He's a married man.'

'Don't worry, I can control myself. If I don't fall in love with him, I won't have any problems.'

'Are you sure?'

'I don't want to talk about it. It seems women are always talking about men . . . Time for lunch.'

As we walked out of the bedroom, Zhu Sha remembered something and said to me in a low voice: 'Next Saturday there's a friendly football match organised by the German Chamber of Commerce at the American School field in Pudong. Mark will be playing. He's a forward on the company team.'

'I'd like to go,' I said quietly.

'Then you're likely to see his wife and child,' she said.

'Great, we're going to see some fun.' I shrugged. Scenes in which the wives and husbands of lovers run into one another are always portrayed very dramatically in films. I had the feeling the director was about to focus the camera on me.

'Have some more,' said Mother, sitting next to me. 'This pig's feet and peanut soup is a new recipe.' Her eyes were filled with motherly love which made me feel warm inside, yet also twice as much under pressure; made me want to leap into her womb where all the anxieties and hurts of adulthood would be ironed out, but also made me want to leap to my feet to escape from the huge space constructed by her love. No matter what happened to me, I wished she'd just leave me alone.

'Still living on take-away food? You look a lot thinner. That boy, Tian Tian, what plans do you and he have?' Mother went on quietly. I kept my head down, eating, deliberately slurping my soup (our family doesn't allow one to drink soup noisily).

Daddy and the students were discussing current international news as if they had personally been to the White House or the Balkans, and knew the developing situation in Iraq or Kosovo like the palms of their hands. They even knew certain details, such as that when Clinton, facing the preliminary congressional investigation of his scandal, proclaimed his innocence, the tie he

*137*

was wearing was a Zoi tie given to him by Lewinsky. This was apparently a bizarre way of asking Lewinsky to stand by him loyally.

'Mother,' I said taking a good look at this still graceful middle-aged woman who always seemed weighed down by anxiety, 'Don't worry about me. If I ever have a problem I can't solve, I'll sneak back here for refuge. Let's make that a promise, okay?' I said, hugging her.

Out came the birthday cake, a gift from the students, with six candles stuck in it. Daddy was in a good mood and blew out the candles in a single breath. He laughed loudly like a grown-up child, cut the cake and shared it out. 'There are going to be some funds arriving soon, and the research project will see some progress,' he said. Then his students spoke one after another about this research topic, 'Research into the Vacation System for Tang Dynasty Civil Servants' (which sounded as bizarre as a person holding a red ball in one hand and a green ball in the other, asking: 'Which hand is holding the yellow ball now?')

I think that a professor's protégés are mainly yes-men, even slaves. First they have to agree with the direction of their mentor's scholarship, and keep any doubts to themselves. Once they've won his favour, they tag along after him to seminars all over the place, publishing in the journals he recommends, getting a post, even marrying and having a family under his watchful eye, until the day when, their position secure, they can speak for themselves.

One of the students asked me about my novel. I thought for sure Daddy had told his students I was writing again. He wasn't proud of his daughter being a novelist, but he still promoted me. The group chatted for a while, and then I wanted to go.

'You can't even stay one night? But I still have so much to say to you.' Mother fixed her eyes on me, and the hurt in them travelled across time, like cosmic dust.

'Oh, I just want to go for a walk. I'll spend the night here, with Zhu Sha.' I smiled, took the keys out of my pocket and jingled them together, learning the sound of a lie.

# 18

# Two Sides of Love

'We're lovers. We can't stop loving each other.'
Marguerite Duras

Two years ago I was sent to Hong Kong to do a series of interviews on its 'Return to the Motherland.' Late each night when I had finished work, I would sit on the stone steps of Victoria Harbour, smoking and gazing at the stars, leaning my head so far back my neck almost snapped. Every so often I would lose myself in thought, forgetting the existence of the universe around me, even of my self. In these moments it felt as though there were probably a few sparsely distributed brain cells left breathing very quietly, like a fine layer of blue mist.

While writing, I entered a state like that from time to time, except that I was stargazing with my head down. The stars twinkled among words that appeared spontaneously, and then I achieved nirvana – that is, I no longer feared illness, accidents, loneliness or even death: I was immune to them all. But real life is never the way we want it to be.

I ran into Mark's family on the field at the Pudong campus of the American School. Mark looked exceptionally handsome that day, perhaps due to the bright sunlight and pleasant surroundings. This elite school for the children of expatriates felt as if it were built in the clouds, far removed from the dust-blown world outside. The entire campus had a newly-washed freshness; even the air seemed to have been sterilised. An unbelievably classy atmosphere.

Mark was chewing gum. Greeting us with perfect composure, he introduced his wife to Zhu Sha and me. 'This is Eva.' Eva was holding his hand. She was prettier and better built than in the photo I'd seen. Her pale blonde hair was casually pulled back into a ponytail, a row of silver studs lined her ear, and her black sweater contrasted with her white skin. In the sunlight that whiteness had a honey scent to it, giving her a dreamlike quality.

A Caucasian woman's beauty can launch a thousand ships. In contrast, the beauty of an Asian woman relies on the knit brows and enticing eyes of a pin-up girl from some erotic bygone era, like the singer Sandy Lam or movie star Gong Li.

'This is a colleague from my firm, Judy. And this is Judy's cousin, Coco, a terrific writer,' said Mark. Smiling and squinting in the sunlight, Eva shook hands with us. 'This is my son, B.B.' Mark lifted his child out of the buggy and kissed him. He hung around for a moment, and then handed B.B. back to Eva. 'It's time to get out there.' He stretched his legs, smiled, threw me a glance out of the corner of his eye, picked up his kitbag and left for the changing-room.

While Zhu Sha chatted to Eva, I sat aside on the grass, realising that meeting Mark's wife hadn't made me as jealous as I'd have expected. On the contrary, I liked Eva. Who made her so beautiful? People always like lovely things. Could it be that I'm actually the sort of decent girl who, seeing a happy family, can feel happy for them? Oh, God!

The match was about to start. My eyes were glued to Mark. He was a picture of fitness and energy running back and forth on the soccer pitch, his golden hair waving in the wind like a dream of exotic love. His speed and power were on exhibition to more than a hundred spectators. In my opinion, many athletic activities are really large-scale orgies. The fans in the stands and the players on the field were jointly excited to the point where they could hardly control their hormones, and the air was filled with their scent.

A few students from the school were drinking Coke and cheering loudly. Eva continued to chat with Zhu Sha (which seemed to interest her more than watching her husband compete), and my panties were already wet. I'd never wanted Mark more than right then. Let me fall into his embrace like an apple shaken from a tree by a strong gust.

'Coco, your story collection,' said Zhu Sha, distracting my attention.

'Oh, yes?' I said, seeing Eva smile at me.

'I'm very interested in it,' said Eva in English. 'I wonder, can I still buy a copy?'

'I'm afraid you can't buy it any more. I have one I could give you, but it's in Chinese,' I said.

'Oh thank you, I'm planning to study Chinese. Chinese culture is very interesting, and Shanghai is the most intriguing city I've seen.' Her face was fair and rosy, that of a tempting young white woman. 'If you're free next weekend, how about coming over to our place for a meal?' she invited.

I concealed my nervousness, looking at Zhu Sha. This wouldn't be a trap masquerading as a banquet, would it?

'Judy will be coming, and our German friends as well,' said Eva. 'Next week I'm returning to Germany. I work in the Environmental Protection Department in the government, and you can't take a long vacation, you know. Germans love ecology so much they're a bit neurotic about it,' she said, smiling. 'In my country, we don't have any smoke-belching three-wheel vehicles, and no one hangs clothes out to dry on the pavement.'

'Oh.' I nodded, thinking that Germany might be the closest place to heaven on earth. 'Okay, I'll come.' I felt that Eva probably wasn't the most intelligent of women, but might be a generous and lovable one.

B.B. in his buggy began screeching, 'Papa, papa.' I turned my head to see Mark waving his fist and leaping into the air, having just scored a goal. From the distance he threw us a kiss. Eva and I looked at one another and burst out laughing.

When we went into the school building to find a washroom, Zhu Sha asked me if I found Eva cute.

'Maybe, which makes one even more pessimistic about marriage.'

'Is that so? From the look of things, Mark loves her very much.'

'Marriage experts say that just because a person loves his mate it doesn't mean he'll stay faithful for life,' I said.

I found an interesting cartoon stuck on the wall in the washroom. It showed a stretch of green forest and a huge question mark: 'What's the most frightening creature on the face of the earth?' Zhu Sha and I blurted out the answer simultaneously: 'Mankind.'

At half-time, everyone drank soft drinks and told jokes. I got the chance to say a few words to Mark. 'You have a lovely family.'

'Yes,' he said neutrally.

'Do you love your wife?' I asked quietly. I didn't feel like beating around the bush, and going for the jugular can give you a rush sometimes. I looked at him in a slightly hostile way.

'Would you be jealous?' he retorted.

'You're joking. I'm not an idiot.'

'Of course I love her.' He shrugged and looked away, greeted an acquaintance, and then turned back to me, smiling. 'You're a beautiful and seductive woman singing in the night. According to a German legend, a siren haunted the Rhine: she would sit on a great rock in the river, and use her song to lure sailors to their deaths there.'

'That's hardly fair. From the word go it was you who seduced me.'

Eva walked over, put her arms around her husband's shoulders, leaned across and gave him a peck. 'What are you talking about?' she smiled, perplexed.

'Oh, Coco was talking about a new story she's writing,' replied Mark smoothly.

Ah Dick came looking for Zhu Sha before the end of the match. He was dressed simply and fashionably, and had gelled his hair; a fringe waved slightly over his forehead. But there was a strange scar on his left cheek; it looked like a new wound from a sharp object. He made polite conversation with me for a moment, and had the sense not to ask about the progress of my novel. I was sick of people asking about my book whenever they saw me. It made me nervous.

'What happened to your face?' I asked, pointing at the scar.

'Someone hit me,' he said simply. My jaw dropped. Who could have been so angry with him? I looked at Zhu Sha, but she moved her hand in a way that indicated that the matter was history and shouldn't be mentioned again.

A light clicked on in my head. Could it have been that crazy woman, Madonna? She had harped on and on about the fact that she couldn't accept their break-up. Would she go so far as to do that to teach her ex a lesson? If so, she really had a thing about violence.

But Madonna wasn't actually in Shanghai just then. She had taken her credit card on a shopping spree to Hong Kong, and would be there for some time. A few nights before she had called, spewing some mysterious nonsense about how she had visited the temple of a centuries-old Buddhist master, Wong Tai Sin, famous throughout Hong Kong, where she was told that she was facing a bout of ill luck, everything was working against her, and it was time for her to travel south or east. So at least her trip to Hong Kong was a move in the right direction.

Zhu Sha and Ah Dick were off to a home-furnishing store to buy paint, as Ah Dick was helping her do up the apartment she'd bought at Ruixin Gardens. They said they were planning to paint the walls retro style in an elegant mahogany colour with a smooth, rich texture evoking the banks of the Seine, because this paint is only made in France and has a 1930s' *shalong* feel to it. Not many stores sold it, but they had heard one place in Pudong did. They left together before the match was over. I stayed till the end. Mark's team won.

Mark came out of the changing-room with his hair soaked, and walked towards us. Eva and I had been discussing the similarities and dissimilarities between feminism in the East and the West. She thought that, in the West, women with some consciousness of women's rights could earn a man's respect. 'Really?' I said. Our conversation ended then, as Eva turned to kiss her husband. 'Let's go shopping, shall we?' she suggested.

In Pudong's *Yaohan* department store Eva went to the gift counter to look at ceramics and silk goods, while Mark and I sat in a corner of the first-floor café, drinking coffee and entertaining B.B.

'Do you love her? I'm sorry, it's a rude question. That's between you two.' I played with a sugar cube, my eyes on a pillar across from us, with decorative graphics painted on a beige background. The pillars effectively blocked the view of the crowds entering and leaving the store.

'She's a kind woman,' said Mark, holding his son's tiny hand, an answer that didn't correspond with the question.

'Yeah, just about everybody's kind, including you and me,' I said a bit mockingly, not really finding my envious mood consistent with the rules of our romantic game. The most important rule being that we should both keep our balance; there should be no sentimentality and no envy. There's a proverb that puts it well: 'Once you've decided to do it, do it, and take the consequences.'

'What are you thinking about?' he asked.

'I'm thinking about what the hell I'm doing with my life. And I'm wondering . . . would you hurt me?' I fixed my eyes on him. 'Might that ever happen?'

He didn't say anything, and suddenly I was swamped by sadness. 'Give me a kiss,' I said softly, moving my body towards the table. He hesitated, then leaned across and left a moist, warm kiss on my lips.

Literally at the instant we separated, Eva appeared from behind the pillar, smiling and laden with brimming carrier bags. In the same instant, Mark's expression rearranged itself. As he took the bags from his wife, he used German to tell her a joke (I guessed it was a joke, since she laughed). An outsider, I watched this married couple's loving behaviour, and then bade them goodbye.

'See you next weekend for dinner,' said Eva.

When I boarded the harbour ferry, the colour of the sky had turned ugly. Lead-grey clouds hung overhead like clumps of old cotton wool. The dirty-yellow river was dotted with rubbish: plastic bottles, rotten fruit, cigarette butts. Wrinkles appeared on the surface of the water, like a skin on hot chocolate, and the light reflected from the waves made me slightly uncomfortable. Behind me were the high-rises of the Lujiazui financial district, clustered like fish scales, and in front were the imposing, swaggering structures on the Bund. An old black cargo ship passed on the right with a red flag billowing from its stern. It looked weird.

I inhaled the bracing, fermented air, and saw the Puxi pier draw nearer and nearer. I had a vague feeling of déjà vu: the yellowish water, the bruised sky, the rust-speckled bow tilting slightly, slowly tilting towards the pier just inches away. It was like approaching a man, like touching another world. A little nearer, nearer still, but perhaps never able to connect. Maybe one draws near only to separate in the end.

I walked down the gangplank and into the crowds on Zhongshan East Road with my sunglasses on. Suddenly I felt like crying. Everyone has an urge to cry at times. Even God.

It began to rain suddenly, but at first the sun continued to shine on the serried buildings until, gradually, it took its rays into hiding and the wind blew up. I slipped into a nearby post office, but it was filled with people taking shelter from the rain, like me. A whiff of rotting tropical vegetation came off their hair and clothes. I consoled myself with the thought that if this smell was unpleasant, it was a hell of a lot better than the one in refugee tents on the border between Kosovo and Albania. I need only think of the countless disasters here on Earth to cheer myself up. How blessed a girl like me should be: young, good-looking and the author of a book.

I sighed. I flipped through the newspaper for a moment at the periodicals counter, and saw a news item from Hainan. The police had cracked a luxury-foreign-car smuggling case – on the largest scale since the founding of the People's Republic – which implicated the top authorities on Leizhou Peninsula, across from the island.

I quickly took out my address book from my handbag. I needed to call Tian Tian. I realised that I hadn't called him for a week; time passed so quickly. It was time he came back.

I paid a deposit at the counter and took a plastic token to Domestic Direct Dial Booth Number 4. I dialled, but for a long time no one answered. Just when I was going to hang up, Tian Tian's fuzzy voice came on to the line. 'Hi, this is Coco . . . How are you?' I said.

It seemed he hadn't yet woken up, and he didn't respond for quite a while. 'Hi, Coco.'

'Are you sick?' I felt concerned. His voice didn't sound right at all. It was coming to me from somewhere out of the Jurassic Era, without warmth or even coherence. A hazy, deep grunt came back.

'Can you hear me? I want to know what's up with you,' I said excitedly, my voice rising. He said nothing. There was only the sound of his slow, light breathing.

'Tian Tian, please say something. Don't upset me.' A long silence, seemingly a half-century long, as I controlled my restlessness.

'I love you.' His voice was like something out of a nightmare.

'I love you too,' I said. '*Are* you sick?'

'I'm . . . fine.'

I bit my lip, staring uncomprehendingly at the smeared pane of clear plastic. Outside the booth the crowd was gradually clearing, so the rain must have stopped.

'Well, when are you coming back?' My voice was very loud, trying to hold his attention. He could fall asleep at any moment, and disappear from the other end of the line.

'Can you do me a favour? Send me some money,' he said softly.

'What? You've used up the credit on your card?' I was utterly taken aback. His credit card was good for thirty thousand RMB. However high prices were in Hainan – and he'd told me it was cheap there – he didn't like to shop and wouldn't spend money on women. He was like a papoose wrapped tight against his mother's back, free of desire. Something must have happened. My intuition, drowned in the fog, deserted me.

'There's a savings account passbook in the right drawer of the dresser. It's easy to find,' he reminded me.

I suddenly became very angry. 'You have to tell me where you spent all that money. You needn't hide anything from me. Believe me, and tell me the truth.'

Silence.

'If you don't tell me, I won't wire the money.' My tone was deliberately threatening.

'Coco, I really miss you,' he murmured. A black tenderness grabbed me.

'Me too,' I said softly.

'You won't leave me?'

'No.'

'Even if you have another man, don't leave me,' he pleaded. He came across as totally without willpower. A sense of confusion flowed through the telephone.

'What's the matter, Tian Tian?' I whispered.

His voice was very weak, but he still managed to tell me the most terrible thing, too terrible for there to be any chance of misunderstanding it. He was taking morphine.

It happened something like this. One afternoon when Tian Tian was sitting in a fast-food restaurant by the roadside, he chanced to meet up with an acquaintance, that guy Li Le from the Shanghai Reproductive Health Treatment Centre. Li Le had come to Hainan too, was living with relatives there, and did odd jobs at a dental clinic they owned.

They really hit it off and, perhaps because Tian Tian had been on his own for some time, suddenly finding someone to talk to made him happy. Li Le took him to a lot of places that he hadn't known about, and even if he had, he wouldn't have gone to them by himself. Illegal gambling parlours, shady hair salons, abandoned warehouses where gangs faced off. Tian Tian was hardly into that sort of thing, but he was attracted by his friend's wide-ranging experience, humour and quick wits.

Li Le seemed very friendly, but under the superficial layer of

warmth floated a sort of detachment, just the kind of personality that Tian Tian could accept. Both of them had black eyes
alternating between cool and warm. No matter what they did –
talking, listening, laughing – their eyes were silent and uninfor-
mative and their expressions melancholy.

They strolled shoulder to shoulder in the soothing southern
breeze, talking of Henry Miller and the beat generation, or sat
on a tiny balcony watching the sun set, sucking up the pure
white liquid from the fresh coconuts in their hands. Not far
from them on the road, a few pale, heavily made-up young
ladies appeared. They were hunting, with whores' hearts,
without romance. Their faces wore insincere smiles, their noses
sniffled pitifully, and their breasts looked hard as pre-historic
fossils. The southern atmosphere was full of clamour, glamour
and illusion.

It was in the clinic of Li Le's relatives that Tian Tian first
experimented with shooting up morphine. Li Le showed him
how, and then asked Tian Tian if he'd like to give it a try. No one
else was there. It was already late at night: people on the street
spoke from time to time in the unintelligible local dialect, large
freight trucks rumbled by heavily on the road and far-off ferries
blew their whistles.

All this took place in another region of the world. Nameless
ravines and hills undulated continuously, forming huge, three-
dimensional shadows. A pleasantly sweet wind blew against
arrow-sharp branches and leaves. Anonymous pink flowers blos-
somed deep in the ravines, one after another, spreading into a
pastel sea. This feeling of intoxication, light as air, warm as a
womb – and toxic – affected every inch of the soil, until it
seeped into the red membrane of the heart.

The moon waxed and waned, and trains of thought were
broken and rediscovered.

Things got out of control. Each night Tian Tian slept in his pink dreams. The pink liquid stuck to his skin, and its poison was like a primeval flood chasing him forward. His body became weak and powerless, and his nerves ready to snap.

Even today I hate to face up to this picture. This is the point of the story when things took an abrupt turn for the worse. Perhaps it was pre-destined from the start, unavoidable from the day the young Tian Tian received his father's ashes at the airport, when he dropped out of school having lost the ability to speak, when he met me at the Green Stalk Café, when his body leaned over mine on our first night, sweating and impotent, when I went to bed with another man. Ever since then, he couldn't shake off those dreams and his relentless pessimism. He was inseparable from them, unable to draw a line between himself and them. He could only live and die in the shadow of his powerless organ.

When I thought about this, I just wanted to scream. That terror, that infatuation, was beyond my understanding or strength. Ever after, when Tian Tian's angelic face flashed before me, I just wanted to collapse behind closed doors. When your heart bleeds, it can bleed badly enough to kill you.

Li Le ran all the errands as Tian Tian's money was exchanged for one clump after another of white powder. The two of them stayed in his hotel room, and the cat slept next to the TV, which was on all day, reporting robberies and municipal engineering projects. They almost stopped eating altogether as their metabolisms dropped close to zero. But the door stayed open, making it easier for the take-out boy to bring food; they were too lazy even to budge. The room emitted a bizarre odour, fresh yet rotten-smelling, like fruit jelly inside a corpse.

Gradually, to save money, or when they couldn't find a drug dealer they trusted, they started to go to the drugstore for cough syrup, which Li Le would crudely cook into a substitute intoxicant. It tasted gross, but it was better than nothing.

One day Fur Ball ran away. She'd had no food for several days, and no attention from her master. So she decided to leave, by which time her stomach was shrivelled, her coat blotched, her bones showing. She must have gone wild, hunting for food in garbage heaps late at night, calling for a mate from some street corner.

I was shocked, and my mind was in utter confusion. Sleeplessness makes your body hot and dehydrated. Shadows float about, recording thousands of shapes and hopeless situations. Throughout that dry, hopeless night, I lay in bed tossing and turning, replaying in any order the days when I first knew Tian Tian. My brain was a screen covered in dust, and my darling and I were the world's most hopeless leading couple.

But we loved one another so deeply that neither of us could leave the other, especially now. The fear that Tian Tian could float away, a gravity-free particle of dust in outer space, tied my heart in knots. I felt I loved him more than ever. I longed for the sun to rise, before I went mad.

# 19

# Going South

'The key is on the windowsill,
In the sunlight before the window.
I have that key, Eileen, let's get married!
Don't get high,
The key is in the sunlight before the window.'
Allen Ginsberg

The next day, carrying an overnight bag, I took a taxi to the airport, where I bought a ticket for the next flight to Haikou. When I'd done that, I realised I had to make some phone calls. No one in Tian Tian's room answered my call, so I left a message at reception saying when I would arrive. As I leafed through my address book, I felt a bit depressed that now, faced with a problem whose solution was uncertain, it seemed I couldn't find a suitable person to share my fears with.

Madonna's mobile was turned off. Zhu Sha's office phone was engaged and so was her mobile; who knew how many people she was speaking with simultaneously? Spider was out of Shanghai on a business trip; his colleague asked if I wanted to leave a message, but I said no thanks. That left my editor Deng, my psychoanalyst David, my lover Mark, my parents, and the phone numbers of a few ex-boyfriends.

Feeling low, I put my magnetic card in the phone slot and pulled it out again and again. I turned my head, and through the plate-glass window saw a McDonnell Douglas plane sliding along the runway. With a burst of speed, it lifted its nose fiercely and shot out of my line of vision. The moment of ascent was extraordinarily elegant, just like a large, silver bird.

I walked into the smoking room and sat down opposite a man. He was leaning slightly forwards, and I could see the lovely Agassi-style goatee he was growing, and the longish leather bell-bottom skirt he was wearing. I hadn't known that a Chinese man could look so good in that style of beard, and he was also the only man I'd ever seen who could board a plane wearing a leather skirt. He was smoking 555 cigarettes: I could smell their distinctive rough tang, like whole-grain flour sticking on the tip of your tongue. He held the hot cigarette between cold fingers.

Then he turned to look straight at me. His eye sockets were slightly shadowed, but his eyes were bright, commanding yet delicate, casting a harmonious image in which *yin* and *yang* were turned topsy-turvy.

We both opened our eyes wide and took a good look at each other. He stood up and smiled, throwing his arms open. 'Coco, is it you?' He was none other than the master stylist I had met in Beijing, Flying Apple.

We embraced and sat down side by side for a smoke. We exchanged a few sentences. It turned out we were taking the same plane, bound for the same place. The lighting in the smoking room made me feel uncomfortable, and I was aware of the dull throb of a headache.

'You don't look very well. Is anything wrong?' He leant over and examined my face carefully, his hand on my shoulder.

'I'm not very well . . . It's a long story. I'm going to meet my boyfriend. He's just about falling apart down there . . . and me, I've no strength,' I muttered, throwing away my cigarette butt and standing up.

'The air in here is terrible,' I said, walking towards the door.

He followed. 'Wait a minute. Say, what's this on the floor?'

*156*

My dizzy head pounding, I just wanted to get outside. 'Coco, did you lose an earring?'

I felt my ear, sighed and took a cobalt pierced earring the size of a rice grain from Flying Apple's hand. Depending on the light, it takes on different colours and shapes. At the time it was the sole point of colour in my sea of black. I thanked him, walking and thinking to myself: 'When bad things happen to you, everything goes haywire. Even taking an innocent smoke can lose you an earring.'

Before I went through the boarding gate, I rang Mark. From what I could hear, he was busy.

'Hello.' He sounded distant. My voice accordingly turned icy. It's only fair to match one cold face with another, for protection's sake.

'I'm at the airport,' I said. 'I won't be able to make it to your dinner this weekend. Please tell your wife I'm very sorry.'

'Where are you going?' I finally had his attention.

'Where my boyfriend is.'

'Will you be gone long?' Anxiety crept into his voice; perhaps he had put down his pen and closed the file in front of him.

'Will you be sorry if I am?' I asked, still coldly. At that moment, I couldn't get any enjoyment out of this. I was sure I looked pale and harsh. I wasn't satisfied with anything. A mass of problems.

'Coco!' He sighed. 'You know I will. Please stop teasing. You'll be back soon, right?'

I was silent for a moment. Of course he was right. I would bring Tian Tian back, and everything would get better. But could things ever be the same again? Could I still have two men, one taking drugs because of his depression, and continue writing my novel with a clear conscience?

I began crying. Mark's agitated voice said: 'What's wrong? Baby, speak to me.'

'It's nothing. Wait till I come back and I'll get in touch,' I said, hanging up. I realised I was contaminating others with my ugly mood, and Mark would be running anxiously about the office. Poor man. And poor me, too.

David Wu once told me, 'Self-pity is despicable behaviour.' When he said this, his expression had a God-like, awesome look to it. His whole face glowed. But I never paid any attention to his advice. I've always found it fairly easy to pity myself. Narcissism is probably my dominant vice.

Flying Apple sat next to me as the plane climbed through the clouds. He chattered away while I read a magazine, put on and took off my coat, read the magazine again, closed my eyes, placed my left hand under my chin, placed my right hand on my chest, coughed, opened my eyes and adjusted my seatback.

The stewardess came to serve drinks and snacks, and when I lowered my pull-down table, I accidentally spilt Coke on Flying Apple's knee. 'Excuse me,' I blurted. Then I began to talk to him, this beautiful man whose eyes flickered like dark fire, like a generator that could flatten a whole bunch of women. Except a sad one like me.

Flying Apple said that he'd absorbed the elements driving the latest trends in Japan, and was now recommending using pink, baby blue and silver to create his clients' images. In several rows behind us sat his fellow professionals, including one video starlet, two photographers, three assistant stylists, and three sporty males in his entourage. They were on their way to Hainan to shoot the starlet's revealing 'photo biography'. I had seen her in a play somewhere; with her plain face, she was neither angelic nor regal, and had little going for her except marvellous breasts.

Flying Apple kept talking beside me, chasing away the

random thoughts in my mind. I listened, thinking that men wearing leather skirts could turn out to be either awful or cute. He talked about a bad tooth that he had had pulled the previous month, his ever-quarrelling parents, and his girlfriends who were always jealous of his boyfriends.

I fell asleep. When I woke he had his eyes closed, and then he came round too. 'Almost there?' he asked me. He opened the blind and looked out to see what was under the plane. 'Still en route,' he said, smiling. 'Don't you ever smile?'

'What? No, I don't feel like smiling just now.'

'Because of me?'

'No, because of my boyfriend.'

He touched my hand and gave it a squeeze. 'Don't be afraid of trouble. Everyone has trouble, big or small, at some time. Like me, I jump from one hassle to another. I don't even know if I love women or men more.'

'Loving and being loved is always a good thing,' I said, smiling sadly. This was what everyone always talked about. Even if I and my story vanished without trace, other people's stories would continue, and the word 'love' would be present in all of them, and revolving around it would be endless dramas, both soul-stirring and bruising.

When we were nearly at Hainan Airport, we hit turbulence. The plane began to shake horribly, and when a stewardess came round to check safety belts, she lost her balance and ended up on the carpet.

The passengers were panic-stricken. I heard the starlet shriek, 'I didn't want to take this flight!' pointing at a man who looked like her agent. 'Great, now I'll pay for it with my life!' Her shriek turned the atmosphere into something rather strange, as if someone was shooting a film, and this dangerous situation wasn't really happening.

Flying Apple gripped my hand tightly, his face pale. 'Just

knowing I can hold your hand as we fall makes me feel a little better.'

'Not to worry,' I said, trying to endure the tossing sensation in my stomach. 'My fortune-teller has never said I'd have an accident, so the plane won't crash. Flying's the safest form of travel there is.'

'I bought insurance. Accident insurance plus life insurance adds up to a tidy sum. I don't know if my parents will be glad or sorry,' he murmured to himself.

Just as he spoke, the shuddering stopped and everything returned to normal.

At the airport Flying Apple and I kissed a hasty goodbye that left my lips wet. Many gay or bisexual men have a special, fuzzy sort of tenderness that one finds in small animals, but I'm always aware of the Aids risk. As Alanis Morissette put it: 'I'm sick but I'm pretty, baby.'

Outside my taxi window the sky was blue, and beneath the blue sky were bright houses. I didn't know where I was. The cabby drove for quite a while, and finally reached Tian Tian's hotel, which didn't look big.

At the desk, I asked if the guest in B405 had picked up my message, and the young receptionist said no. Her lips were smothered in bright red lipstick, and there was a smear on her teeth too. I had her call upstairs, but Tian Tian wasn't in. There was nothing to do but sit and wait on the sofa in the corner of the lobby.

The three o'clock sunlight shone down on the street beyond the picture window, and the alien throng and traffic were bustling. But it wasn't as congested as Shanghai, nor did I sense any elegance or foreign atmosphere beyond the brash business hum of the city. Everybody looked much the same, except for the occasional tall female beauty, obviously immigrants from the north. Their bodies have an assertive beauty that Shanghainese women lack, and their eyes are bolder, but they don't have our elegant reserve.

I was starving. I picked up my bag and went out. There was a fast-food restaurant opposite, and I chose a window seat facing the street so I could see who went in and out of the hotel.

A few trendy kids were in the restaurant, jabbering away in a language I couldn't understand. The radio alternated between Cantonese and English songs. Two policemen came in, and both separately turned and looked me over. They bought their Cokes, but as they turned to leave they gave me another look. I touched my face, and it didn't seem to be smudged. My black, tight-fitting top hadn't burst a seam, nor had my bra-strap slipped, my zip was fastened, and my belly was firm and flat. Evidently, I looked either very pretty or very suspicious.

Suddenly, I had no appetite at all. I couldn't eat anything, and just sipped a few mouthfuls of coffee, which had a chemical taste, like drinking furniture polish.

I went into the washroom and looked at my pale face in the mirror. I straddled the flushing toilet and urinated like a man. (I always do that in a public lavatory. Used by countless people, the toilet seat has known any amount of body fluids, germs, smells, memories and history.) This toilet looked like a giant white fly, doleful yet uncomplaining, perched under the hips of women of all kinds.

A dull pain shot through my abdomen, and I noticed a smear of red on the tissue. What rotten luck. Virtually every time I left Shanghai for anywhere, my period would arrive. And now of all times, when I was facing a life-or-death situation, my body had to get bogged down in its own predicament.

Wave upon wave of pain battered me as my anxiety deepened the contractions of my uterus. I had imagined that my last act of sex with Mark had seeded a foetus, and had even been thinking of telling Tian Tian everything, and then having the baby. Just who had given me the child would be irrelevant, so long as it had love's blood coursing through its veins, so long as its smile could brighten the sky, disperse the haze and the sadness.

I hurt so much my whole body felt chilled. I pulled down a good thick wad of tissue from the toilet paper roll, and stuffed it inside my panties, hoping the roll had been sterilised. Now what I needed was a big glass of hot water, and a hot-water bottle placed tight against my belly.

Mother once told me most women who have given birth no longer suffer this monthly agony, because the cervix has loosened. Which means that if I never have a baby I'll have a lifetime of suffering. If menopause comes at fifty-five, I've still got thirty years to go, with twelve periods a year. My brain was moving at lightning speed. When I get like this, I'm more neurotic than a sick cat.

Zhu Sha had the same problem, but not so badly; Madonna's was even more extreme. Men left her one by one, and of course there were many reasons, but one of them was not being able to stand her fluctuating moods during those seven days each month when she lost control.

Cruelty and neurosis tortured her and them. For instance, she would send her boyfriend to the supermarket to buy pain-killers and sanitary towels, but when he returned he either hadn't bought them fast enough or he hadn't bought her preferred brand, and she would throw a tantrum and hurl clothes and ornaments around. Her memory would fail her and she would contradict herself, cancelling dates, parties and plans. No one could lean back and have a good laugh in front of her, nor be silent either. If she looked round and found her boyfriend behind her, she'd scream.

She would also have nightmares all night. Once she dreamt that some gangsters she knew from Guangzhou stuck their hands in her uterus and extracted something priceless, and screamed in despair. When she woke, she found that blood had soaked through her towel, seeped through the sheets to the mattress, and even stained her boyfriend's underpants. So she went to wash it off and put on a new towel in the bathroom. But obviously her boyfriend couldn't take much more of that sort of thing.

The influence of a woman's period affects both the body and the mind. The media have covered the topic exhaustively. In film and fiction a woman's destiny takes a turn for the worse as soon as her periods stop. After a while this seems a bit stupid, but it gives feminists a platform from which to ask men: Is this fair? When will women really be liberated?

Stuffed with toilet paper, I walked bow-leggedly, like a toddler in a nappy. By then I had already lost my grip on what was happening. I wanted to see my baby right away. I imagined the bone-penetrating warmth that would come when we embraced and melted into one, the warmth travelling from one heart to the other. Utterly unrelated to sexual desire, it was yet another type of madness born of the chemical reaction between love and kinship and an irrational God's curse.

With my left hand tight against my stomach, I drank one cup of boiling coffee after another, until I spied a familiar figure through the window.

I got up and hurried out of the door. Crossing the road I called his name loudly. He stopped, turned round and we exchanged smiles. Because there was no other choice, with the compassion and sorrow born of our intense love, we yet again attracted and absorbed one another. Love existed from the very beginning, just as death opposed it from the start. I heard him clear his throat. My womb grew warm, my pain lightened, and I realised we were fated to hunger after the very last drop of joy like bees harvesting nectar.

Because there was no other choice.

That night I went with him to the dental clinic where Li Le worked. I found it a frightening place, dirty and sickly sweet, with a cold gleam like a metallic shell. Li Le was as thin and straggly as ever, as if his growth had been stunted by some accident. I kept my mouth shut. I admit I was scared, but I had promised to go with Tian Tian to the school playing field where an illegal deal would take place, in exchange for which Tian Tian would leave with me the next day for Shanghai and go to a detox centre run by the Public Security Bureau. I told him this was the only way. I needed him to be well, because we had to live together for a long time to come. I held his hand, my other hand stuck in my pocket where the money was. My tummy began to ache faintly, even though an o.b. tampon was tightly stuffed into my body like a sluice gate.

We walked in through an unguarded gate, and I saw the playing field with its oval athletics track, a small jungle gym for kids to climb, and a tennis court and basketball hoop. We withdrew into the shadow of the wall.

Tian Tian hugged me lightly and used a filthy handkerchief to wipe the beads of sweat from my forehead. No matter how bad things were or where he found himself, Tian Tian always had a handkerchief ready, like a well-behaved child or an aristocrat.

'Does it hurt a lot?' he asked me tenderly. I shook my head and rested it on his shoulder. The moonlight cast a deep, dark shadow above him. He was much thinner, and there were dark purple circles round his eyes. I couldn't bear to examine his face in detail, or tears would cloud my eyes and I'd feel utterly helpless.

Two men in jeans and dark glasses appeared, and our clasped hands suddenly iced over.

Li Le stepped out to meet them and said something in low

tones. The men walked towards us. I was kneeling against a corner of the wall, breathing evenly and concentrating, not moving at all. Tian Tian stood up, grasping in his hand the money I'd supplied.

The man threw me a look and asked: 'And the money?'

Tian Tian held out his hand. The man counted it, then smiled. 'All right. Minus what you owe from last time, I can give you this much,' he said, quickly stuffing a small packet into Tian Tian's hand. Tian Tian crammed it into his left shoe.

'Thanks,' he said quietly, then hauled me up. 'Let's go.'

We left very quickly. Li Le was still talking to the dealers when Tian Tian reached the main road bustling with people. We waited silently at the kerb for a taxi to appear. A group of sleazy-looking youths walked past, casting lewd looks at me out of the corners of their eyes. One of them said something I couldn't understand, no doubt something crude. His mates laughed, pleased with themselves, and someone kicked an empty paper Coke cup, hitting Tian Tian's leg.

Tian Tian's hand in mine broke out in a sweat. I looked at him, and consoled him quietly, 'Pay no attention. It's nothing.' Then a taxi came by and we hailed it. It stopped and we dived in.

We hugged each other tight inside the taxi. He kissed me and I was speechless, silently pressed against his face. His hand lay warmly on my stomach, and the warmth melted the tension in my womb and my clotted blood.

'I love you,' said Tian Tian softly. 'Don't leave me, don't stop caring for me. You're the best, the most beautiful girl in the world. You have all my love.'

Late that night, I vaguely heard the sound of a cat's cry, fine as silk in motion. When I turned on the light, Fur Ball was there. I leaped out of bed and put the plate of leftover salt-and-pepper roasted pork on the floor. She came over, put her head down and wolfed it up. She looked totally run down. Her coat was so dirty you couldn't make out her colour and her face was thin and fierce.

I sat on the bed smoking and watching her eat. I didn't know how she'd found her way back. Maybe she'd seen me from some corner, like her lucky star, and knew that meant she could go home to Shanghai. The thought made me emotional.

I jumped off the bed, gathered Fur Ball in my arms, and went into the bathroom, where I bathed her in shower gel and warm water. She kept obligingly still as I rubbed her with my fingers, docile as a child. Then I dried her off and brought her over to the bed. Tian Tian was still sleeping, and Fur Ball went to sleep at our feet.

We awoke to sunlight and to find Fur Ball licking us. The soles of our feet were covered in her saliva, and itched slightly.

Tian Tian and I looked at one another for an instant, and then he began to remove my pyjamas. I opened my eyes wide in the bright morning. The warm air lifted my naked body; I saw my pink nipples rising like graceful buoys on the tide and my lover's lips were tiny fish, tenderly and adorably playing in the water. I closed my eyes and accepted everything. His fingers caressed my bleeding wound. Lubricated by blood, I exploded. I heard Fur Ball miaow in the distance and at the same time felt her rough tongue on the soles of my feet.

That morning's lovemaking with my lover and a cat remains clear in my mind. It was a little crazy. That white-coloured drug and sickly-sweet, horrific smell will always be stuck in my nostrils. On date after date with men, shopping with girlfriends, writing alone, or even walking on Gierkeziele Street in Berlin, I can't forget that morning of death and love, that sweet and terrifying flavour.

# 20

# Boy in a Bubble

'And don't cry, baby, don't cry.'
Paul Simon

Outside the window dark skies turned to rain, and Aaron Kwok's Pepsi advert ran on endlessly. It was Wednesday, and having seen Mickey Mouse cartoons, I knew that anything could happen on a Wednesday.

When he awoke, early, Tian Tian had had a change of heart. He didn't want to go to the detox centre today.

'Why?' I asked, eyeing him squarely.

'I want to spend some more time with you.'

'But we aren't parting for ever. All right . . . don't worry. I understand how you feel. But what happens if you start feeling ill?'

He took a little packet out from his shoe, and waved it.

'Tian Tian!' I moaned. 'You actually brought that stuff back with you?'

For the first time ever, Tian Tian went into the kitchen to make me breakfast. I lay in the bath in a daze. I could hear fried eggs sizzling in the wok and the clang as the wok cover hit the floor. For all his good intentions he was probably making a terrible mess. And one breakfast wasn't enough to buy me off. I couldn't forgive his relapse.

I didn't eat it. He sat silently on the sofa, feeding Fur Ball. My

*167*

manuscript in front of me, I hit a momentary dry spell, and then panic came over me, like a sorceress who discovers her magic has vanished. I couldn't throw myself into the distant world of words. Real-life changes could happen at any moment, like ripples surging on the water. I'd always hoped for instant success: like Ali Baba, who had only to say 'Open sesame' for the gates to the treasure trove to swing open; like Bill Gates who became a billionaire overnight; like Gong Li who, at my age, had already subjugated tens of millions of white men with her stunning beauty, all without learning a word of English.

Now, it seemed, I wasn't strong enough. My dreams would never be realised in this city. There was nothing to do but grab myself by my hair and yank myself off the planet (before Nostradamus' prediction came true), or leave society with Tian Tian for the African jungle or a South Pacific island where we would grow marijuana, raise little chickens and dance primitive dances around a fire for the rest of our lives.

'Want to go for a walk?' Tian Tian threw a paper aeroplane on to my desk. Every one of the planes he folded was lovely. They had illustrations painted on them, and aphorisms and famous quotes from famous people written all over them: 'Hell is other people,' 'Loneliness is for ever,' 'Life happens elsewhere,' 'Live poetically,' and so on.

We drove into the city centre, along Yan'an Road, where the elevated highway hadn't yet been completed, past a long row of old houses with little gardens and walls around them. Shanghainese take pride in embracing both new and old simultaneously. Rising here and dipping there, the city's engineering projects use steel-reinforced concrete pillars to raise its massive torso, whereas the fragmented historical remains use fine rain and moss to embellish delicately the face of the city. Each time I sit in a taxi and cross this metropolis divided between new and old, I feel I can hear the city's endless chatter all the way.

I may remember that sound for the rest of my life, and may never understand it. Mark told me that every city in the world has a unique sound. In the sounds of Paris, London, Venice, Vienna and Shanghai, he found a certain quality, ethereal, hard to pinpoint, resonating in the heart of each city, and linked to the essential character of its people.

Sounds a bit metaphysical, doesn't it? The men in my life simply must have a few ingenious synapses in their brains, because sex and love make a person more sensitive and more likely to generate the spark of inspiration.

Perhaps a good meal at Benny's would start the day off well. Benny's is a restaurant decorated by a mad Belgian designer to look like a massive lobster. There's a long silver window, and along the upper portion of the wall is a round mirror, so guests may, if they wish, lean back and spy on everyone around them. What keeps tongues clicking is the fact that in the mirror you can watch – risk-free – women wearing low-cut dresses, revealing cleavages of every shape and size.

Eating hot-and-sour soup and baked clams, Tian Tian and I began a difficult conversation of a sort we rarely had.

'Do you like me the way I am now?' The bluish whites of Tian Tian's eyes were like a question mark on his pale face. He seemed to have stored up a reserve of courage in preparation for this chat. 'Naturally, you needn't lie.'

'How long have we known each other? It's almost a year, but it seems much longer, and we'll last a century, ten thousand years, because I love you. But if you don't hurry up and get well . . . I can't think.'

'If one day I die – no, don't interrupt me, I mean when I die, at that instant when I close my eyes never to open them again, what kind of person will you think I've been?'

I didn't want to eat any more. My tongue had lost all feeling and my stomach was numb too. Separated by the plates, glasses and forks, we held each other's eyes for a long time. The whites of his eyes turned bluer until, as the playwright Joan Hawkes put it, 'they oozed a misty liquid.'

'I will h-a-t-e you,' I enunciated clearly.

'Death is the expression of exhaustion, a solution arrived at rationally once one has known the deepest depths of tiredness. I've thought about it for a long time, perhaps all my life, and having thought it through, I'm not ashamed of dying. A person like me can't go on constantly polluting himself, annihilating his soul.' He jabbed the left side of his chest with his finger, but he'd have looked a bit more natural if he'd used a dagger.

'It's an impulse in the dark of the soul. Psychologists always say impulses are dangerous and discourage them, but an impulse comes uninvited.' His voice was crystal clear and cool, his lips pale and unemotional. Despite the impersonal pronoun, he was talking about himself.

'The weaker my will, the brighter my eyes, because I've seen the great black hole in the belly of the sun, and the cross formed by the major planets of the universe,' he said.

My despair turned to anger. 'I'm not going to bullshit you. In one word, you're degenerate.'

'Perhaps. The dying never have the chance to explain themselves to the living. Actually, a lot of people are even more degenerate.'

I clutched his hand. Cold as ice.

'What are we talking about, for God's sake? Don't go on. Why do we have to talk about something so horrible here and now? Don't tell me about life and death, love and hate, the ego and the id. We're alive together, aren't we?

'If there's something you don't like about our life, get specific: I don't get the washing clean enough, I talk in my sleep, my novel isn't profound enough, it's utter rubbish – whatever. OK! I can change; I can try to do things perfectly. But for heaven's sake, don't say such horrible things . . . It's absolutely irresponsible. I'm always dreaming of finding wings and soaring in the sky with you, but you're always thinking of abandoning me and leaping alone into hell. Why?'

A lot of people were looking our way. I raised my head and saw myself in the mirror: frantic, tear-filled eyes, and a fierce expression. I felt really idiotic. We so obviously loved one another.

'Coco.' Tian Tian's face remained absolutely sombre. 'Right from the start we were two different sorts of people, I said so at the time. But that hasn't stopped us loving each other; you full of energy and ambition and me devoid of desire, drifting with the tide. Philosophers say "Everything originates in nothingness," and nothingness accentuates everything.'

'Whoever said that can drop dead! Don't read those books any more. You need to be amongst living, breathing human beings. You need to do more physical work. My dad often says "Work makes a person healthy". You need sunlight and grass, and dreams of happiness and all the joy that goes with them,' I said rapidly, like a sewing machine struggling and thundering in the night.

'For starters, tomorrow you should just go to that damn detox centre, and take part in some light manual labour like gardening, and sing songs with everyone. When you've made it through the worst, I'll make sure you get out more with girls, but I absolutely won't let you fall for them. I'll even find prostitutes for you, if you'll just get well, like a normal person,' I said, crying. The mirrors on the walls above were a blur.

Tian Tian hugged me. 'You're crazy.' He took out a handkerchief and gave it to me to dry my eyes.

I looked at him through the fog of my tears. 'I *am* crazy, because you are too.'

A gaze was fixed intently on me from another corner of the restaurant and reflected in the mirror opposite, and in a distracted moment I saw it was Mark's. He was sitting with a middle-aged foreign woman who seemed to be a friend. He must have been looking at me for some time by then.

I pretended I hadn't noticed him, and told the waiter to bring the bill. Today was Wednesday, a day when anything could happen.

Mark was still looking in my direction, his expression confused and agitated. When he finally stood up, I turned my head away. The waiter came and handed me the bill. I took out my wallet, but the more I hurried, the less able I was to dig out the RMB notes.

Mark came over, feigning surprise. 'What a coincidence! I didn't expect to see you two here.' He offered his hand to Tian Tian.

All of a sudden I despised the scene taking place in front of me, and I despised this German. He had no right to extend that hypocritical hand of his to Tian Tian. His hands had once caressed every inch of my body. In this moment of deceit, those hands of his were extraordinarily offensive. Don't tell me he couldn't see how weak and helpless Tian Tian was just then. My God, we'd just finished a cruel and bitter conversation, he was about to go into detox, and we were both in despair. But the man who had known me secretly in a shameless, carnal debauch came over and politely and hypocritically asked Tian Tian, 'How are you?'

Even if he had a hundred reasons to desire me, he should have controlled himself and stayed right where he was, far away from us, and let us go in peace.

My nerves were taut as a bowstring. I pulled Tian Tian by the hand, quickly moving to the door. Mark followed and handed me a book we had left behind on the table. I thanked him in a low voice, and then in an even fainter voice said: 'Get lost.'

That night we barely closed our eyes. We kissed through the night, and the bitterness of our saliva filled the room. Our bed drifted in the boundless sea like a lonely island in imminent danger. We took refuge in each other's love. When the heart breaks there's a crackling sound, very light and very fine, like the splintering of wood fibres. I promised Tian Tian I would visit him often, and that I would take good care of Fur Ball and myself. I would write seriously and finish my novel. I wouldn't let myself sink into nightmares. I had to believe I was the luckiest and most beautiful girl alive, and that miracles do happen. It was all I could do. I swore I would await his return with my blue eyes flecked with purple.

I love you. And that's how my love is.

First thing the next day, I took him to the detox centre in a daze. They found his name in a record book, there because I had already registered him. After a few items they deemed unnecessary had been rejected, the steel door slowly closed and we scarcely had a chance for a last look.

# 21

# Cocktails

'Come writers and critics
Who prophesy with your pen.'
Bob Dylan

'Love will tear us apart.'
Ian Curtis

'A different kind of dame
gets a different kind of fame.'
Sally Stanford

I stayed in my room writing for a week, not even bothering to comb my hair. No phone calls disturbed me, and no one knocked at the door (except the delivery boy from Little Sichuan and an old lady from the Residents Committee collecting a street-cleaning fee). I was in a daze, like slipping on mud: from this door to that, from reality here to fiction there, I hardly needed to try. It was my novel that pushed me on.

I gave up embellishment and lies. I intended to put a completely genuine version of my life before the public's eye. This didn't require too much courage, just obedience to that mysterious force. As long as it felt good, that was enough; I didn't have to play naive or cool. This is how I discovered my real self, and overcame my terror of loneliness, poverty, death and all other potential disasters.

I often fell asleep on top of my manuscript, and woke with a swollen cheek. Sometimes, when the wall clock's silver hands pointed past twelve, I would imagine I was hearing things. Those sounds would recur, like the snoring of the electrical repairman next door, the boom of a crane on a far-off building site in the dead of night, or the hum of the refrigerator in the kitchen.

Several times when my patience was exhausted I put down my pen and walked quietly into the kitchen and opened the fridge. I hoped a tiger hidden inside would pounce on me, cover my mouth and nose with his golden fur to stop my breathing, and then rape me without hesitation.

Actually, in the middle of this reclusive life, I discovered the *tao* and attained a state of grace. To my mind, heaven is no more than this: being at ease and completely free of worry. There are no men to notice your hairstyle and clothes, no one to fuss about whether you're full-breasted or your eyes are sufficiently elegant. There are no dinners to rush off to, no police to restrain your merry-making, no supervisors to check the progress of your work, no distinction between the dark of night and the light of day, and no one to reappear and squeeze you dry of affection.

I was hypnotised by my novel. In order to convey one torrid scene as authentically as possible, I tried writing naked. Many people believe that there's a connection between the body and the mind. (The American poet Theodore Roethke allegedly dressed and undressed repeatedly in front of a mirror to get a sense of what it was like to dance naked.) I certainly believe there's a secret connection between writing and the body. When my body shape is relatively full, every sentence I write is pithy and poignant, whereas when I'm thinner, my writing is full of over-long sentences like dense clumps of silky-soft seaweed.

I reached beyond the limitations of my own life and tried to write about grander, even universal themes. This may seem like a slogan from God, but that's what I tried to do.

In my novel, a couple hold each other close as a raging fire spreads through their room. They know they can't leave. Fire has sealed off all windows and corridors, leaving them only one thing to do: make love madly in the heart of the blaze.

One of my ex-boyfriends told me this story, which happened near his home.

When they carried the lovers out on a stretcher, the charred bodies were so tightly fused together they couldn't be separated. The boy and girl, not yet twenty, were studying at one of Shanghai's top universities. It was a weekend evening, and her parents had gone to Tian Chan Theatre to watch Chinese opera. The boy came round to her place, and they watched TV, listened to music, chatted, and predictably, like all young people, were tender and touching too.

The fire started in the communal kitchen downstairs, and took hold rapidly. The wind that night was especially strong, so they had no hint of danger until the air in their room burst into flames. They realised there was no way out, so there was only one thing left for them to do: make love madly in the heart of the blaze. Afterwards, my nose really smelled burning and the dry hot air of desperation.

I put down my pen, wondering: what if I and my lover had been in that room? Without a doubt, we would have done the same thing, because there would have been no other choice. Only through that intense bonding could we have faced the extreme terror of imminent death. The only theory of Freud's I find convincing is the mystical link between the instinct to live and the instinct to die.

I remembered our picnic on the grass, when Madonna asked me: 'If Nostradamus' prediction of the end of the world were to come true now in 1999, what would you choose as your last act?' Then she answered her own question: 'Fuck, of course!'

While my right hand gripped the pen, my left hand crept down to my sex, which was already moist, my clitoris like a sticky, swollen jellyfish. I put one finger in to explore, then a second. If I had eyes or some optical instrument on my fingers, they'd discover a beautiful, pink and carnal universe, the swollen blood vessels stuck close to the tender, pulsating inner walls of the vagina. For thousands of years, women's exotic gardens have awaited the invasion of the opposite sex just like this, awaited the most primitive joy, the battle which would carry the sperm inside, and then within the pink, fertile palace there would be a tiny new life to carry on. Isn't that perfect?

I satisfied myself with a slight sense of disgust. Yes, my satisfaction is always accompanied by a hint of disgust. Other people use the loss of home and family, being reduced to living like a vagabond, to stimulate themselves to write a masterpiece. But me, I apply Opium perfume and lock myself away for seven days and seven nights to the sound of Marilyn Manson's destructive songs.

Perhaps this will be my last book, because I still feel that despite all my efforts I haven't created anything unique. I've shamed my parents and disappointed my innocent little butterfly of a lover.

Seven days later, a phone call scooped me up from the depths. The sunlight outside the curtains was beautiful, and the wind carried the refreshing scent of violets and orchids from nearby Changfeng Park. On the phone, editor Deng had unexpected news: they had decided to reprint my collection of short stories, this time grouped together with others in a series called *Winds of the City*.

'How many will be printed?' I enunciated each word with

great care, because seven speechless days and nights had left my mouth clumsy.

'It's been settled at ten thousand. Not enormous, but you know the market's very sluggish because of the financial crisis in Southeast Asia. To be frank, ten thousand isn't bad at all. At first the publisher was doubtful, but I pointed out that the first edition sold out almost at once.' She laughed modestly, leaving it to me to jump in and thank her.

'Payment by royalty or by the word?' I asked, my brain slowly coming back into play. It's like opening a window: heat, noise and disorder from the outside, including the airborne germs which cause tuberculosis and diarrhoea, all stream pell-mell inside. This chaotic energy invigorated my brain, and once again I left the prison of my novel, on temporary parole.

'Let's fix a date when you can come out. I've a few friends in the book business who'd like to get to know you,' said Deng in friendly tones. 'I told them you're writing a novel at the moment, and they'd really like to talk to you, see if there's a way of working with you. I'd say the more opportunities like this, the better. What do you think?'

She seemed to have thought of every angle for me, and she knew how to manage all the details in a way that fitted in with the rules of publishing. All I needed to do was accept the gift I was offered. I didn't know if she was really keen on my writing, but I didn't think this was the moment to ask, so I thanked her and promised to ring her later and agree a time and place.

Afterwards I rang Madonna. She was still in bed and her voice was muffled and sleepy. When she realised it was me, she made an effort to clear her throat. In a low voice she said to the person (obviously a man) by her side: 'My dear, could you please get me a glass of water?'

Then she asked me what I'd been doing lately. I told her the whole story: how I'd gone to Haikou to look for Tian Tian, Tian

Tian had gone into the detox centre, and now I had my head buried in my book.

She was obviously astonished. 'How did that happen, for God's sake?' She took a deep hit on her cigarette, and exhaled lengthily.

'Things are beginning to look up. I'm confident he'll recover,' I said. 'How about you?'

She grunted. 'How would you expect? I live on booze and men. It's all a mirage. One day I'll lose my bearings and float away on the wind – and when that day arrives, I'll thank the Lord for it. Hey, if you're free this afternoon, let's get together. I'll bet you're feeling awful, and I haven't seen you for ages. How about going for a swim? Let's go to Donghu Hotel and swim in their open-air pool. I've got a gold membership card. You know, the good thing about swimming outdoors is you can amuse yourself and others at the same time. If a woman wants a quick and easy way to attract men, apart from dirty dancing, swimming outdoors is the way to do it!' She laughed out loud, like a woman in a Hollywood thriller.

'Excuse me, darling, at the moment I'm like a panting she-dog. This little bastard has just about done me in. He's sucked all the life out of me. Okay, enough of this. I'll drive over and pick you up. I've got a present for you.'

Beside a sheet of blue water, Madonna and I stretched out on sunbeds, clear sky above our heads, a light breeze brushing our faces, and the sunlight like a smattering of honey making our exposed flesh sticky. After being covered up for a season our skin was pale and unappealing. I draped a towel over me and focused on a man in the water. His name was Ma Jian-Jun, and he and Madonna had met in dramatic circumstances.

Madonna was racing her car through the streets late one night when the roads were empty, one of those moments when it's safe to go crazy. As she turned the wrong way up a one-way street lined with parasol trees, her path was blocked by a police car that shot out from the shadows.

Two policemen got out of the car, one with broad shoulders and long legs who looked like the latest Agent 007, Pierce Brosnan. 'You've made a mistake, miss,' he solemnly announced, sounding like a dead ringer for 007 – except he wasn't holding a gun and he lacked the hint of menace.

Madonna looked him over under the dim glow of the street lamp, and three seconds later she'd fallen for him. She obediently paid her fine, and handed over her mobile phone number too. What made this handsome cop decide to get involved with a lonely woman who drives recklessly in the middle of the night is hard to guess.

'He said he found my hands attractive. When I passed the money through the car window, he noticed a pair of enchanting hands, slim and fair, with fingers set off by the gleam of a diamond ring as if they'd been touched by magic. A pair of fake hands like those on a plaster mannequin,' whispered Madonna, laughing heartily. There was a huge contrast between her face and her hands, which were amazingly youthful, like those of a teenager.

'Who cares what he says, he's happy to fuck with me anyway. And he does it well. Every time he knocks at my door wearing his uniform, I'm wet in three seconds flat.' She looked over at me, but my mind was elsewhere.

'Hey there, try to cheer up. Let's go for a dip,' she said, walking towards the pool and plopping into the water. The pool was gradually filling up with swimmers, and a pair of Japanese men with black body hair and turnip legs were soaking in the water and looking at me.

I took off my sunglasses, unwrapped my towel and revealed a red bikini. Under the sun, the red colour contrasting with white skin made me think of strawberries and cream. I leapt into the water, and a gentle, transparent force lifted my body. In the sunlight I had nowhere to hide; even if I shut my eyes, the eyes of everyone else could see this strawberry fool through the water.

I didn't know why my reaction was so odd. Usually the expressions of strangers looking at me half-naked gave me an instinctive sense of satisfaction, but as soon as I thought of myself as a dessert exposing myself in broad daylight I became uncontrollably angry. Feminism reared its head. What was it that made me seem so like an empty-headed Barbie doll? Those men probably couldn't guess I was a novelist who'd just shut herself in a room for seven days and seven nights, and they probably couldn't care less either. In public when one notices an unknown woman, one needs only to check out her three key measurements; one needn't consider what she's got upstairs any more than the number of steps up to the White House.

When I'd finished swimming my mood hadn't improved much, particularly when I saw Madonna and her policeman boyfriend flirting. I felt depressed, and sneezed in the changing room.

'Poor thing! Your worries have used up all your endorphins. You need to watch your health!' Madonna wrapped me in a large towel and leaned towards my ear. 'Look at me. Since I got a new boyfriend I haven't had a cold,' she said softly. 'Know why? The experts' answer is that sex raises your resistance to illness, so I don't sneeze or get a runny nose.'

She gave me a little kiss, and then remembered she had a present for me in her handbag. 'Wait a sec. I'm going to give you a surprise.'

'What?'

'Close your eyes.' She laughed. I shut my eyes, imagining it wouldn't be anything special. She was forever playing pranks.

'Okay, open your eyes now.' She thrust an object under my

nose, and I stepped back before realising it was a female sex toy, a genuine plastic vibrator. But that wasn't all. She even unwrapped it, pulled out the pink phallic device, and demonstrated it in detail against her palm.

'Uh, thanks. I don't need one,' I said hastily.

'It's new. After that little bastard Ah Dick left me, I thought I'd be needing one, but I never used it after all. It just can't fill that hole in your heart.' A strange smile emerged on her face, hurt yet lewd. 'I mean, psychological consolation. But now I've got a man again, while you're twice as depressed. You must be desperately lonely. Poor you. You could use this.'

'No, no thank you.' My face was all red. The thing was thumping outrageously, and frighteningly large. I thought to myself I'd rather use my own fingers. They're softer and more reliable.

'Take it, I beg you.' She was still laughing.

'No.' I was laughing too.

'All right. You're such a proper young lady, but really, deep down, we're alike.' She gave me a look as if she could see right through me, opened her mouth wide and made a face.

'We really should make a date to visit Tian Tian. As long as I've known him, it seems like he's been living a nightmare. Of course, he was lucky to meet you. I know how much a boy like that needs affection.'

'But I always feel guilty about him, as if I were another of his nightmares,' I said. 'We cling on to each other as if we were travelling together through the darkest night.'

'Darling, don't let it drive you crazy. I know you're taking it hard, but it isn't the kind of thing another woman could handle. Actually, you're unique. If you feel lonely, give me a call. I can lend you my boyfriend, or maybe we could have a threesome.' She went into another fit of laughter. This was a typical Madonna snook cocked at convention. I believed she was capable of doing it too, even though it was outrageous. Just the words made me feel slightly sick, the way you do when you eat something very sweet.

We had dinner together at Yang's Kitchen, which is run by a Taiwanese. Her policeman boyfriend seemed to approve of me, since as he sipped his wine he pressed his knee against mine. I didn't bat an eyelash. While my mouth was full of the tasty juice of razor clams, my brain was busy wondering how a policeman's performance in bed would differ from that of any other man. He'd probably treat each woman under his body as a law-breaking citizen and crack down on her fiercely. But would his organ be as fierce, and his endurance as great?

As I thought about that, the tip of my tongue produced a satisfying stream of saliva, and my stomach felt warm, as if held by a large hand.

Madonna yelled, 'What the hell's this?'

Fuming, she threw down her chopsticks violently. I couldn't help laughing as the knee was jerked away.

The waiter rushed over.

'What is this disgusting thing doing here? I'll bet your chef's nearly bald. He won't have one damn hair left soon,' she said, gesticulating rudely at her bowl of soup.

The restaurant manager came over too, apologised several times, and had the waiter remove the bowl of black-boned chicken and wolf-berry soup in which a strand of hair was floating. In no time, a new bowl of soup turned up, and a free dessert was promised.

When I got home, I discovered Madonna's present in my bag, no doubt put there on the sly. 'She's really a crazy woman,' I recalled Tian Tian's words, shook my head and put the thing in a drawer. I washed and got into bed.

Drowsiness engulfed my body like the tide under the moon at mid-cycle. This was my easiest descent into sleep for days. My

Tian Tian, my novel, my anxiety, and even my damn problems making a living – all were jettisoned into a bottomless pit. I'd get a good sleep and deal with it later.

Dear Coco, you needn't worry. When you wake up, tomorrow is the day after the one before.

Early next morning, the fat woman next door discovered a letter and a postcard in our letterbox. As always, she brought them to me enthusiastically. I thanked her, walked over to the sofa and sat down. The letter was from Tian Tian, and the post-card from Mark, in Mexico.

I hesitated a second and decided to read the postcard first. On the front was a cactus the size of a huge pagoda, towering in the desert. On the back were scrawled some words in English.

'Honey, I've come to Mexico on business. It's rather dirty but very intriguing. Everywhere you look there's marijuana, trishaws, and sad black-haired, blue-eyed women. In the hotel, I ate quite a few of the world's spiciest jalapeno chillies. I bet next time I see you you'll be knocked out by my hot kisses.

'PS: A client of ours, who makes unbreakable glass, is being a nuisance. From here I have to go to our HQ in Germany to look into the market for it, and into a competitor he's asked us to see. Back in maybe a fortnight.

'PPS: I can't get through to you. Please think about going on-line. I can help you apply for a free e-mail address.

'Kisses! Mark.'

I kissed the postcard. For a while I had taken the phone off the hook. I assumed he'd guess I was writing. I didn't need to worry about him, anyway. He was a pillar of society, handsome and intelligent with an enviable job, a skilled handler of complex relationships, and good at keeping on an even keel (typical Libra). And he took to women like a fish to water.

As long he wanted to, even if I ran off to the South Pole, he'd manage to make contact.

Mark's abilities seemed to have been a gift from the gods, whereas Tian Tian was the total opposite. They were like beings from two different universes. Their existences met in inverted images of themselves projected on to my body.

I found a silver letter opener on the table. I didn't generally use anything so pretentious to rip open a letter, but this time it made me feel a bit less nervous.

Tian Tian had written just one page:

'My dear Coco,

'Writing to you from this place feels a bit like a fantasy. I don't even know if this letter will reach you safely. Now I'm far away from you, very far, hundreds of millions of light years away. When I think of all the things between us, my mind is flooded with thoughts of you. I keep having nightmares.

'In one of the dreams, I keep running. Above and below me are pink blossoms and fruit. The flowers have thorns and I bleed as I run, until I jump into a deep, deep hole. There isn't a glimmer of light. I can vaguely hear your voice, as if you're reading your novel. I begin to call your name in despair, and then my hand brushes against a hot ball of something. It's soaking wet and throbbing.

'I guess it must be a heart, but I don't know who'd throw their heart into this black hole.

'This dream replayed again and again, making me hysterical, so that now I haven't got an ounce of strength. The doctor says this is a normal physical reaction to the treatment, but I really don't want to stay here any longer. Everywhere there are dismal, hopeless faces.

'After the first course of treatment I'll come home. Right away. Pray God gives me a pair of wings. A kiss for you. One thousand, ten thousand kisses. If there's a reason to live, loving you is it.

Sad Tian Tian

June 30'

On the back of his letter he'd drawn a cartoon of himself with the corners of his mouth drooping in a crescent moon and a few hairs glued to his scalp. I couldn't help crying. Scalding tears poured down my face like lava.

I thought, God, what does it all mean? What kind of fate has been arranged for this boy and me? My tears always fall for him, my heart always aches for him, and it's for him that my soul soars. I don't know if what we had between us was love, but it was hopelessly tragic, the purest poetic expression of doomed passion, like a prisoner locked in a hidden cell, like lilacs swaying in the wilderness, like fish swimming in the abyss of despair.

Back before we began, we'd lost the chance of a chance. Time's high-speed train whistled and rumbled through modern tower blocks into the distance. My tears meant nothing. The joys and sorrows of any one person meant nothing, because the train's massive steel wheels never stop spinning for anyone. This is the secret that terrifies everyone in the cities in this fucking material age.

# 22

# A Rendezvous with Publishers

'Let us be together. Our lonely hearts, exposed under the lamplight.
The train is shifting quickly in the darkness.
These are the only methods created
by God to sway the framework of time.'
Tori Amos


Deng called again, enquiring thoughtfully how I was eating and sleeping, and how my writing was going. Then she asked if I could meet her and her publishing friends at a café on Shaoxing Road.

I said that'd be fine.

I took a cab. Shaoxing Road is a small street with a strong literary ambience; several publishing houses and bookstores are based there. The café is called Old China Hand Reading Room in English, and is famous for its wall-to-wall library and its 1930s furnishings. The owner is a well-known photographer, Deke Erh, and his patrons include plenty of famous media types – journalists, publishers, writers, TV and movie producers, Chinese opera stars and scholars from the West – who shine and sparkle stars against its elegant backdrop. The books, jazz music, smell of coffee and antique furnishings fit in with both Shanghai's erotic past and its consumer-orientated present.

I pushed the door open and saw Deng and a few men seated round a corner table. As I sat down, I realised one of the publishers looked familiar, but it was only when he smiled and handed me his card that I remembered who he was.

When I was studying Chinese at Fudan U., he was Activities Chairman in the department's Student Union. Two years ahead of me, he was one of the people I secretly admired then. He was nicknamed 'Godfather' because he usually wore a hat and dark glasses, like a mafioso.

Fudan U. was putting on the first intimate drawing-room comedy ever staged by a Shanghai university, called *The Trap*, and Godfather was the director. I overcame all sorts of difficulties, triumphed over other candidates, and won the heroine's role. With a script conference as my excuse, I often went to Godfather's Number 3 Dormitory, where I would sit with him at the Heart-to-Heart Table (so-called because people regularly gathered around it for heart-to-hearts). I would focus my eyes, misty from shortsightedness, on his eloquent face and fantasise that he'd suddenly shut up, lean across the table and clamp on to to my lips like a magnet.

This scene was far more moving and memorable than any drawing-room comedy, but it never took place. I was too young, and terribly afraid of embarrassment. And as for him, he fell for the stage designer. She went around with a string of silver keys hanging round her neck, and when she walked her long legs seemed to waltz. When she smiled, two dimples formed on either side of her mouth. She often ordered boys about bossily, sending them scurrying every which way with hammer and nails in their hands. She seemed to be an expert on paper stage props, and was always phoning the Huifeng Paper Company. I secretly called her 'Huifeng'.

Huifeng totally mesmerized Godfather. On the eve of the performance I saw them walking hand in hand in the moonlight along a tree-lined boulevard. I felt like the 'Song of Heartbreak Moonlight'.

The play was a huge success. My performance was excellent, and at the moving moments tears flowed like raindrops and feverish applause broke out.

And two months later, on the grass behind Chairman Mao's statute, I made the acquaintance of the Christian/Shakespeare-worshipping sex maniac. As I've said, we soon dropped all pretence of friendliness, and I even had to call on my Public Security Bureau contacts to warn him off.

Remembering these events made me feel foolish, but also pleased me. Had I fallen for Godfather rather than that fanatical Christian, would things have turned out differently? Would I have so many problems now? Would I be writing so intensely, and living such a strange life? Who knows?

'Hi, Godfather.' I happily shook the hand he held out.

'You're more beautiful than ever,' he flattered me. This line may be a cliché, but it never fails to please a girl. Deng introduced the other men to me. All were mutual friends who had set up an imprint called *La Rive Gauche* at the publishing house where Deng worked. It'd take a graduate of Fudan U. to come up with a name like that. But I knew from Deng that *La Rive Gauche* had published a series called *A Thousand Paper Cranes* whose sales broke records at the China National Book Fair and the intangible assets of which already exceeded ten million RMB.

My mood lightened. Time and again, in one city or another, I run into Fudan graduates, and that makes me happy. An air of freedom, wit, youthful frivolity and aristocratic decadence floats over Fudan U.'s Yanyuan Garden, Xianghui Auditorium and the rows of parasol trees on Handan Road. This is the naive and romantic stage of a student existence, before we set off on the long road of real life, and its traces are the tell-tale sign by which we recognise our fellow alumni.

'It's great that you already know one another. Coco, tell us about the novel you're working on,' said Deng, keen to cut to the chase.

'I read your short story collection, *Shriek of the Butterfly*, and it made me feel quite marvellous. It was like going into a room with mirrors on all four walls plus the ceiling and floor – everywhere the light was like a cornered snake striking here, then there. At the heart of this chaos was a touching and insightful yet bizarre sense of reality. And the language is dark and erotic. Reading your stories was like' – Godfather lowered his voice – 'like having fantastic sex.'

He threw me a meaningful glance. 'That sort of book can be a mesmerizing read, particularly for the educated reader.'

'The writing mirrors the writer,' interjected Deng.

'Your target market could be defined as university students and white-collar workers, especially women, who would probably react strongly to it,' said one of Godfather's friends.

'But I don't really know how it'll turn out, because I haven't finished . . .'

'All passions are a source of inspiration,' said another.

'Thank you for your kind words.' I took a sip of coffee, and dragged my eyes back from an antique telephone across from me. Something made me smile and add softly: 'At last I've discovered the meaning of being a writer. At least it's more impressive than being a hundred-RMB note.'

Outside, the sky darkened, and orange wall lights came on. Godfather suggested going somewhere for dinner. Deng declined, as her eighth-grade daughter was waiting for her to come home. 'She's preparing for her high-school entrance exams. Time's tight and I've got to keep a close eye on her,' she explained to us.

\* \* \*

After dinner Godfather asked where I lived, and offered to take me home. I'm not stupid, and I could see what was on his mind. That wouldn't do; things had changed. I particularly wanted to be alone that night, even though he was as attractive as ever.

We hugged and went our separate ways, I promising to tell him as soon as the novel was finished. 'I'm very glad to see you again, and I'm very sorry I never asked you out back at Fudan,' he said softly into my ear, half in earnest, half playfully.

I walked alone down Huaihai Road at a leisurely pace. It had been a long time since I'd strolled like this. It occurred to me that I was, after all, only twenty-five, still rather young; I was like a credit card with a healthy line of credit which could be used now and paid for later. The neon streetlights were no more dazzling than I, the ATMs no richer.

I walked to the subway station entrance at Parksons department store. Downstairs there's a huge bookstore franchise, Ji Feng Bookstore, famed for its wide range of stock and die-hard stand against discounting. I browsed aimlessly, and stopped for a moment in front of a shelf of fortune-telling books. According to one, women born on January 3rd – dubbed 'Pretty-Legged Girls' – are exceptionally charismatic and have strong mental and physical recuperative powers. It predicted the year 2000 would be a year of rich harvests for me. Didn't sound too bad.

Then I walked over to the subway station's PhotoMe booth. In Mark's apartment hung a long row of beautiful, artsy pictures he'd taken at the PhotoMe. Four of them were self-portraits in four different poses, naked to the waist: standing, kneeling, crouching and from the side. Each featured a section of his body – head, chest, stomach, legs – and when pieced together they had a particularly exciting visual effect, like a robot, or a dismembered body.

And there was what he liked to call his 'Orang-utan Series'. He'd taken a dozen shots of his arms, and another dozen of his torso together with his long arms, like a modern version of Tarzan; so bizarre, so sexy. The first time I made love with Mark at his place, the photos on his walls really turned me on.

I inserted enough money into the slot and, after four bursts of the flash and about five minutes of time, took out a row of four pictures. The faces on them showed, respectively, sorrow, anger, happiness and detachment. For a brief moment, I couldn't tell who this girl in front of me was. Why did she feel such intense emotions? Which corner of the world did she live in, what sort of people did she know, and how did she make a living?

Another five seconds and my mind had returned to normal, as if I'd released my soul and then put it back inside my skull. I glanced at my self-portrait photo, and put it carefully in my handbag.

The station clock said it was already 10.30 p.m., but I still wasn't sleepy. There was still half an hour before the last train would leave Shanghai Station. I bought a ticket from the vending machine, slid it into the automatic gate, and the turn-stile ceased resisting. I walked downstairs, chose a relatively clean-looking seat in a row of red plastic ones, and sat down.

I could snooze, or I could check out the strangers around me. I once wrote a short story, *Subway Lovers*, about a frail beauty who, whenever she takes the last subway from People's Square, always runs into the same neat and tidy businessman, who smells of tobacco, cologne and air con. They never speak, but a certain tacit understanding exists, and occasionally when one of them fails to appear, the other feels inexplicably sad and disoriented.

Then one day, when the weather has turned cold and it's snowing, the subway car floor is slippery. A sudden jolt sends the woman accidentally sliding into the embrace of the man. They press close, and none of their surrounding passengers notice anything unusual. Everything happens spontaneously. The man doesn't get off at his usual stop, but travels to the terminus with her. He kisses her there on the platform late at night, and then, like a true gentleman, wishes her goodnight and walks away.

I wasn't sure whether it was right for them to have no intimate contact, or whether having them go to bed and become lovers would satisfy the reader more.

When the story was eventually published in a trendy magazine, it generated quite a reaction among professional women. Speaking on behalf of many of her colleagues, my cousin Zhu Sha expressed their dissatisfaction with the compromise that ends the story.

'You should have them either not touch at all, or else let them release their passion. But he kisses her and then politely says goodbye and leaves. What does that mean? It's like scratching an itch through your boot, an awkward, incomplete feeling, worse than a drizzling summer day. We can all imagine how they both toss and turn sleeplessly in bed that night. Love stories are all like that nowadays. It's depressing.'

Zhu Sha was still married then, but she was already awkwardly stuck in limbo. Beneath their dignified and refined exteriors, she and her sisters hide a warm and sensitive heart. They're scrupulous and meticulous workers, and have high standards for their personal lives as well. They aspire to the image of the modern, independent new-style female, confident, wealthy and attractive. They like Andy Lau's line in that Ericsson ad, 'Everything is within your reach', and the image of the professional woman in the De Beers ad, smiling confidently, a diamond ring on her hand, with the male voice-over: 'It's self-confidence twinkling, it's charm glistening.' But they like security too.

The last train chugged up to the platform, and when I stepped into the car I smelled a pleasant male body odour. It was just like I'd written in *Subway Lovers*: 'Intermingling smells of tobacco, cologne, air con and his body wafted about, and this enchanted air made her slightly dizzy.' I couldn't stop myself turning to check out my surroundings. I wondered if the story's hero might actually appear to its author of his own accord. But I had no way of confirming which male body near me was giving off these smells, and abandoned my dream. Yet I did feel that in our urban lives (especially at night) there is a beautiful sense of mystery wafting subtly throughout everything.

# 23

# The Mother from Spain

'You never listen to a word I say.
You only see me for the clothes that I wear,
or did the interest go so much deeper? It must have been
the colour of my hair.'
Public Image Ltd

'The weather is getting hot. Cicadas chirp among the poplars of the old foreign concessions. Stone stairways, spotted with dirt and soot from car exhausts lead into the city's secret gardens. Ancient mansions and fashionable people hide by day and come out at night. High-heeled shoes walk down mossy alleys, down streets lined with skyscrapers, past fantasies in all directions. The clack of high heels is the perfect echo of materialism ringing in the city's ears . . .'

One afternoon, without warning, when I'd had just written that lyrical passage, the clack of high heels sounded outside the door, followed by a discreet knock. I opened the door to a middle-aged woman I didn't know. But her overdone outfit and her accent, with its twang and exotic flavour, made me realise instantly who this surprise visitor was.

'Is Bi Tian Tian in?' She eyed me rather worriedly for a few seconds, and then smiled. 'You must be Coco.'

I automatically ran a hand through my hair, which I'd left loose, and noticed a few inkstains on my fingers. Worse, I was wearing a skimpy negligee, and even someone half blind could see through the white cotton that I had nothing on underneath. I folded my hands over my stomach, trying to act as if this was quite normal, invited her in, and ducked into the bathroom to slip on the panties I'd put in the washing machine the night before. I had to make do with that. I pulled my hair back and inspected my face for smuts in the mirror. I'd never dreamed Tian Tian's mother would appear unannounced in our apartment.

I was wrong-footed from the start. My mind was still on my writing, and I'm sure any girl whose boyfriend's mother burst into the place where they were cohabiting would be just as shocked, especially when said boyfriend had become a drug addict and was locked up in an isolated, frightening detox centre. How should I tell her what had happened to her son? Would she be hysterical, would she faint? Would she scream at me and demand to know why I hadn't taken better care of her son? Why was I was so irresponsible, still living so carefree, writing my novel? She'd probably wring my neck.

I went into the kitchen and spent ages looking round. The fridge was empty, and there was only a scraping of coffee left in the jar. Edgy, I set out a cup, spoon and sugar cubes, scraped some brown powder out and made a cup of coffee. White foam floated on the surface, like the crummy coffee you'd get at a bad café. I sampled a mouthful. At least it didn't taste bitter.

She was sitting on the sofa, still measuring up the decor. Her gaze rested at length on Tian Tian's self-portrait, the most remarkable of his works. It caught the chill of his eyes, clear and cold as ice. The feeling in his painting was hard to fathom. It made you feel that when he looked in the mirror and sketched his features he'd started to enjoy his loneliness.

I gave her the coffee and she thanked me. She eyed me up openly. 'You're prettier than I expected. I didn't think you'd be so slight.' I laughed, my heart thumping. 'Oh, I'm sorry, I haven't introduced myself. I'm Tian Tian's mother. You can call me Connie.'

She took a smart box of Cuban cigars out of her bag. I passed her a lighter and she carefully lit her cigar. The room was suffused with a bluish-grey smoke, a slightly pungent smell, but one which created a pleasantly exotic mood. We both relaxed a bit.

'I didn't tell you in advance when I'd be coming, since my son wrote that he hoped I wouldn't.' A hurt smile surfaced. Her well-preserved face was virtually unlined, and her permed hair was jet black and lustrous and cut in the child-like style of Yue-Sai Kan. Chinese women who've lived abroad for a long time all seem to favour this hairstyle, as well as that kind of brown eyeshadow, that kind of burgundy lipstick, and that kind of professionally tailored dress. Perhaps the lifestyle overseas encourages them to dress up, to make up for the way mainstream Western society has always disdained and marginalised the Chinese race.

She gazed for some time at Tian Tian's self-portrait, with its gloomy water-drenched expression. Then her eyes moved towards the big bed we never made. I sat next to her feeling helpless, preparing myself for a maternal interrogation. Indeed, she began to talk.

'When will Tian Tian be back . . . I should have called or written beforehand,' Connie had finally asked. Her eyes were filled with hope and anxiety, like a young girl awaiting an important moment.

I began to speak, but my mouth was dry and my tongue burning. 'He . . .'

'Oh, yes.' She took a photo out of her bag. 'This is a picture of my son ten years ago. Back then he still had a baby-face and was quite short. In a minute when I see him, I'm afraid I won't recognise him.'

She handed the photo to me. I saw a frail youth with a peaceful look in his eyes, wearing a brown jacket, long corduroy trousers and white trainers. He was standing in front of a fiery-red canna plant, and under the bright sun his hair was as soft and wispy as a dandelion – so light it could be blown away by a breeze at any moment. Tian Tian in the autumn of 1989. The colours and a certain atmosphere about the photo reminded me of a dream I vaguely remembered. It gave me a feeling of déjà vu.

'Actually, Tian Tian hasn't been here for a while now . . .' Although it was hard to say the words, I told her the whole story truthfully. In my mind, one floating image after another flashed by, each emitting a faint light, sentimental and passionate pieces of my memory.

Connie's cup fell to the floor. It didn't break, but her dark red skirt was soaked through. Her face went pale and for a moment she said nothing.

I felt oddly comforted that another important woman in Tian Tian's life was sharing my pain. She seemed to be trying hard not to lose control. I jumped up to get a towel to dry her skirt, but she waved me away, as if to say that it didn't matter or that she didn't want the towel.

'There are clean skirts in my wardrobe. You can choose one that matches and put it on.'

'I'd like to visit him. May I?' She lifted her head towards me, her eyes powerless.

'The rules don't allow it. But in a few days he can come out,' I said carefully, and once again suggested she dry or change her skirt.

'No thank you,' she murmured. 'It's all my fault. I should never have let him get like that. I hate myself. For so many years I've given him nothing. I should have taken him to Spain with me. Even if he hadn't wanted to go, I should have made him . . .' She started crying, blowing her nose into a tissue.

'Why did you never think of coming back to see him before now?' I asked her frankly. Although I was touched by her tears and there was a choking feeling in my own throat, I'd never considered her a competent mother. Whatever unspeakable secrets this unknown woman from Spain might have in her past, I had no right to criticise her. But I'd always understood that Tian Tian's rootless existence, filled with lost souls and dark shadows, was fatally linked to her. Their relationship was a rotting umbilical cord linking the infant to its mother's womb forever. Ever since she'd abandoned her family, and her husband's ashes were flown home in a McDonnell Douglas jet, her young son's chaotic fate was sealed. That was when he started to lose his faith in talent, enthusiasm and happiness, just like an organism whose molecules slowly lose the ability to resist certain kinds of cold or corrosion. Mother, son, smoke, death, terror, indifference, grief – everything hung together, there was cause and effect, like the Buddhists' eternally revolving Wheel of Transmigration.

'He must absolutely detest me. He keeps his distance from me, shuns me,' she mumbled to herself. 'If I come back to live, maybe he'll hate me even more. He's always suspected I caused his father's death . . .' A harsh, cold light suddenly glinted in her eyes, like a drop of winter rain hitting a window.

'It's all because that old woman is always slandering me without cause, but my son believes her and won't speak to me any more than absolutely necessary. We hardly communicate. Sending money to him is my only consolation. I've been so busy running the restaurant. I've dreamed of how one day I'd give all the money I've earned to my son, and that day he'd understand that the person who loves him most in the world is his mother.' Her tears were falling like raindrops, suddenly revealing the depths of her fragility.

I kept handing tissues to her. I couldn't bear to watch her

sobbing openly like this. A woman's tears are like a rain of silver drumbeats; their special rhythm is catching, drumming on a special part of the onlooker's brain and driving her to the verge of tears as well.

I got up, walked over to my wardrobe, and took out a narrow, knee-length black skirt which I'd never worn in the year since I bought it. I laid it in front of her, the only way I could think of to stop her tears and her increasingly sad reminiscences. 'Even though I've come back now, he may not want to see me,' she said in a low voice.

'Would you like to wash your face? There's warm water in the bathroom. This skirt looks as if it'd fit you perfectly. Please put it on.' I looked at her worriedly. There were tear streaks in her powder, and the coffee stains were horribly obvious on her crimson skirt.

'Thank you!' She blew her nose. 'You're a nice, thoughtful girl.' She reached up and smoothed her fringe. A uniquely feminine elegance had returned to her movements. 'I'd like another cup of coffee, if I might.'

'Oh, I'm sorry.' I smiled awkwardly. 'That was the last of it. There's nothing left to drink in the kitchen.'

Before she left she put on my skirt, and it was a perfect fit from every angle. I brought out a carrier bag and helped her put her skirt in it. She hugged me and said she'd be waiting for the moment when she could meet her son. At present she and her husband were working with a real estate agent, viewing buildings in the city centre to find one suitable for a restaurant. She gave me a slip of paper on which were written her room and phone numbers at the Peace Hotel on the Bund.

'We'll see each other again soon. I've a gift for you which I forgot to bring. I'll be sure to give it to you next time – and there's also one for Tian Tian too.' Her voice was very faint, and there was an appreciative gleam in her eyes.

There was an empathy and a tacit understanding between us. There were deliberate and accidental wrongs, regrets and emotional pain, on all sides. They were in every fibre of my body, in every nerve. But even if the wrongs of her dead husband could be laid squarely at the door of this woman called Connie who had appeared out of nowhere, even if her heart had once been infected by evil spirits, even if there were thousands and thousands of truths which would stay hidden until the end of time, even if she were everything you despise, resist, denounce and condemn in your heart . . . there's still that moment of common feeling when a fragile, innocent impulse seizes a person's heart, like the hand of God reaching down in an empty gesture to the world.

# 24

# Dinner Ten Years On

'You had the key to your soul
And you did open that the day you came back to the garden.'
Van Morrison

On a hot, dry day, an hour after Mark rang (saying he was back in Shanghai, wanted to see me as soon as possible, and would I like to go to an avant-garde German film with him), Tian Tian came home. Like the light and dark sides of the moon, complementing one another, the two key men in my life had returned into my orbit.

When Tian Tian opened the door, I froze for an instant, then without a word we fell into each other's arms. Our invisible antennae reached out to one another, sensing physical impulses that came from a love in the mind not the body.

Then he suddenly remembered that the taxi was still parked outside, waiting for him to pay.

'I'll do it,' I said, grabbing my bag and heading down the stairs. I gave the cabby 40 RMB. 'I haven't any change,' he said. 'Then forget it,' I told him, and went back into the lobby followed by his thanks. The melted white sunlight behind me abruptly faded, and my eyes re-adjusted to the darkness of the stairwell. When I came into the apartment I was greeted by the sound of running water from the bathroom.

I walked over and, leaning in the doorway, smoked and

watched Tian Tian bathe. The hot water turned his body pink, like a strawberry milkshake or a newborn baby. 'I'm falling asleep,' he said, closing his eyes. I went to the side of the bath, picked up a sponge and scrubbed him lightly. Watson's bath oil emitted a faint and refreshing herbal scent, and a bee buzzed, bumping against the bathroom window dyed champagne colour by the sunshine. The tranquillity was palpable and visible, occasionally overflowing like a liquid.

I smoked and watched his delicate and pretty face and body, deep in sleep, as if I could hear Kreisler's *Liebesfreud* nocturne. He seemed to have regained his health.

Tian Tian abruptly opened his eyes. 'What shall we eat tonight?'

'What would you like?' I smiled.

'Tomatoes with sugar, celery fried with lily root, garlic-fried broccoli, potato salad, quail braised in soy sauce and a big bowl of chocolate ice cream, vanilla ice cream, strawberry ice cream . . .' His face lit up with longing as he smacked his lips.

I gave him a kiss. 'Wow, your appetite's never been so good.'

'Because I just crawled up out of the ground . . .'

'Where shall we go to eat?'

He grabbed my arm and took a bite, like a tiny carnivore.

'Let's have dinner with your mother.'

He was dumbstruck. He dropped my arm and leapt up out of the water. 'What?'

'She's back, and her Spanish husband's with her.'

He crossed the bathroom barefoot and headed straight for the bedroom without drying.

'You're unhappy, aren't you?' I said, chasing after him.

'What do you think?' His voice was quite loud. He lay down on the bed, his hands cradling his head.

'But she's here.' I sat at his side, focusing on him as he

focused on the ceiling. 'I understand it upsets you. But you shouldn't be afraid of this sort of complicated situation. Don't hate or avoid it; now's the time to face up to it. This is just what you need.'

'She's never loved me. I don't know who she is. She's just a women who sends me money from time to time, and that's only fooling herself. It's just a way to exonerate herself, make her feel less guilty. Whatever, she's only ever been interested in her own feelings and her own life.'

'Whether you like her or not isn't important. All I care about is that you're not happy, and it's your mother's doing. The sooner you straighten out your relationship with her, the sooner I'll be able to see you create your own happiness,' I said, bending down to hug him. 'Please, get rid of your inhibitions, just like a pupa biting its way out of a cocoon and becoming a beautiful butterfly. Love yourself. Help yourself.'

Silence. There was an odd spaciousness to the room, like a wide meadow. We kissed, and our bodies grew increasingly lighter and smaller until the fantasy of a tiny flower bud occupied every inch of our brains.

Afterwards we made love calmly in a way which, while unable to achieve perfection, would always be irreplaceable. His stomach was white and smooth, almost capable of reflecting my lips like glass. The fuzzy hair about his sex, like larkspur, smelled of the warm, sweet hormones of a small creature (like a rabbit, his sign). Where I used my other hand to caress myself, I gradually began to feel swollen and hot. Tiny, secret blue sparks were lit where fingers and tongue lingered, bringing with them sticky, wet saliva and chasing away chaos, emptiness and regret.

I don't think I'd ever kissed anyone so madly. I simply wasn't thinking what I was doing. I only knew he was the joy I had lost and found once again. He was the fire of my life, the impetus behind my work; he was inexpressible sweetness and pain, a perfectly beautiful rose resurrected by alchemy in a remote ancient Persian garden.

As he burst, I climaxed too. I withdrew my juice-soaked hand and brought it up to my mouth. I smelled my scent, and he grabbed my hand in his teeth and sucked on it. 'It's sweet with a slightly musky flavour, like aniseed and cinnamon duck soup.' He sighed, turned over and was fast asleep in no time, one hand still gripping mine tightly.

At seven thirty in the evening, Tian Tian and I arrived at the Peace Hotel on the Bund. There under the bright lobby lights we saw Connie and her husband waiting anxiously.

Connie was wearing her best, dressed in a gold-brocaded red *qipao*, very high heels, painstakingly and heavily applied make-up, with a glamorous and poised air, in the style of Hollywood starlet Lisa Lu forty years ago. As soon as she saw Tian Tian she began crying and reached out to him, but Tian Tian retreated. Her Spanish man moved a step closer to her, and she took advantage of this to lean against his chest, wiping her tears with a handkerchief.

She quickly regained her composure and smiled. 'I had no idea you'd grown so thin and so handsome, I'm really . . . terribly happy. Oh, let me do the introductions,' she said, approaching us on her husband's arm. 'This is my husband Juan.' Then she turned to Juan. 'This is Tian Tian and Coco.'

We shook hands. 'Everyone must be starving,' said Juan in Spanish-accented English. 'Let's go and get some dinner.' He was the image of the typical matador, fortyish, tall, healthy, dashing, with a full head of chestnut-brown hair, light brown eyes, and a beaked nose. Under his full lips he had a cleft chin, characteristic of Westerners, which almost seemed to have been carved by a knife, and this made his jaw forceful and sensual. He and Connie were well matched, the middle-aged version of a beauty and her hero, with Connie perhaps three or four years his senior.

We took a taxi to Hengshan Road. No one said anything en route. Tian Tian sat in the back seat between Connie and me, his body as stiff as a lead weight.

Juan occasionally praised something faintly in Spanish, probably the city's night scenery outside the window. It was his first time in China. In his small Spanish town, he wouldn't have seen mournful Chinese women and Chinese men wearing traditional gowns except in films. His Chinese wife rarely spoke of her homeland, I later learned, so the modern, dazzling Shanghai now before his eyes was a far cry from what he had expected.

We walked up a small alley between ivy-covered walls lit by streetlights for a few minutes, and then saw a short row of old European-style houses. We entered a courtyard illuminated by a back-lit advertisement. It was Yang's Kitchen, a Chinese restaurant. The decor is low-key, the cuisine simple, light home-style cooking. I wasn't sure how Connie, who hadn't been in Shanghai for long, had found this little restaurant deep in these lanes and alleyways. But without a doubt it's a great place to talk and eat in peace.

Connie asked me to order. The restaurant owner, a Taiwanese, came over and chatted with Connie as if they already knew one another well. Juan announced that there were two dishes, in his crude Chinese, Phoenix Claws (chicken feet) and Pork Tripe, which he didn't want to eat because right after arriving in Shanghai he had tried them and got diarrhoea that very night. 'He had to be taken to Huashan Hospital for an I.V.,' added Connie. 'It was probably because he'd just arrived and wasn't acclimatised yet. It wasn't necessarily the food.'

Tian Tian sat beside me seemingly oblivious to our conversation, just smoking in a daze. For him to have agreed to meet his mother that night hadn't been easy, and no one could force him to greet her with a smile or burst into tears.

The meal progressed rather slowly. Connie kept recalling the time she was pregnant with Tian Tian, his birth and their life up until he was thirteen. All sorts of minutiae were still perfectly clear in her mind, and she recounted them one by one as if she were counting the family treasures. 'When I was pregnant I often sat at the head of the bed staring at a calendar. It had a picture of a little foreign girl playing with a balloon on the grass, and I thought she was the cutest thing. I kept imagining that I would bear a little child as lovely as her, and lo and behold, I had an extraordinarily beautiful baby. Granted, it was a boy, but he was delicate and beautiful.'

As she spoke she focused her eyes on Tian Tian, but Tian Tian's eyes remained expressionless while he extracted a bamboo shrimp from its shell. To her husband, she explained briefly in Spanish what she'd said. Juan nodded agreement, and said to me: 'He is very good-looking, and a little girlish.' I declined to comment, sipping my wine.

'When Tian Tian was five or six, he could already draw. He drew a very amusing picture called *Mama Knitting a Sweater on a Sofa*. The balls of wool on the floor had grown eyes like a kitten, and Mama had four hands doing the knitting. He was always asking how I could watch TV and knit at the same time, with my hands moving so fast . . .' Connie's voice was very low, but her laughter was loud, as if someone had ordered her to laugh loudly.

'I only drew Papa repairing a bicycle,' interrupted Tian Tian unexpectedly. I shot a glance at him, and reached out my hand to squeeze his, which was a bit cold. The gathering suddenly fell silent. Even Juan seemed to have understood what Tian Tian was implying. His words inadvertently broke a taboo no one wanted broached; anything to do with his dead biological father was touchy and unlucky.

'I still remember the year when Tian Tian was nine he took a

liking to a six-year-old girl next door, to the point that . . .'
Connie used Shanghainese to continue a story out of the past. A
gentle, disapproving expression appeared on her face, as it
should when any mother recalls the exploits of her son when he
was young, though her eyes were filled with foreboding. She
kept talking as if she were facing a life-or-death challenge, and
had to concentrate her strength to meet it.

'. . . he took our pretty little trinkets, the alarm clock, vases,
glass marbles, comics, a box of chocolates – he even stole my
lipstick and necklace – and gave them all to the young mistress
next door. He was a terror, stealing just about everything in the
house.' She made a wild gesture and laughed loudly, generating
a panicky vibration in the air, like someone playing a piano with
broken keys.

'My son is capable of ignoring everything for the one he
loves,' said Connie in a low voice, looking at me and smiling
faintly. The light wasn't bright, but I could still sense a trace of
mixed emotions, of envy and of love.

'Can we go home now?' asked Tian Tian, turning to me and
yawning.

Connie seemed a bit nervous. 'If you're tired, why not go
back and rest?' she said. Then she signalled for the bill, and
indicated to her husband to take something out of her bag,
two gifts carefully wrapped in colourful paper. 'Thanks,' said
Tian Tian faintly. Over the years, Tian Tian had accepted the
money and gifts Connie gave him as the norm: you couldn't
say he loved or hated them. They were like eating and
sleeping to him and he instinctively needed them, that was
all. I thanked her too.

'Juan and I will see you home, and then we'll go on somewhere else,' said Connie.

Juan spoke in English: 'I saw in the English-language
*Shanghai Now* magazine that a luxury liner called Oriana is

permanently docked at the Bund, and open to visitors. Wouldn't you like to go with us to take a look?'

'Darling, there'll be plenty of chances, let's go together another time. Tian Tian's tired.' Connie tugged at her husband's hand. 'Oh,' she said, as if she'd suddenly remembered something. 'On the way out we can take a look at the house we've chosen for our restaurant. It's in the courtyard next door.'

The moon hung round and shining in the sky, and in the moonlight everything was permeated by a faint trace of mystery and cold. Walking into this courtyard, with a round lamp encircled by an ornamental iron railing, and paved with pale red tiles, we found an old three-storey, western-style house which appeared to have been renovated. The entire structure still looked proud, and the elegant grandeur accumulated over seventy years of history emanated from it once again, undimmed by the vagaries of time – something that a new building would be hard-pressed to emulate. To the eastern and southern sides of the building stone stairways meandered upwards, occupying an extravagant amount of space for Shanghai's pricey old Foreign Concession area.

A few hundred-year-old camphor and parasol trees adorn the courtyard and house like a colourful lace frill on a skirt. There was a massive balcony on the second floor, which could be converted into a superbly romantic café in spring and summer. Juan said that when the time came they could hire young red-skirted Spanish women to dance flamenco there. You could imagine the rich, exotic atmosphere.

We only stood on the balcony briefly, without going inside, because the interior wasn't decorated and there wasn't much to look at.

The electric light and the moonlight mingled together against the ground and our bodies, and for an instant there was a vague, dream-like feeling. A taxi took us home, Connie and Juan waving as the car drove off. Tian Tian and I held hands walking slowly up the stairs, entered our apartment, sat on the sofa and opened our presents.

Mine was a gem-studded bracelet, his a book of Dali's art and a Ravel CD – Tian Tian's favourite artist and best-loved composer.

# 25

# Love or Passion?

'The man's happiness: I will.
The woman's happiness: He will.'
Nietzsche

'Making love with a woman and sleeping with a woman are
two separate passions, not merely different but opposite.
Love does not make itself felt in the desire for copulation (a
desire that extends to an infinite number of women) but in
the desire for shared sleep (a desire limited to one woman).'
Milan Kundera

Tian Tian was back, filling an important space in my life
again. Each night we fell asleep inhaling each other's
breath, and early each morning we opened our eyes and
kissed, as our stomachs growled with hunger. The more we
kissed the hungrier we grew. It must have been love that
famished us.

The fridge was stuffed full of fruit, every brand of ice cream,
salad and vegetables. We wanted to live a simple, frugal vege-
tarian existence, like ape-men in the jungle tens of thousands of
years ago – but not without refrigerators, ice cream, mattresses
or flush toilets.

Our cat Fur Ball remained incorrigibly wild, maintaining two
homes, in our apartment and among the street-corner rubbish
bins. She commuted between the two, snoring at the foot of our

bed on Fridays and Saturdays, her body smelling sweetly of body wash (Tian Tian was responsible for bathing and disinfecting her), and as soon as Monday arrived, like an office worker she would tuck her tail in and leave the apartment right on time, to wander the streets as she pleased.

As night fell, she would gather her cohorts and begin her ritual mating calls. Even though she was strolling amid the filth and stink of garbage, she still found her own very special pleasure in it.

Sometimes, late at night, you could hear the shrieking of a band of cats downstairs, rising and falling. The local Residents Committee organised people to clean up all the places where cats could be hiding, particularly rubbish. As a result there were a lot fewer stray cats, but Fur Ball kept right on doing her thing unmolested. It was as if she had an uncanny ability to outwit fate. The gods were powerful, but she was pretty resourceful herself, occasionally even bringing a tomcat home for the night. We imagined that if there were a 'Cat Gang', she would be its Queen, conferring her sexual favours on the males of her choice.

And as for me, I hit a bout of writer's block. Twenty-five thousand or so words away from the end, my brain went utterly blank, as if all my imagination, wit and fire had oozed out my ears overnight. The words that came from my pen were lousy and obscure; I wrote, tore it up and tossed my pen into the dustbin too. I even began to stutter a bit. Whether on the phone or chatting with Tian Tian, I did my best to avoid adjectives, favouring subject + verb + object constructions, and imperative sentences, such as 'Don't console me,' and 'Please torture me.'

Tian Tian hid himself away in another room, absorbed in painting illustrations for my temporarily broken down novel. Most of the time he stayed in there with the door shut. When some suspicion or other worried me I would suddenly push open the door and go in, but I never smelt that strange smell or saw him doing anything unusual.

After he came back from the detox centre, I thoroughly swept out the room, taking all morning to check each corner for marijuana or other suspicious stuff. Once I'd made sure there was nothing left of his past there, I constructed a haven for him within its walls. He installed himself there with a heap of paints, like Da Vinci seeking the true nature of things in a chaotic world. Like Adam in the Garden of Eden, using his rib to create a miracle of love.

'I can't do anything,' I said. 'I think I'm really losing it. No enthusiasm, no inspiration. I guess I'm just an ordinary girl – more ordinary than most – infected with a mad desire to get famous by writing a book.' I felt even more useless when I looked at the desk piled with his lovely illustrations. I felt truly sad, knowing that I was failing to live up to his love and my own dreams.

'No you're not,' he said, without looking up. 'You just need to rest for a while, and have a bit of a moan, and play the spoiled child.'

'Do you think so?' I looked at him, surprised. His words sounded unusual. Interesting.

'Complain about yourself, and you win a bit of attention from your lover,' he continued perceptively. 'That's one way of letting off psychological steam.'

'That sounds like Dr Wu's logic. But I'm really happy that you see it that way.'

'Will your publisher agree to use these illustrations?' asked Tian Tian, putting down his pen. I walked over to his desk and flipped through them. Some were just drafts, but others were fine, finished pieces. The colours were light and soft, the figures clean yet slightly exaggerated. The necks were all longish,

Modigliani-style, but the eyes were Asian, narrow and delicate, melancholy as well as comic and naive.

And those characteristics are just what my words and his paintings have in common.

'I love them. Even if I don't finish my novel, they have a life of their own, we can show them. People will like them.' I reached over and kissed him on the lips. 'Promise me you'll keep on painting. I have faith you'll become a great painter.'

'I haven't given any thought to that yet,' said Tian Tian calmly. 'And I don't necessarily want to be a famous painter.' That was true. He never had any ambition, and never would. There's an old saying: 'At the age of three one can tell the person at eighty.' It means that in all the years one lives, from three to eighty, there are some things in one's core that never change. That being so, many people can tell very early on what their future will be like.

'It's not a question of fame. It's a way of giving yourself something to cling on to, a reason to be happy,' I argued. But there was another sentence I didn't say out loud: 'And it would drive you to break for ever from your drugs and your dissociation from life.' The desire to be a great painter would give him a focus. I once wrote: 'Life is like a chronic illness, and finding something interesting to do is a kind of long-term cure.'

'The solution to all problems is never to try to fool yourself,' he said simply, giving me a sharp look (he rarely used to look like that, but since his return from the detox centre, I'd begun to notice a few subtle changes in him), as if to imply that I was using the great truths of life to mislead us both, somehow trap him.

'Okay, you're right,' I said as I walked out. 'That's why I love you.'

'Coco,' he called after me, using a tissue to wipe wet gouache off his hand, 'you know what I mean. Early every morning when

I open my eyes and find you next to me, I just feel one hundred per cent happy.'

Before meeting Mark I spent a while trying to think up an excuse for going out, but in the end I didn't need one. Tian Tian was at Madonna's place watching *The Emperor Strikes Back*, and said he'd be at it all night. I hung up the phone, put on a long waist-hugging, see-through top and black, low-slung pants, rubbed some silver powder on my cheekbones and went out.

At the corner of Yongfu and Fuxing Roads I saw my long-limbed Mark. Neatly dressed, fresh and standing under a streetlight, he looked like a film star who'd drifted over the Pacific. My foreign lover had a pair of wicked blue eyes, a cute bum, and that monstrous plaything. Each time I saw him I imagined I was willing to die for him, die under him – and each time I left him, I thought that he should be the one to die.

When he slid off my body, and picked me up, wobbling with unsteady steps into the shower; when he put his hand covered with body shampoo between my legs, gently washing away our mingled juices; when he got excited again and grabbed me, pulling me down on his crotch; when we made love again, lubricated by the body shampoo; when I saw him catch his breath between my spread thighs, calling out my name; when all the sweat, all the water, all the orgasm hit our bodies at the same instant, I would just think to myself: This is the one who should die.

When you close your eyes, the instincts of sex and death are only separated by the finest line. In my story *Pistol of Desire* I arrange for the heroine's father to die as his daughter climaxes while making love – for the first and last time – with her lover, an army officer. That story won me male admirers and harsh criticism in the media.

Mark and I kissed and went hand in hand through a metal

gate and a garden of gloriously scented purple hydrangea to a tiny cinema suite. I stood in a corner far away from the seats, watching Mark as he greeted and chatted in German with his blond-haired friends. One of them, a woman with short hair, occasionally looked my way. Foreign women always look at the female Chinese lovers their compatriots bring as if they're intruders. In China they have a much smaller pool of potential mates than do foreign men; they generally don't care for Chinese males, but countless Chinese women are competing with them for their Western men.

Sometimes when I was with Mark I felt deeply ashamed, afraid I'd be mistaken for one of those cheap women who go fishing for rich foreign boyfriends because they'll do anything to get out of China. So I always stood in a corner, put on a serious expression and returned the amorous looks he threw me with a scowl. Pretty silly.

Mark came over to suggest having a drink with the female director after the film. There were too many people so we ended up standing. I had to admit that I didn't really understand the dream-like images of glaciers and trains, but I felt that the director was experimenting with a terror all humans share, a feeling of helplessness. She chose a powerful medium. The colours in the images were mesmerizing, with a subtle purple-and-blue harmony amid the strong black and white contrast. Even wandering among Shanghai's boutiques, you wouldn't find such a collage of pure art and compelling colours. I like a director who can shoot that kind of film.

When the film was over I met Shamir, the director, an Aryan woman in a short black skirt with a close-cropped butch haircut. Her blue-green eyes radiated enthusiasm and her legs were long. Mark introduced me. She looked at me in a peculiar way and offered her hand in a slightly reserved way. But I reached out and hugged her. She seemed a bit surprised, though pleased.

As Mark had told me beforehand, Shamir was a true lesbian. When she looked at me, there was something in her eyes – a subtle flirtiness – that one doesn't find in most women.

We sat on the second floor of Park 97 by the cast iron balustrade, drinking in an atmosphere of shimmering light, smoke-veiled wall paintings and background music. Downstairs Tony, one of the owners of the Park, was running back and forth greeting customers. When he looked up and saw us he waved a hasty 'Hi there'.

Shamir coughed once, picked up my embroidered red satin bag, looked at it closely for a moment, gave me a little smile and said, 'It's sweet.' I smiled back.

'I have to admit I didn't really understand your film,' Mark said to her.

'Nor did I,' I said. 'But I was mesmerized by the colours. Those rays of light clashing with one another, and yet attracting each other too. You'd be hard put to find such colour combinations in another film, or even in a clothes shop.'

'I'd never thought of a connection between a clothes shop and my film,' she laughed.

'After the film I felt as if it was a dream I'd had before, or a story someone once told me. Maybe it's like a sensation I had for a moment reading Coco's book,' said Mark. 'At any rate, it's a really good feeling . . . like smashing something to bits and then piecing it back together.'

'Really?' said Shamir, putting her hand to her chest. Her voice had a strange child-like quality. One moment her movements were as calm as a lake's surface, then she'd suddenly do something impetuous. When she agreed with you she would stick out her hand and grab you by the wrist, saying with great conviction: 'Yes. That's exactly right.'

This was a woman you could not be indifferent to. She'd done so much – even been to the North Pole to shoot a film, where she'd climbed a huge frozen waterfall called 'the Wailing Wall' because it seemed as if it were made from a cliff of tears. She was currently working for Germany's biggest cultural exchange organisation, DAAD, where she was in charge of cinematography, and knew all the underground film-makers and avant-garde professionals in Beijing and Shanghai. Every year her organisation held a festival in Germany to which they invited all kinds of artists, including Chinese ones. A lot of people liked her, but the upbeat impression I had of her came directly from *Flight Itinerary*, the film we'd just seen.

She asked about my stories. I told her that they were all true and chaotic stories of what happened in Shanghai, this flower garden with a post-colonial flavour. 'One of my stories was translated into German. If you're interested, I can give you a copy,' I said truthfully. It was translated by a student of German who fell for me back at Fudan U. He was a top student who left to study in Berlin before he even graduated.

She smiled at me like a flower blossoming in a spring breeze. Handing me her card, complete with mail and e-mail addresses, telephone and fax numbers, she said, 'Don't lose it. We'll be meeting again.'

'Oh dear, you've fallen for Coco,' joked Mark.

'So what?' Shamir laughed. 'She's an unusual girl. Not just bright, but very pretty too. A frightening *baobei* . . . I'll bet you she'd say and do anything.'

Her words moved me, freezing my body for an instant like an electric shock. I still don't understand why it is women – without exception – who best understand other women can unfailingly uncover another woman's most subtle, most secret characteristics.

Thanks to those words of appreciation, before we parted we stood at the entrance to Park 97, kissing intimately in the shadow of the trees. Her moist, inviting lips attracted me like an exotic flower, and I felt a sudden carnal pleasure as our tongues intertwined smoothly and perilously, like silk. I can't explain why I overstepped the bounds of ambiguity with this unfamiliar woman – from chatting to kissing, from a goodbye kiss to a passionate one.

A street light suddenly went out. A feeling of heaviness, like a blow, and yet one of detachment too, came over me. Her hand touched my breast, and through my bra lightly twisted my nipple – firm as a flower bud – while her other hand slid down to my thigh.

The street light came on again and I snapped back to reality, as if waking from a dream, tearing myself away from a mysterious temptation. All the while, Mark had stood there silently enjoying the scene.

'You're so cute – too bad I have to go back to Germany tomorrow,' said Shamir softly. Then she hugged Mark. 'Goodbye.'

Sitting in Mark's BMW, I still felt a bit dazed. 'I really don't know . . . what that was all about,' I said, lightly fingering my hair.

'First of all, you were bewitched by her film,' said Mark, taking my hand and giving it a kiss. 'A sensitive woman kissing another sensitive woman takes one's breath away. That kind of sensitivity is sensual.' The words didn't sound at all male chauvinist; rather the reverse, they were understanding.

Touched by his words, my underwear dripping wet, I floated on a cloud all the way to his cavernous apartment – so big you can go crazy anywhere in it. I turned on the stereo and put on a record of Xu Li-Xian singing a Suzhou ballad, took off my clothes and walked towards the bedroom.

He suddenly remembered there were the blueberry jellies I especially love in the fridge, and signalled to me to wait. He went into the kitchen where I heard dishes clattering, and then came out stark naked, carrying a plate of fruit jellies and a silver spoon over to the bed. 'Have a bite, honey,' he said, putting the silver spoon to my lips.

Both enjoying our delicious jellies, one mouthful at a time, we suddenly burst out laughing. With one shove, he pushed me down, and then like a caveman he buried his head between my legs and began kissing my sex with his sweet, icy tongue. 'You have a really lovely pussy. There isn't another of such quality in Berlin and Shanghai together.' Eyes wide open and staring vacantly at the ceiling, pleasure anaesthetised my brain, robbing me of my wits. *Loveliest Pussy* sounds neat, perhaps even more moving to a woman than *Best Novel of the Year*.

He ate a mouthful of fruit jelly and then a mouthful of me, looking for all the world like a cannibal chieftain. When he straightened up and went inside I quickly lost control and exploded. 'Do you want to have a child?' he muttered irresponsibly, ramming forcefully into me. In that instant, sexual pleasure swept over me as if mountains were being toppled and seas emptied, until it seemed I was making love with every man in the world.

# 26

# Early Summer

'We look for a sign, but it is not revealed.'
Suzanne Vega

'Happiness, happiness. What is youth?'
Suede

On May 8th an American air strike hit the Chinese Consulate in Yugoslavia. Three bombs tore through five floors all the way to the basement, killing reporters who worked for Reference News and Guangming Daily and injuring twenty other people. That day at 5:30 p.m. students from universities all over Shanghai gathered outside the US Consulate at Urumuqi Road, carrying banners and shouting: 'Oppose superpower violence, support sovereignty and peace.' A few eggs and bottles of mineral water flew into the consulate compound, as if they'd grown wings. More and more students came, and the protest continued into the next day.

Madonna led a group of Western friends there for a look, and brought back photos to show us. The shot which left the deepest impression was of a couple from the Shanghai Academy of Drama, each holding a placard aloft with both hands: 'Sovereignty' and 'Peace'. Madonna said they stood absolutely motionless, like statues, for more than an hour. They were wearing matching his-and-hers clothing, like something out of the 1950s or 1960s, and the girl had thick eyebrows and big eyes.

One of Madonna's friends, called Johnson, even gave a wad of American dollars to the students to burn.

'Let's hope there isn't a war,' said a worried Tian Tian. His mother Connie had become a Spanish citizen, my secret lover Mark was German, and both nations belonged to NATO, not to mention Madonna's coterie of fun-loving, easy-going Yankees.

On May 9th, the Shenzhen and Shanghai stock markets both dropped sharply, and the KFC in east Shanghai's Wujiao Plaza was closed. Overnight, an army of hackers attacked hundreds of US sites, and the US Department of Energy, Department of the Interior and others were disabled. The home page of the Department of Energy had photos of the bomb victims and the Chinese flag inserted into it. NATO's website was closed down.

On May 10th, I unexpectedly saw Mark's face on a special evening broadcast by IBS, Shanghai TV's English channel. On behalf of his firm he expressed deep regret for the bombing incident, and solemnly apologised to the families of the dead and injured. Spokespersons for other large foreign firms in Shanghai also appeared, including Motorola, Volkswagen and IBM.

After the programme, while Tian Tian was bathing, I called Mark. He said he loved me, gave me a kiss and told me to get a good night's sleep.

My attempts at writing remained virtually non-existent. It felt like trying to talk business to someone in a café when you can't concentrate; you keep right on talking but your mind isn't there, and unconsciously you watch the people and scenery outside the window. Of course, writing – which is my life – can't be compared to a business meeting with a stranger in a café. How could it be? If my writing ever just becomes a job, I hope I'll give up.

Deng and Godfather both called. The second print-run of

*Shriek of the Butterfly* was due out soon and the publicity arrangements were in hand. Seminars, book sales and book-signing events were planned at Fudan U., East China Normal U., and Shanghai Normal U. There would also be coverage in newspapers and magazines. Deng gave me a long list of editors from popular magazines, who she said had all approached her in the hope that I'd write some short, trendy pieces for them. The money was good, and appearing in those publications wouldn't hurt my image.

Deng had already unofficially begun to act as my agent, but so far she hadn't mentioned it and I hadn't paid her. I didn't know why she was working so hard on my behalf. I could only think it was because she was kind and foresaw a good future for my work (a novelist is like a stock which rises or falls depending on developments).

Though I couldn't write, Tian Tian was turning out illustrations at a good clip. Soon he'd have to wait for me to pick up my pen again.

Spider sold me a Pentium II PC and installed a modem and a lot of games free. So when I had nothing to do I would play computer games with Tian Tian (who was already addicted to *The Empire Strikes Back*), write poetry and send e-mail to friends, including Shamir and Mark.

'Let's have a get-together. I miss my darling Tian Tian so,' said Madonna over the phone in her gravelly voice.

'I'll read you a poem: "The days pass damn slowly/A heart steeped in lukewarm water suffers the torments of beautiful time/My lover's pitying eyes count each new wrinkle in the mirror/Waking, I can no longer speed at 180 to the beach/I am alive but dead too".'

She burst out laughing, amused with herself, as she finished reciting it. 'I wrote that right after I woke up today. Not bad, eh?

Real poets are to be found going crazy in their beds, not on the literary stage.'

'I've had it. I haven't been able to write a word recently,' I admitted.

'So you should give a party to get rid of your bad luck. When you want to fend off bad luck and chase away gloom, what could be better than good booze, music, friends and partying?'

I made a string of calls. Nothing interesting ever happens in August. 'In honour of Tian Tian's new series of paintings, the novel I'm stuck on, and everyone's friendship, health and happiness, you are invited to our one plus one plus one party,' I repeated over and over again.

The day before the party I got an unexpected call from Beijing. It was that bisexual make-up artist who claims to be constantly heartbroken over his boy- and girlfriends, that handsome *baobei* Flying Apple. He said he would be flying to Shanghai the next day as stylist for the models in a Vidal Sassoon promotion. 'Then come here,' I said gaily. 'It'll make my party even more interesting.'

At eight thirty that evening the '1 + 1 + 1 Party' kicked off in our apartment.

What I'd called '1 + 1 + 1' meant '1 person + 1 rose + 1 poem'. I had carefully planned every detail of the party. I slaved over the invitation list: we needed a balanced male–female ratio, and people without a sense of humour were completely banned or they'd ruin the atmosphere. Luckily my friends were mostly very cool – hard-core pleasure-lovers and romantics. I cleaned up the room a bit. No need to overdo it. The next morning I'd wake to utter chaos.

Tian Tian was looking quite happy in a traditional Chinese shirt and glossy taffeta trousers, like a lovely youth from a moonlit island in ancient Greece. The door was wide open, and as each friend arrived they hugged him, then I checked they'd brought the presents we'd asked for.

Zhu Sha and Ah Dick were the first to arrive. Zhu Sha was in high spirits, wearing a pale red dress with spaghetti straps, and looking a bit like Gwynneth Paltrow. She looked younger than the last time I'd seen her. The work on her new apartment was finished, and Ah Dick had moved in with her.

'Ah Dick's paintings are selling very well at the Qingyi Art Gallery, and next month he's going to Venice and Lisbon for an international exhibition.'

'For how long?' I asked Ah Dick.

'Probably three months,' he said. His ponytail had been cut, and except for the skull ring on his right hand he looked as clean and neat as an office worker, no doubt partly the influence of Zhu Sha. I'd originally thought they wouldn't last three months, but now it seemed that they were made for each other.

'I'd like to see your paintings,' said Tian Tian to Ah Dick.

'Let me see yours first,' said Ah Dick, pointing to a row of gouache paintings on the wall. 'It's a real pity not to show them publicly in a gallery.'

'We will one day,' I said, smiling at Tian Tian.

Madonna turned up with a young American. Apparently the policeman Ma Jian-Jun had already become a full stop to a sentence on a page already turned in her long romantic history. Her love life was built on one break-up after another.

Madonna's face was as fair as usual, and a cigarette dangled from her hand. Her tight-fitting black top, sapphire-blue brocade capri pants, and even her thick rubber-soled shoes carried the Gucci logo. Wearing sunglasses at night made her stand out, even if it was a bit affected (wearing sunglasses at night really is rather affected, don't you think?). She introduced the blond American youngster who was a dead ringer for Leonardo DiCaprio as Johnson – one of the gang she'd taken to the protest at the consulate. And, pointing to us, 'Coco and Tian Tian.'

Johnson hadn't brought a poem. 'I'll get him to write one immediately,' said Madonna. She smiled naughtily at me. 'Know how we met? On Shanghai Oriental TV's dating show, *Saturday Rendezvous*. He was head of the cheering section for Male Guest Number 6, and I was head of the team for Female Guest Number 3. Yeah, it's only a silly TV game for bored people, but flirting in front of an audience of millions is quite a turn-on. Anyway, she knew me and wanted me in her cheering section. So we spent a whole day shooting the programme, and I met Johnson. He speaks Chinese very well. Give him a minute and he'll write a pithy Chinese poem in the Li Bai style,' she said, smiling.

Johnson was a bit shy, precocious and cute like DiCaprio before he made the big time. 'Now, you're not allowed to fall in love with my baby. I'll get very jealous,' she smiled again. Meeting Zhu Sha and Ah Dick wasn't at all awkward for Madonna and Johnson. Madonna gave Zhu Sha a generous hug and chatted to Ah Dick. I guess if you give any woman a new, adorable lover, she'll become broadminded and let the past go. (When it comes to inconsistency, women are right up there with men.) New love is the key to recovering self-confidence.

Next came Spider with a *laowai*, an overseas male student from Fudan U. Spider hugged Tian Tian, hugged me too and kissed me like a madman. 'This is Yisha,' he introduced. 'He's from Serbia.'

As soon as I heard this my ears pricked up. He looked as if he'd never be very happy, but he kissed my hand graciously and said I was quite famous at Fudan, where many girls had read my works and dreamed of becoming writers like me. 'And I've read *Shriek of the Butterfly*,' he added.

I was touched by his words and by his face, which reflected the painful destruction of his home and family. I instinctively began to worry whether, if he realised there was a Yankee in the room, he'd fly into a rage and get into a fight. The Americans had dropped tens of thousands of tons of high explosive on Yugoslavia, blowing countless women and children to smithereens. In his place, I'd knock down the first American I saw.

'Please sit anywhere,' said Tian Tian, gesturing. 'There's plenty of food and drink, but try not to smash the plates and bottles too quickly.'

Spider whistled. 'If you used plastic ones, they wouldn't break so easily.'

Then Godfather and a group of his friends approached, holding roses. From their pockets they dug out old poems published in Fudan U's *Fields Ploughed for Poetry* four years ago, and recited them. I introduced them to Tian Tian. I'm not bad at introducing people to one another, a skill similar to mixing a cocktail or rushing from one cinema to the next.

The last to arrive was Flying Apple, accompanied by several glistening models, all colleagues of his: beautiful young women from the catwalks, TV programmes, cocktail parties and other places far away from the man in the street, in sight but out of reach, like goldfish in a bowl.

Flying Apple's hair was as colourful as a peacock's plumage or a three-dimensional oil painting. He wore a pair of handsome black-framed glasses (though he isn't short-sighted), a D&G tee-shirt and black-and-white checked, straight-legged trousers. Wrapped around his trousers was a piece of dark-red calico from Thailand, like a skirt yet somehow sexier. His skin was fair but not cold, sweet but not cloying. We hugged and kissed – our lips met with a smack. Tian Tian sipped his drink and didn't come over, watching from a distance. He had a strange fear of bisexuals and gays, only being able to accept heterosexuals and lesbians.

Conversation buzzed amid the soft lighting and electronic music. Drinks in hand, the guests repeatedly pointed at Tian Tian's paintings, and time and again Flying Apple made exaggerated faces as if looking at them might actually bring on an orgasm.

'I'm falling in love with your boyfriend,' he murmured to me.

I tapped a silver spoon against a glass and pronounced the official beginning of the 1 + 1 + 1 event. Everyone had to offer a rose to the person they thought the most beautiful (regardless of gender), dedicate a poem to the person they considered the most intelligent (regardless of gender), and the most beautiful and most intelligent person would be determined by the numbers of roses or poems received. If you wanted, you could also offer yourself to the person you most adored (regardless of gender). But that could, of course, be left for after the party. The room was big enough, but no way did I plan on our party turning into an orgy.

After I'd clearly stated the rules of the party, a frightening series of sounds – a shriek, whistling, stamping of feet and a glass smashing on the floor – filled the room. It almost took the roof off, and just about gave Fur Ball a heart attack. She shot like an arrow off the balcony. 'She'll kill herself!' screamed one of the girls who'd come with Flying Apple.

'No she won't,' I said, throwing them a look. I don't take to girls who shriek; it's a misuse of the vocal cords. 'She's just climbing down the water pipe to go for a stroll in the street.'

'Your cat's really *ku*,' chuckled Flying Apple, like a mouse in a bucket of lard. This titillating scene was just what he liked; he's a bona fide member of the New Generation who never ceases to seek new thrills.

'How did you come up with those rules?' asked Spider, grinning impishly, a snow-white cigarette stuck behind each ear like a young carpenter on a construction team.

'And what if the person I wished to offer myself to were you?' said Madonna, teasingly narrowing her eyes into a smile.

'Well, why not give it a try?' I said, my expression following hers.

Sipping wine, smoking and listening to electronic music can make you feel great all over.

'And if the person I wanted to devote myself to were your boyfriend?' said Flying Apple charmingly, biting his lip.

'I have the right to refuse,' said Tian Tian calmly.

'That's right. Everything must be acceptable to both parties, but no one should refuse a rose or a poem.' I smiled. 'It's safe here, just like in heaven. Everyone should mellow out and try to be happy. Where shall we start? Madonna darling, let's start with you.'

Wearing sunglasses as usual, Madonna had taken off her shoes and was barefoot. She pulled out a rose from the large vase into which they'd all been put. 'I present this rose to most beautiful Tian Tian, this poem to most intelligent Coco, and as for myself, I'll wait and see how I feel before I decide. I just started drinking, so how should I know who I'll spend the night with?' She giggled. She tossed the rose to Tian Tian, who was sitting on the floor, drew out a sheet of paper from her handbag, temporarily placed her sunglasses on top of her head, went down on one knee and read her poem in an exaggerated, theatrical manner: 'That is not yours/Kiss it not/Lay it down . . .' Everyone clapped when she finished, and I blew her a kiss of thanks.

Next up was Johnson, who gave his rose to the most beautiful woman in his eyes, my cousin Zhu Sha, and dedicated his poem to the woman he found most intelligent, Madonna. It was certainly short: 'Lovely maiden/Let's travel together afar/A penguin invites us to drink water from the South Pole/Why not be happy?' As to whom he would choose to offer himself, he said he'd decide that later too.

'Have you fallen for Ms Zhu?' Madonna asked him. 'We Chinese say "A lover sees beauty in his loved one". If you find her the most beautiful, you must be in love with her.' Johnson blushed.

Zhu Sha and Ah Dick were quite calmly canoodling in a corner of the sofa. Drinks in hand, they remained relaxed as flowers in a courtyard, elegant and charming, no matter how boisterous anyone else got; utterly different in temperament from Madonna, as different as water and fire.

'No problem. You're a free American citizen, you have the right to love whoever you please,' said Madonna in a strange voice.

Hearing this, Ah Dick couldn't help but laugh. He pulled Zhu Sha forcefully into his embrace. 'Darling, it's always good to have others attracted to you, because you're a truly enchanting woman.'

'We'll have no envy or dislike at our party,' I said. 'We're playing a game; let's enjoy ourselves.'

'Agreed,' chimed in Flying Apple, taking advantage of the moment to put his hand around my waist and rest his head on my shoulder. Tian Tian pretended not to see, concentrating on snipping off the end of his cigar, soggy from too many puffs.

I tapped Flying Apple on the head. 'It's your turn, sugar.'

'I give my rose to my most handsome self, my poem to most intelligent Coco, and offer myself to anyone who can arouse me, male or female,' said Flying Apple. As he spoke, he looked in the wardrobe mirror and rearranged the colourful sarong-like vestment wrapped around his trousers.

'I really think I look quite lovely,' he added.

'We think so too,' agreed several of the models, gathering

around and hugging him like a troupe of half-women, half-snakes wrapping themselves about a big apple.

'No one else gave me a rose. To avoid losing face, I suppose it's best to give myself one.' Flying Apple dangled the rose from his mouth and, in rhythm with the music, stretched out his arms as if to take flight. He looked utterly bewitching and delicate, and his goatee added to his demonic good looks.

'I present you with my rose because I also find you the most beautiful,' said Yisha the Serb suddenly in fluent Chinese. 'My poem goes to my friend Spider, who is Numero Uno on the computer, and has the highest IQ of anyone I've met. As to offering myself, naturally I dedicate myself to the person I consider the most beautiful.' All eyes fluttered in the direction of Yisha, as if he were a visitor from outer space.

A peal of laughter erupted from Johnson, the American. Yisha jumped up from his seat on the floor and brushed himself down. 'You find that funny?' he asked, staring straight at Johnson.

'I'm sorry,' said Johnson, still smiling. 'I'm sorry, I can't help myself.'

'Just like your country's planes can't help flying over our country and dropping bombs on it? Just like your army can't help killing so many of our innocent civilians? What a lie! You Americans!' shouted Yisha. 'Just thinking of you people makes me sick. You all have to stick your noses into everybody's business. You're shameless and greedy beyond belief. You're vulgar, stupid and uncivilised, but you're full of yourselves and arrogant. You deserve to be spat on, motherfucker!'

Johnson got up quickly. 'What the hell are you talking about? What do I have to do with those damn air strikes? Why are you insulting me?'

'Because you're a motherfucking American.'

'Forget it, forget it. You've had too much to drink. Don't get upset,' said Spider, jumping to separate them. Godfather, seated among a group of beautiful models, continued quite unperturbed to do card tricks to attract their attention. But from time to time they glanced over at the two *laowai*, red-faced from arguing. From an ethical point of view they supported the Serb, but from an aesthetic point of view they were sympathetic to the Leonardo DiCaprio look-alike Johnson.

'If you have the guts, fight it out to prove who's right,' encouraged a giggling Madonna, whose only fear was the absence of chaos. Flying Apple came forward and grabbed Yisha's hand, since the argument had begun because Yisha had announced he fancied him, which touched him.

'Why not both take a cold shower?' asked Tian Tian. He wasn't being sarcastic. The question came straight from his well-intentioned, simple nature. In his view, bathing was the best way to solve all problems. The bath was a warm, safe haven, like a womb. Cleansing oneself in clean water could distance you from loud rock'n'roll music, from gangs and gangsters, from all sorts of problems and pain.

The international incident over, the show went on. Tian Tian offered his flower, poem and self to me, and I did the same to him.

Madonna smiled sarcastically. 'You play the devoted couple in public. Isn't that a bit sick-making?'

Tian Tian smiled faintly. 'Sorry, we didn't mean to make you jealous.' But I felt a twinge of remorse. Madonna and Zhu Sha both knew about my affair with Mark, but how could I come clean to Tian Tian about it? Especially since the feeling he gave my body was different from Mark, so the two couldn't be compared. Tian Tian used his unique closeness and his affection to get to a part of my body Mark couldn't reach. I don't think that I was being greedy and selfish about this, but I'll admit I was unable to control myself and was forever looking for excuses.

'I can't forgive myself,' I once said to Zhu Sha. Her

response was, 'Actually, you've been forgiving yourself all along.' True.

Zhu Sha and Ah Dick each gave all three items to each other, while Spider, Godfather and two of Godfather's friends gave me their poems (fortunately, I thus became the evening's most intelligent woman. I received a long string of fragrant or odoriferous poems, such as: 'Your smile brings people back to life/A thing of great quality.' This was flattering, while 'She resembles crimped steel/Not a living creature . . .' was disparaging. 'She laughs, she cries/She is real, she is fantasy' was just right.) Of the four men who gave their roses and bodies to Flying Apple's models, three-and-a-half were grads of Fudan U., the half being Spider, of course, who never graduated. The Fudan grads and glamorous models were mutually ogling one another, and since the guestroom had a sofa, bed and carpet, it would be able to accommodate them.

While Ah Dick was looking at Tian Tian's paintings, Zhu Sha and I chatted over a plate of strawberries. 'Have you seen Mark lately?' she asked quietly, not looking directly at me.

'Yeah,' I jiggled my legs: Tian Tian had just changed the record to acid jazz. The room was in chaos, and everyone's eyes were beginning to look like egg yolk leaking into the white. Everybody was busy doing their own thing.

'Why do you ask?' I turned my head to ask her.

'There's a rumour going round the office that he's going to be leaving China soon to go back to head office.'

'Is that so?' I tried to act as if this didn't matter, but a wave of very tart strawberry juice spread across my tongue, turning my stomach.

'He's probably been promoted because he's done so well here, and he'll go back to a top job in Berlin.'

'Who knows? Maybe it's true.' I stood up, kicking aside a

magazine and a brocaded red satin cushion, and walked over to the balcony.

'Try not to think about it,' she said quietly.

'So many stars. It's awfully pretty.' I raised my head to look at the sky. The stars in the deep, cold heavens were like small cuts from an explosion; flowing out from them was silver blood, and if I'd had wings I'd have flown up there to kiss each one. Every time our bodies touched, I felt the same pain followed by a soaring sensation. Once, I'd convinced myself that a woman can separate her heart and her body – a man can, why not a woman? But in reality, I found I was thinking more and more of Mark, of those deadly and divine moments we spent together.

Zhu Sha and Ah Dick said their goodbyes, but before they left Zhu Sha made a point of going over to Johnson to shake hands with him, and thank him for his rose. Johnson didn't look happy. First he'd had a row with the man from Serbia, and now the beautiful Zhu Sha was going.

The evening began to get chaotic and out of control. At 3:00 a.m. Flying Apple took his Serbian to the New Jinjiang Hotel, where he was staying. Spider, Godfather and his two friends and four of Flying Apple's models were fooling around in the guestroom. Tian Tian, Madonna and I slept on the big bed in our bedroom, and Johnson on the sofa.

At 5:00 a.m., I was woken suddenly by the noise of several people tossing about at the same time. From next door came a woman's hysterical shrieking, like an owl on a rooftop. Madonna had slipped out to the sofa. I could see her snow-white, naked body, fine and slender, entwined about Johnson like a large white snake. She even had a cigarette in her right hand, taking an occasional puff as she enveloped Johnson.

I watched them for a moment, feeling Madonna was really very *ku*, very special. She changed her position and noticed me.

She blew me a kiss and gestured to show that I could join in if I liked.

Suddenly Tian Tian held me tight: he'd woken too. Drifting in the air were the smells of adrenalin and smoke and booze, strong enough to suffocate a cat.

The sound system played the song 'Green Light' over and over again. No one could really sleep. Tian Tian and I kissed deeply and calmly, as if there were no tomorrow. After Madonna and Johnson's grunts and sighs had died down, we hugged again and fell asleep.

When I woke the next afternoon, everyone and their shadows had vanished without trace. Not even a message was left behind. The floor and table were littered with leftover food, cigarette ends, empty pill containers, dirty paper towels, one smelly sock and a pair of black panties. A ghastly scene.

Since my lifeless, dreary mood had completely vanished during the party, a swing in the opposite direction was inevitable. I threw out the rubbish, cleaned up the room and prepared to start my life anew.

Then I realised, with no surprise whatsoever, that I could write again. That impalpable, enchanting ability to manipulate language had come back to me, thank God!

I focused all my attention on finishing my novel. As usual Tian Tian stayed in the other room amusing himself, occasionally going to Madonna's to play computer games or for a spin in her car. The kitchen became empty and dirty again; we gave up dreaming up new recipes to cook. Little Sichuan's take-away boy began coming to our door with food. Little Ding had quit. I wondered if he'd begun writing, as he'd dreamed, but when I asked the new boy, he didn't know.

# 27

# Chaos

'Between the deep blue sea and the Devil, that was me.'
Billy Bragg

'It is fatal for anyone who writes to think of their sex.
It is fatal to be a man or woman pure and simple.'
Virginia Woolf

A sudden call from home. Mother had broken her leg. The elevator wasn't working because of a power cut, and she'd slipped on the stairs. I was stunned for a moment, then I hurriedly got my things together and took a taxi over there. My father was at college teaching, and an amah was running about, but apart from her the apartment was so silent I felt giddy and could hear my ears ringing.

Mother was lying in bed with her eyes closed, her pale, gaunt face shining as if it had been polished, like the furniture around her. A thick cast had already been applied to her left ankle. I approached her, walking as quietly as possible, and sat down in the chair at her bedside.

She opened her eyes. 'You've come,' she said simply.

'Does it hurt?' I greeted her equally simply.

She reached out a hand and stroked my fingers. The vivid polish on her nails had faded, which made them look odd.

She sighed. 'How's your novel going?'

'Not so good . . . I write a little each day, but I don't know how many people will want to read it.'

'Since you're set on being an author, there's no point worrying about that.' This was the first time she had spoken to me like that about my novel. I looked at her silently. I actually wanted to lean over and hug her tight, and tell her how much I really loved her and needed her encouragement to strengthen my resolve.

'Would you like something to eat?' I asked, not reaching out to hug her after all.

She shook her head. 'Is your boyfriend well?' She knew nothing about Tian Tian's time at the detox centre.

'He's done a lot of paintings, excellent ones. Perhaps I'll use them in my novel.'

'You wouldn't move back in for a little, would you? . . . Even a week would do.'

I smiled at her. 'Fine. My bed's still in the same old place, right?'

The amah helped me put my room in order. It had been vacant ever since Zhu Sha moved out. The bookcase had a thin layer of dust on it, and the furry orang-utan still sat on the top shelf. As the glow of the sunset came through the window, the room was filled with brushstrokes of warm colour.

I lay down on my bed for a moment and had a dream. I dreamt I was riding the old bike I had at high school down a street full of familiar faces. Then a black van suddenly drove towards me, and a group of masked men jumped out. The leader waved a pink mobile phone, ordering his underlings to throw me and my bike into the back. They shone their torches into my eyes, and tried to make me tell them the whereabouts of an important person. 'Where's the general?' They stared intently at me, asking me loudly. 'Spit it out. Where's the general?'

'I don't know.'

'Don't lie, it's no use. Take a good look at the ring on your finger. What kind of woman doesn't even know where her husband is hiding?' I looked vacantly at my left hand. I was indeed wearing an extravagant, eye-catching diamond on my ring finger.

'I really don't know,' I said, waving my hands desperately. 'Even if you kill me I won't know.'

When I awoke, Daddy was back. Everything was still quiet in my room, but I realised he was in and that it was almost dinner-time by the smell of cigar smoke drifting in from the balcony.

I got up, walked out to the balcony and greeted him. He'd changed into casuals, and in the dusk I saw his slightly chubby tummy protruding and his greying hair lightly ruffled by the wind.

He looked silently at me for a moment. 'You fell asleep?'

I nodded, a smile emerging. 'I feel very energetic now, fit enough to go tiger-hunting in the mountains.'

'Good. Time for dinner.' He leaned on my shoulder and came inside.

Mother had already been helped to her seat in a chair with a velvet cushion. The dinner table was laden with dishes that exuded warmth and filled my nose with spicy fragrances.

In the evening, I played chess with Daddy for a while, and Mother lay on her bed, occasionally watching us. We spoke about everyday things in a distracted way, until the topic turned to that most important event in one's life – marriage. Not wanting to get into that, I quickly put the chess set away, bathed, and went back to bed.

I phoned Tian Tian to tell him I needed to stay here for a week, and then described my afternoon dream to him and asked him what it meant. He said that I was having a premonition of success in my writing, but that I had yielded to existential anxiety. 'Really?' I said sceptically. 'Check it with David Wu,' he responded.

That week passed very quickly, keeping my mother company, watching TV, playing cards, and eating a hodge-podge of such favourites as green bean and lotus root soup, yam and sesame pudding, and grated turnip pancakes. The evening before I was to leave, Daddy called me into his study for a heart-to-heart talk.

'Remember how you liked to go out all alone when you were young? In the end, you always lost your way. You've always been a girl who loses her way,' he said.

Smoking, I sat in a rocking chair opposite him. 'That's true,' I said. 'And I still get lost often.'

'To put it plainly, you like taking risks too much, and you expect miracles to happen. Those aren't fatal flaws . . . but many things aren't as simple as you imagine. To your mother and father, you'll always be an innocent child . . .'

'But . . .' I started to explain, but he waved me down.

'We'd never stop you from doing anything you wanted, we couldn't do that . . . But remember one very important thing: whatever you do, you must take responsibility for the conse-quences. You're always talking about freedom according to Sartre, but "freedom of choice" is a freedom based on certain conditions.'

'I agree.' I exhaled a mouthful of smoke. A window was open, and the study was subtly scented by a Casablanca lily in a vase.

'Parents always understand their children. Never use words like "old-fashioned" to put down your elders.'

'I don't,' I said disingenuously.

'You're too emotional. When you're down, you see nothing but darkness; when you're up, you're thoroughly overexcited.'

'But to be honest, I like being that way.'

'One condition necessary to be a truly great author is to abandon vanity, and learn how to be independent in a precar-ious profession. Don't become complacent about your status as an author; first of all you're a human being and a woman, and only third an author.'

'That's why I always go dancing in sandals and strappy dresses, befriend psychoanalysts, listen to good music, read good books, eat fruits rich in vitamins C and A, take calcium tablets, and try to be a smart, exceptional woman,' I explained.

'I'll come to see you and Mother often, I promise.'

Connie invited Tian Tian and me to dinner to admire her nearly completed restaurant. We ate at a wood and rattan table on the balcony. The sun had gone down but the sky was still quite bright, and the poplar and scholar-tree leaves and branches wove and swayed above our heads. The newly-hired trainee waiters in their eye-catching black-and-white uniforms trailed up the broad marble staircase, bringing the dishes one by one to our balcony.

Looking slightly tired, Connie was nonetheless beautifully made up. A Havana cigar in her hand, she had the waiter snip the end and serve it to her in order to check his cigar-cutting skills. 'I only employ quick-witted youngsters with no previous experience whatsoever, so they won't have picked up any bad habits and can start learning straight away,' she said.

Juan wasn't there, as he'd gone to Spain to bring a team of Spanish chefs back to Shanghai. The plan was for the restaurant to open at the beginning of June.

As she'd asked, we'd brought a section of my manuscript and some illustrations for her to see. Puffing on her cigar, she was full of praise as she slowly examined Tian Tian's paintings. 'Look at these extraordinary colours, and these amazing contours. I knew my son was gifted even when he was a baby. Your mother's delighted with these pictures.'

Absorbed in eating his cod baked in paper, Tian Tian said nothing. The paper had now been sliced open, but it had preserved all the aroma of the snow-white meat and sauce, which was cooked to perfection and smelt divine. 'Thanks,' popped suddenly out of Tian Tian's mouth as he ate his fish. There was no longer outright antagonism between mother and son, but a sort of stubborn wariness and disappointment remained.

'The second floor of the restaurant has two walls which haven't been decorated. Would Tian Tian help out by painting a little something on them?' suggested Connie unexpectedly.

I threw Tian Tian a glance. 'You'd do a great job of it,' I said.

After the meal, Connie showed us round the many interconnected rooms and foyers. Attractive light fittings and custom-made mahogany tables and chairs were nearly finished. In two of the rooms red-brick fireplaces had been built, with wooden mantels, bearing a display of wine and whisky bottles. The wall opposite each fireplace was still bare.

'What style of painting would be appropriate here?' asked Connie.

'Matisse? No, perhaps Modigliani would be best,' I said.

Tian Tian nodded. 'His paintings have a subtle glamour and a coolness that make you want to get close to them, but you can't . . . Sipping wine and smoking a cigar while viewing a Modigliani by a fireside would be like a trip to paradise.'

'Will you do it?' asked Connie, a winning smile on her face as she looked at her son.

'I've been living on you all this time, so I should do something for you in return,' he replied. We stayed in Connie's restaurant, listening to Latin music and drinking late into the night.

Tian Tian began wearing overalls and, brushes and paints in hand, going to his mother's place to work on the murals. Since it was a long way away, to save trouble he often slept there, in a comfortable room that Connie had prepared for him.

In the meantime, I kept my head down, writing madly,

writing and then trashing what I wrote, trying to find the right ending to my novel. Last thing at night I'd check my e-mails from friends all over. Flying Apple and the Serb, Yisha, were wildly in love. They'd been to Hong Kong for a *tongzhi*, gay, film festival. Flying Apple sent me some photos over the web: him with a group of seductive boys on the beach forming a multi-layered sex cocktail; they were stacked on top of one another, stripped to the waist, and some had pierced their nipples, navels and tongues with silver rings. 'Our beautiful mad world,' he wrote in crude lettering.

Shamir wrote, in English, saying I had left a deep impression on her heart, like a delicate yet passionate oriental watercolour which aroused an ephemeral, indescribable emotion in her – like a rose in a night garden which blossoms and perishes in an instant. She couldn't forget the marvellous yet treacherous fragrance of my lips, like a storm, an undercurrent, or a flower petal.

It is the most uninhibited love letter I've ever received, and the fact that it was written by a woman left me feeling odd.

Spider asked if I was still planning to set up my own home page. He would be at my service at any time, as business had been poor lately and he had nothing else to do. Madonna said sending e-mails was more of a pain than phoning, and this would be her first and last message. She only wanted to tell me that my party was totally rotten and totally enjoyable. She hadn't been able to find her mobile phone the next day and wondered if I'd seen it.

I replied in whatever beautiful or frank terms came to mind. My friends and I, a tribe of the sons and daughters of the well-to-do, often used exaggerated and *outré* language to manufacture life-threatening pleasure. A swarm of affectionate, mutually dependent little fireflies, we devoured the wings of imagination and had little contact with reality. We were maggots feeding on the city's bones, but utterly sexy ones. The city's bizarre romanticism and genuine sense of poetry were actually created by our tribe. Some call us *linglei*, others damn us as trash; some yearn to join us, and imitate us in every way they can, from clothes and hairstyle to speech and sex; others swear at us and tell us to take our dog-fart lifestyles and disappear.

I turned off the computer and a line flashed on the screen, then extinguished itself. 'Green Light' by Sonic Youth had just finished on the sound system with the last line 'Her light is the night, uh, uh, uh'. I stepped into the bath and lay down in the warm water. At one point I fell asleep, surrounded by water and bubble bath as I dreamed, and in my dream I composed a poem about the night. But I only remember this: 'Before the day disappears I never know what the night is/Never know what the lines on the bedsheets are/Never know what the longing on the lips is/uh, uh, uh . . .'

One muggy evening, when there was no wind and the barometric pressure was low, Mark, with no forewarning, drove to my building and called me from his car downstairs. 'I hope I'm not disturbing you, but I really want to see you now.'

Distorted by interference, his voice was indistinct and buzzy, making a buzzing sound. Just as he finished his sentence, the line disconnected. Perhaps his handset's battery had run down. I could imagine him throwing the phone down in the car and saying 'Damn it!' I put down my pen and for the first time ran downstairs without putting on any make-up.

I looked at him, neat as a pin, and then at myself: bare feet in sandals, and my nightgown grotesquely rucked up. I convulsed with laughter despite myself.

He began to laugh too, but quickly stopped. 'Coco, I have to tell you some bad news: I have to go back to Germany.'

I touched my suddenly frozen facial muscles. 'What?' I stared at him for a moment, and he returned my look silently. 'Looks like it wasn't just a rumour,' I murmured. 'My cousin told me you might be transferred back to head office.'

He hugged me. 'I want to be with you.'

'Impossible!' screamed my heart, but my mouth said nothing, using its lips and tongue and teeth to meet the raging torrent Mark unleashed on me. That's the way it was. Even if I pounded my fists against his chest, or schemed to steal every cent, credit card and ID he owned, it wouldn't change one fact: my German lover, the Westerner who gave me more excitement and ecstasy than all my other men put together, was going to leave me, and that was that.

I gave him a shove. 'All right. When do you leave?'

'No later than the end of next month. I want to be with you every moment, every second.' He lowered his head and buried it in my bosom. Like a last desperate flowering before night, my nipples firmed as his hair rubbed against them through my nightgown.

We drove fast and smoothly and the colours of our dream turned dark, its edges slowly curling up like the cracked valleys and black cliffs on the dark side of the moon. Night-time in Shanghai always has a passionate and nerve-racking quality. We flew along the smooth streets through neon lights and gold dust, while the speakers played Iggy Pop's lyrics: 'We're just visitors passing by/visitors in a rush/See the sky full of stars/Waiting for us to disappear together.'

You can make love passionately, worry endlessly, create truths or destroy your dreams. Whatever. But what makes you really wonder, is why God thinks he can put out all the stars with his tears whenever he wants. It was then that I thought some catastrophe was bound to happen that night – a car crash, a random accident to puncture our passion and obsession.

But there was no accident. The car arrived at Pudong Central Park. Since it was closed, we made love outside the park wall in the shade of a clump of trees. The collapsible seat smelt of frivolity and leather. I had a cramp in my foot, but I didn't say anything, just bore the discomfort until my thighs were soaked with the juices of our dream.

Right until I awoke up in his apartment early next morning, it all seemed like a dream. Sex bleeds easily, like an ink brushstroke on a traditional Chinese painting; but sex can't change anything, especially not the black bags under your eyes in the mirror.

To reach its ending, every story must pay a price. The human body extends its antennae to engage with another body, only to draw back when disaster strikes.

Mark announced that, as of now, every day was our farewell party and he needn't knot his tie and leave for the office at 9:45 a.m. on the dot. He was determined to enjoy each day to the full, and he begged me to spend more time with him. My boyfriend was painting Modigliani frescoes at his mother's restaurant, my novel lacked only its final pages, and after a few weeks he might never see me again.

For the rest of our lives! My head hurt fit to burst.

He turned down the volume of the Suzhou ballad and brought me an aspirin tablet from the medicine cabinet. He massaged my back and my feet with the amateur skills he'd acquired from visits to 'pure massage' parlours. He teased me in his tacky Shanghainese. From start to finish he went to every length to wait hand and foot on the oriental princess of his dreams – his gifted girl with waist-length black hair and sad, sensitive eyes.

And I – I finally realised I'd fallen into the trap of love and passion set by this German man who wasn't supposed to be anything more than a sex partner. By way of my vulva he had reached my vulnerable heart and then the intimacy behind my eyes. Since feminism began the hypnotic quality of this kind of sex has been demystified, but I discovered through my own body a woman's inherent flaw. I'd fooled myself by saying it was all just a game, amusing for us both; life's just an amusement park, and we can't stop searching for pleasure.

And my boyfriend would still be at the restaurant, lost in his own world, using colours and lines to salvage himself and the world which were both, in his eyes, out of step.

I stayed in Mark's apartment. We lay naked in bed, listening to Suzhou ballads, watching videos and playing chess. When hungry, we cooked noodles or wonton in the kitchen. We rarely slept, and no longer read each other's eyes; it would only have added to our troubles.

When semen, saliva and sweat had glued shut every pore in our bodies, we took bathing suits, goggles and VIP card to the Hotel Equatorial for a swim. There were virtually no other guests at the poolside, and we were like two rare fish swimming to and fro in a huge nothingness bathed in orange light. The tireder we were the more beautiful we grew, and the more debauched, the happier.

Back in bed, we tested our reserves of sexual energy with fiendish zeal to see just how far they'd go. We discovered it was a crazy, demonic force. If God said all was dust, then we would revert to dust; if God said Judgement Day had arrived, then we were living our last day on earth. That plaything of his seemed to be made of rubber: it was erect throughout, and showed no signs of flagging even when I began to bleed from its pounding.

A phone call from his wife saved me. He rose unsteadily from the bed and went to answer it. Eva wanted to know why he hadn't been answering her e-mails.

I thought to myself: God, quite apart from going at it non-stop, we didn't have the strength to turn on the computer.

Eva couldn't do anything but call and ask her husband, and after they had talked for a bit they agreed a date for his return to

Germany. They spoke in German, and though their voices rose, they didn't argue.

When he put the phone down and crawled into bed, I gave him a kick that sent him tumbling to the floor.

'I'm going crazy. This isn't right, sooner or later something'll will go wrong,' I said, and began to get dressed.

He grabbed my foot and kissed it, found a cigarette in a pile of tissues on the floor, lit it and stuck it in his mouth. 'We've always been crazy, ever since we met. Do you know why I'm am so bewitched by you? You're utterly unfaithful, but you're totally trustworthy. They're opposites but they meet in you.'

'Thanks for putting it like that.' I felt depressed seeing myself as I dressed; like a doll that's been raped too often – but whose body, were she to undress again, would start the magic of it again. 'I'm going home,' I muttered.

'You look perfectly horrible,' he said tenderly, hugging me.

'Yes, I do,' I said. My emotional state couldn't have been worse. Like going to hell, that's all. I felt like crying. I despised and pitied myself. He hugged me, his golden body hairs stroking me like feelers.

'Sweetheart, I'm sure you must be worn out. The more energy your body expends, the greater the love you generate. I love you.'

I didn't want to hear that. I wanted to run away like a gust of wind and get back to where I once belonged. Perhaps nowhere could make me feel safe, but I still ran home like a rat.

The sunlight out on the street pierced my eyes like a white blade. I could hear my blood thumping round my body, and for an instant, facing the shoulder-to-shoulder crowd on the street, I didn't know what to do, what day it was, or who I was.

# 28

# My Lover's Tears

'All the jokes, all the lost cartoons.'
Allen Ginsberg

'From then onwards, when the dark night ended,
it was already too late to refuse. It was too late to stop loving you.'
Marguerite Duras

I opened the door, before me all was emptiness and silence. A daddy longlegs scampered from the wall to the ceiling. Everything in the apartment was the same as ever. Tian Tian wasn't in. Perhaps he was still at the restaurant, or perhaps he'd come back and, not finding me in, gone out again.

I'd already realised that my sudden disappearance might have been a fatal mistake. It was the first time I'd gone off without trying to cover up. Tian Tian would certainly have called me, and if he'd found I wasn't there . . . I didn't have the strength to think about it. I bathed, forced down two tranquillizers, and went to bed.

I dreamed of a broad, muddy-yellow, frightening river. There was no bridge, only a leaking bamboo ferry with a white-bearded, foul-tempered old man guarding it. I was crossing the river with someone whose face I couldn't see. Halfway across, a huge wave hit us. I yelped, but I was already wet from the water that had leaked into the boat. The person whose face I couldn't see hugged me tightly from behind. 'Don't be afraid,' he (she?) whispered in my ear, and used his (her?) body to balance us.

Just as the next threat loomed, my dream ended. The ringing of the phone woke me up with a jump.

I didn't want to pick up the phone. My dream had mesmerized me. Who was my companion in danger in the boat? There's an old proverb: it takes ten years to build a partnership and a hundred years to share a pillow.

My heart was thumping uncomfortably fast. I finally picked up the handset. It was Connie, sounding very worried, asking if I knew where Tian Tian was.

My head began to hurt badly. 'No, I don't know either.'

I despised the phony sound of my voice. If Connie knew where I'd been and what I'd been up to these last few days, she would never speak to me again. She might even find someone to beat me to death, if she really had plotted to murder her ex-husband in Spain. If she truly had a heart, ruthless yet filled with maternal hormones, she must sense that her only son, about whom she was so worried, was being betrayed by the girl he adored.

'I called a few times and no one answered. I was afraid you'd both vanished.'

There was more to that than met the ear, but I pretended I didn't get it. 'I've been at my parents' place for a few days.'

She sighed. 'Is your mother's leg healed?'

'Thank you for asking. She's better.' Something occurred to me. 'I thought Tian Tian was painting at your restaurant?'

'There was only a bit left to do, but he just left. I thought he'd gone home. He wouldn't be in trouble, would he?' she asked anxiously.

'No way. He probably went to a friend's house. I'll call right away and ask.'

The first person I thought of was Madonna. I phoned her, and her voice sounded hoarse at the other end. Tian Tian was indeed at her place.

'He says he wants to stay here for a few days.' Madonna's voice was implying something. Didn't Tian Tian want to come back? Perhaps he didn't want to see me. Since I'd disappeared for a few days without telling him, I guessed he might have called my parents, in which case my fib wouldn't stand up.

Agitated, I walked in circles, smoked several cigarettes and, in the end, decided to go to Madonna's. I simply had to see Tian Tian.

In the taxi, my head was empty. I created 101 reasons to absolve myself of blame, but each was less solid than the next. Who would buy the idea that I'd suddenly taken off for a wedding in far-off Guangzhou? Or been taken captive by a masked man who came to burgle the apartment?

So I didn't plan to tell a lie. I'd tell him what I had been up to. I just couldn't lie to a boy with the eyes of a child, the intelligence of a genius and the love of a lunatic. I couldn't insult his heart and mind like that. And in telling him the truth, I'd already accepted, I had to be prepared for the worst – that in the space of just a few short days I would lose my two most unforgettable men.

I was always giving ground, compromising, lying. Yet I always had such a romantic attitude to love and reality. I reckoned that of all the university-educated girls in the world, there couldn't be one as screwed up as me. The President of Fudan U. should rescind my diploma, and the Chairman of the Fantasy Association should pronounce my epitaph while God smiles and clips his fingernails.

On the way I spoke silently to myself: 'All right. Go on and say it. All right, I can't stand it. Tian Tian, I love you. If you think I'm despicable, come right here and spit in my face.' All the way, I desperately wanted the journey to end. I was exhausted. The woman in the make-up mirror was a stranger

255

with chapped lips and dark circles under her eyes, sick but impervious to medical treatment due to her multiple personalities and cowardice in love.

Madonna's white villa was set amongst red flowers and green willows. She'd had an incredibly long and winding drive specially built – according to the American magazine *Style*, a long drive with the house invisible from the entrance implies privilege and class. But the conventional prettiness of the landscaping, azaleas and willow trees undermined that symbol.

Speaking into the intercom, I announced myself and asked them to open the gate.

It opened automatically, and a guard dog leapt out fiercely. I immediately saw Tian Tian, lying on the grass and smoking.

Avoiding the dog, I went over to him. He opened one eye and looked at me: 'Hi!' he said, still hazy with sleep.

'Hi!' I greeted him, standing there and not knowing what to do with myself for a moment.

Dressed casually in bright red, Madonna came down the steps from the arched veranda. 'Would you like a drink?' she asked with a big, lazy smile on her face. The amah brought a large glass of apple juice spiked with red wine.

I asked Tian Tian how he'd been the last two days. 'Fine,' he replied. Madonna yawned and said they had everything here, and I could come and stay too; there was a lot going on. Several silhouettes appeared one after another on the veranda. Only then did I discovered there was a whole gang of people there, including a bunch of *laowai* with Johnson among them ,and Number Five, his girlfriend, and several tall, slender young women who looked like models. They all seemed as laid-back as a slew of snakes slithering about their noxious lair.

I could sense the presence of marijuana from their spacey look and the general atmosphere. I went over to Tian Tian, but he laid his head on the grass in a pose that suggested he was half-asleep and communing with the soil; as if he were Titan, son of the Earth in the ancient Greek myth, whose separation from it would mean death. Sometimes, being face-to-face with Tian Tian was like being confronted with utter sadness. At the same time he had an incredible store of hidden anger.

'Don't you want to talk to me?' I held his hand.

He removed it, and looked at me with a puzzled smile. 'Coco, don't you know? If your left foot hurts, my right foot hurts.' This was the definition of Catholic love expressed by his favourite Spanish writer, Miguel de Unamuno.

I watched him, speechless. His eyes were suddenly shrouded in layers of mist, each of a different depth, and at their centre, enveloped within the layered mists, was a painfully unyielding diamond. That unyielding ray of light made me aware that he already knew what he should know. He was the only person in the universe who could deploy his wayward intuition to enter my world. We were tied to the tip of the same nerve. When my left foot hurt, he would immediately feel pain in his right foot. There was no room for lies.

Everything went black in front of me, and I fell, completely exhausted, on to the grass next to Tian Tian. At that instant my body went out of control. I saw Madonna's pointed, thin face glowing cold, cold white, and suddenly tilting to one side like a broken sail; a series of grey waves lifted me up; and a huge shell emitted Tian Tian's voice: 'Coco. Coco.'

When I opened my eyes, silence surrounded me. I was like a pebble randomly washed up on the seashore, lying heavily on a mattress. I recognized one of Madonna's countless bedrooms, filled with luxurious and utterly meaningless decorations all in brown.

There was a cold towel on my forehead. My eyes passed over a glass of water on the table at the head of the bed and fell on Tian

Tian on the sofa. He walked over, touched my face gently, and removed the towel. 'Feeling a bit better?'

I flinched at his touch. The dizziness was still pressing down on me and I still felt very tired and depressed. He sat at my bedside, motionless, looking at me intensely.

'I've been lying to you all along,' I said weakly. 'But there's one thing I've never lied to you about.' I opened my eyes and looked at the ceiling. 'That is, that I love you.'

He didn't speak.

'Madonna told you, didn't she?' Blood was surging in my ears. 'She promised not to breathe a word to you . . . You think I'm quite shameless, don't you?' I couldn't shut my mouth. The closer I was to collapsing, the more I needed to explain, but the more I spoke, the more idiotic I became. Tears poured down, soaking strands of hair on either side of my face. 'I don't know why. I just wanted you to make love to me perfectly just once. I want you so much, because I love you.'

'Yes, dear, love will tear us apart.' So sang Ian Curtis, who committed suicide in 1980.

Tian Tian leaned over and hugged me. 'I despise you!' He squeezed these words out from between his teeth, and each word seemed to explode. 'Because you make me despise myself.' He began to cry. 'I can't make love. My whole existence is just a farce. Don't pity me. I should disappear.'

If your left foot hurts, my right foot will begin to hurt. If you're suffocated by life, my breathing will cease too. If, when you want to express your love there's nothing but a black hole, then I won't be able to make love either. If you sell your soul to the devil, a dagger will stab my chest too.

We held each other close. We exist, we really do exist; apart from us nothing exists.

# 29

# Nightmares Revisited

'Oh Lord, please hear our prayers.'
Mother Teresa

Tian Tian began taking drugs again; flirting with the devil. I descended into a world of nightmare. Again and again I watched Tian Tian being led away by the police, watched him use blood oozing from his wrist to write his epitaph on a white canvas, watched an earthquake, watched the sky fall in like a stone wave that explodes on impact. I couldn't stand it.

One evening, when he threw down his syringe, loosened the rubber tube on his arm and lay down on the bathroom tiles, I took off my belt, walked over to him and tied his hands.

'No matter what you do to me . . . I, I'll never blame you. I love you, Coco, do you hear me? Coco, I love you,' he babbled. Then his head lolled to one side and he passed out.

I plonked myself down on the floor, buried my head in my hands, and tears slipped through the gaps in my fingers, slipping away like the happiness that simply happens to people and can't be deliberately searched out. Looking at this unconscious boy, whose willpower had gone, my broken-hearted lover lying in this ice-cold bathroom, I could only cry until my throat closed up. Whose fault was it all? I wanted to find someone to blame for everything, so I'd have an object to hate and to rage against.

Begging him, threatening him, throwing things or leaving home – none of these were of use. He always wore that aggrieved yet innocent smile. 'Coco, no matter what you do to me, I won't blame you. I love you, Coco. Remember that, please remember that.'

At last, one day, I broke the promise he'd demanded of me and told Connie the truth about Tian Tian. I told her over the phone that I was terrified, that Tian Tian was flirting with disaster, and I might lose him at any moment.

Not long after I put the phone down, a pale-faced Connie walked into our apartment.

'Tian Tian,' she said, trying to smile warmly, but the way her wrinkles pushed up against one another made her look as if she was crying, which made her look older. 'Your mother is begging you. Your mother knows she's made a lot of mistakes. I should never have left you for such a long time. I've been a selfish mother . . . but, but now we're together again. We can start again. Give your mother and yourself a chance, won't you? Seeing you like this is worse than death itself . . .'

Tian Tian turned his head away from the TV screen and looked at his pale, anxious mother. 'Please don't cry,' he said kindly. 'Since you've been happy for the past ten years, you can go on being happy. I'm not a great problem for you, nor an obstacle to your happiness. I hope you'll always be beautiful, rich and trouble-free. Whatever you desire, you can achieve.'

Stupefied, Connie hid her face in her hands as if she did not understand Tian Tian's message. How could a son speak to his mother like that? She burst into tears again.

'Don't cry, it'll age you quicker. Anyway, I don't like to hear people cry. I feel fine about the way I am.' Tian Tian stood up and turned off the TV. He'd been watching a programme about a French couple who'd spent their lives researching volcanoes around the world, and been swallowed up by a sudden lava flow during a trip to Japan. A quote from these scientists was broadcast in the programme: 'We are in love with volcanoes. That red-hot torrent is like blood flowing from the heart of the earth. In the deepest interior of the earth life is quaking and exploding. If the day comes when we are buried in it, that too will also be an inexpressible joy.' And at the end of the programme, their words were realised, and they had both died within the boiling, blood-like lava.

Tian Tian spoke as if to himself. 'Can you guess how that French couple felt just before they died? I'm sure they were glad,' he said dreamily, answering himself. Even now, I don't believe Tian Tian's death can be compared with the deaths of those scientists. But at the same time, I understand that something like the same irresistible, indescribable force took him away. If the earth can angrily gush out its lethal blood in an instant, why can't we destroy ourselves, faced with so many lost souls, faced with our materialist age.

It cannot be avoided and it cannot be explained. When your lover leaves, you can cry out all the tears in your body, but he won't come back. He's gone for ever, taking with him your broken memories, reduced to ashes, and leaving behind a soul, alone.

# 30

# Auf Wiedersehen, My Berlin Lover

'They pass through your sorrow and leave you quite still . . .
sitting among souvenirs.'
Dan Fogelberg

The rest of the summer will always be with me. Mark did everything he could to stretch out the few days he had left in Shanghai, but they finally came to an end.

On his last evening, we went to the buffet in the revolving restaurant on the top floor of the Jinjiang Tower Hotel. Mark chose this place suspended above the city because he wanted to get a last panoramic view of the lights, streets, skyscrapers and movement of the crowds in night-time Shanghai, and to breathe once more its debauched, mysterious and fragile atmosphere. Then he would board his 9:35 a.m. flight for Berlin and home.

We didn't have any appetites and we both felt flat.

Mark had a dark tan, like an African mulatto – he'd just been on a trip to Tibet, where he'd been very ill with a fever and just about died. He said he'd brought back presents for me but didn't have them with him.

'I'll come to your place for them,' I said, because we both knew that after dinner we'd make love one last time.

'I haven't seen you for two weeks,' he said tenderly, 'and you've got so much thinner.'

'Have I?' I touched my face. 'Am I really so thin?'

I turned to look out of the picture window. We'd done a complete revolution from our original position facing The Garden Hotel, and now the hotel's flat, slightly curved shape, like a UFO, towered before us again.

'Tian Tian's begun taking drugs again. He seems determined that I'll lose him one day,' I said softly. I gazed into Mark's Danube-blue eyes. 'Is it because I did something wrong and God is punishing me?'

'No, you didn't do anything wrong,' he said definitely.

'Perhaps I should never have met you, and I certainly should never have gone to bed with you,' I said, smiling a bit. 'Even coming out with you this evening meant telling a lie. He probably guesses who I'm with, but I can never come right out with it. Piercing that last paper-thin layer wouldn't just be hard, it'd be shaming,' I said, falling silent.

'We're so close. We're utterly obsessed with each other.'

'Okay, let's not talk about that. Drink up!' Both of us drained our wineglasses. Alcohol is wonderful, it warms your stomach and banishes the cold from your blood. A truly faithful companion.

Every diner was surrounded by fresh flowers, lovely women, silver cutlery and fine food. The band struck up the *Titanic* theme song – the music before the ship sank – but the ship we were in, revolving in mid-air, was not going to sink, because the nocturnal happiness of Shanghai will never sink.

We sat in his car speeding through the night, past parasol trees, elegant and enchanting cafés and restaurants, and gorgeous buildings whose beauty takes your breath away. We kissed along the way. He was driving recklessly. Balanced on the brink of desire as we were, kissing was like dancing on a knife's edge.

At the junction of Wu Yuan and Yong Fu Roads, we were stopped by a police car.

'This is a one-way street. You can't go that way. Do you understand?' said a policeman gruffly. Then he smelled the alcohol on us. 'And you're driving under the influence.' We pretended not to speak any Chinese, until a torch was shone on us, and someone said: 'Coco, is that you?'

I put my head out the window and tried to focus for ages before I finally recognised Ma Jian-Jun, Madonna's former boyfriend. I blew him a kiss and said, 'Hello,' still in English. Then I saw Mark and the other policeman whispering something on the other side of the car. I heard something like, 'Forget it. These two just came back from abroad. They don't know the rules here, and the girl's a friend of a friend. . . .'

The other policeman whispered something I couldn't hear, and in the end Mark paid 100 RMB. 'That's the best I can do for you,' said Ma Jian-Jun in my ear. 'And 100 RMB is half price.'

When we took to the road again we had a laugh. But then I said: 'There's no fun in this. Let's go back to your place.'

I forget how many times we made love that night, but in the end, even using lubricant I still hurt so much it was hard to bear. He was like a pitiless beast, like a soldier breaking through enemy lines, like an enforcer giving a beating, but we continued to inflict and receive pain all the same.

Yes, women like to have the fascist with the boot in the face in their beds. Separated from its brain, the flesh has a memory of its own. It uses a high-precision, physiological system to retain each encounter with the opposite sex. Even when months and years have flown by and everything has become part of the past, the uncanny radiance of sexual memories remains. While dreaming, lost in thought, walking on the street, reading a book, conversing with a stranger, making love with another man – at any of these times the memory suddenly jumps out. I can count all the men I've had in my life . . .

I told Mark about this when we said goodbye. Mark hugged me tightly, and his wet eyelashes brushed against my cheeks. I didn't want to see wetness on the eyes of the man I was never going to see again.

I lifted the huge bag crammed with records, clothes, books and things Mark had given me. The bin bag of the love which drove me mad.

I waved goodbye. When the taxi door closed he came running over impulsively. 'You really don't want to see me off at the airport?'

'No.' I shook my head.

He clutched his hair. 'What shall I do for the next three hours? I'm afraid I'll end up driving over to see you.'

'No, you won't.' I smiled at him, although my body felt like petals trembling in the wind. 'You could ring Eva, or someone else, or try to visualise your family's faces. They'll be in front of you in a dozen or so hours. They'll meet you at the airport.'

Agitated, Mark kept touching his hair. Then he leant forward to kiss me. 'Okay, okay, you cold-blooded woman.'

'Forget me,' I said softly. I closed the window and told the driver to get going. These moments are best kept to a minimum in anyone's life. They're just too hard to bear, especially for a couple with no future. He had a wife and child, and would be far away in Berlin, and I couldn't go to Berlin. Berlin was just an impression, taken from films and novels. An industrial, senti-mental city with a bluish-grey backdrop. It was too remote, too alien.

I didn't turn to look at Mark towering by the roadside, but I didn't return to Tian Tian's apartment either. The cab took me to my parents'.

The lift wasn't working again, so I lugged that huge bag of

assorted items all the way from the ground floor to the twentieth. My footsteps were weighed down by lead; man's first steps on the moon couldn't have been more difficult than mine. I felt like I might collapse at any point, fainting midway through my journey, but I didn't want to rest. I just wanted to get home.

I banged at the door, and when it opened, my mother couldn't believe her eyes. I threw down my bag and hugged her. 'Mother, I'm so hungry,' I said, crying.

'What's wrong with you? What's wrong?' She ran to Daddy's bedroom. 'Coco's here, hurry up and give us a hand.'

My parents led me to my bed to rest, their eyes filled with surprise. They couldn't know what their daughter had been up to. They would never really understand the impulsive, noisy world and its futility from their daughter's point of view. They didn't know their daughter's boyfriend took drugs, that their daughter's lover would soon be on a plane home to Germany, or that the novel she was writing was chaotic, revealing, and full of metaphysical thoughts and raw sex.

They would never know the terror deep in their daughter's heart, and the desire that death can't overcome. Her life would always be a revolver of desire, capable of going off and killing at any moment.

'I'm sorry. I just want to eat some congee. I'm hungry,' I murmured repeatedly, trying to smile. Then they disappeared, and I threw myself head first into the dark.

# 31

# The Colour of Death

'Whether he is alive or dead, conscious or unconscious, has
become irrelevant to me because he has already disappeared.
It was then, in that instant when the sound of music was
hurled out over the seas, that she discovered him, and found
him at last.'

Marguerite Duras

**M**y novel is coming to an end now. After going through
one pen after another, at last I've found that feeling of
release – like when you shoot from a mountaintop
down the ski slopes towards the bottom. Release, and a strange
sense of sadness.

I don't believe I can predict the fate of this book. It's part of my
fate too, and I haven't the means to control it. Nor can I take any
further responsibility for the characters and story created by my
imagination. Now they've been put down on paper, it's time for
them to live and die on their own.

Tired and weak, I don't want to look at myself in the mirror.

It's been two months and eight days since Tian Tian's death, but
for a long time now I've had an eerie sense of being able to
communicate with his spirit.

When I'm in the kitchen making coffee the sound of rushing
water suddenly fills my ears, and for an instant I think it's Tian
Tian in the bath. I rush there, but the bath is empty.

When I'm at the desk turning a page of my manuscript, I suddenly sense someone on the sofa behind me. He is watching me silently and tenderly, but I'm afraid to look back and frighten him away. I know Tian Tian still keeps me company in this room. He will wait stubbornly until I finish this novel which he was once so enthusistic about.

The night is the hardest, when someone whispers in my ear. I toss and turn and hug his pillow, and pray for the spirits to send him into my endless dreams. A grey mist slips in through the window and presses gently yet heavily on my skull. I hear a distant voice calling my name. Dressed in white, he comes towards me with his beautiful face and his eternal love, and we soar upwards on transparent wings. Grass, buildings and roads speed past beneath us. Rays of light make gashes in the jade sky.

Dawn approaches, as if to warn that the spell is waning. Night is banished from every corner of the earth. I wake from my dream, and my lover is nowhere to be seen. Only tenderness in my heart and traces of moisture in the corners of my eyes remain. Since the death of Tian Tian at my side that early morning, every dawn has been like a cruel and overwhelming avalanche.

The day Mark left Shanghai, I stayed hiding at my parents'. The next day I left for the apartment on the western outskirts of the city. I didn't take Mark's gifts, except for a platinum wedding ring inset with a blue sapphire, which I wore. I'd taken it from Mark's little finger when he was asleep.

He was so distraught when he left he wouldn't notice on the flight that I'd stolen it. And it was no big deal. Perhaps I was playing a final trick on him, or perhaps I wanted a souvenir.

The ring was lovely but a bit large, so I put it on my thumb. Before I reached the apartment I took it off and put it in my pocket.

Tian Tian was watching TV. The table was heaped with popcorn, chocolate and Coke. He flung his arms wide when he saw me. 'I thought you'd run off and I'd never see you again,' he said, hugging me.

'My mother made some wonton. Would you like me to cook you some?' I shook the bag of food in my hand.

'I want to go out for a ride, and lie on the grass for a while.' He leant his head against my chest. 'With you.'

We took our sunglasses and a bottle of water with us, and a taxi transported us to Fudan U. where I had studied. The lawn there was luxurious, and the atmosphere more relaxed than in a public park. I've always remembered the campus atmosphere fondly – a place with a sense of freedom, but elegant and refreshing too.

Under the deep shade of a camphor tree, Tian Tian wanted to recite a poem, but couldn't recall any. 'Wait till your stories are published. We can recite them aloud here, louder and louder! University students like that kind of thing, right?' he said.

We lay there for a long time, and even had dinner in the student cafeteria. There's a bar on Zhengtong Road near the overseas student dormitory called the Hard Rock Pub, where a rock band called The Maniacs often appears; Zeng Tao, the guitarist, is the owner of the bar. Thinking of having a beer, we went in.

The faces at the bar were familiar. Our friends were growing old. The lead singer for The Maniacs, Zhou Yong, hadn't made an appearance for a long time now. Last summer, Tian Tian and I had been to a concert they gave at the A-Gogo at the East China University. Their post-punk music blew our minds, and we'd danced till we dropped.

Spider came in with a few people who looked like overseas students. We embraced, greeted one another with *ni hao, ni hao*, and agreed this was indeed a coincidence. Recently Spider had been hanging around with foreign students because the computer business was growing more difficult, and he'd lost interest in it, deciding instead to go somewhere abroad to study.

*271*

He already spoke decent English, and passable French and Spanish.

The music was 'Dummy' by Portishead. People were dancing, but the faces at the bar were blank, as usual. People who hang out in bars day and night are all like that, cool and expressionless. I listened to the music as Tian Tian slipped into the toilet and, after a long while, wobbled out.

I knew what he was doing, but I could never deal with it head on, deal with his dulled, vacuous expression, as if his soul had flown far far away. Afterwards I got drunk. His drug high required a matching alcoholic high on my part, and with each of us inside our own high we resisted our egos, ignored our pain and jumped about like rays of light.

Having danced inside the music and soared inside our own euphoria, at one in the morning we returned to our apartment. We didn't wash, just threw off our clothes and lay down on the bed. The air con was on full blast, and even in my dreams I could hear its buzz, like an insect's cry. My dreams were empty except for that one troubling sound.

Early the next morning, as soon as the first ray of sunlight showed, I opened my eyes and turned to kiss Tian Tian. My hot, hot kiss was imprinted on his cold, cold body, which was glowing white. I shook him hard, called him, kissed him and pulled his hair. Then, I jumped out of bed naked and ran on to the balcony. Through the glass I stared at the bed inside the room, at my lover's body lying there. I stared for a long, long time.

Tears flooded my face and I bit my fingertips. I cried out: 'You fool!' He didn't react. He was dead, and so was I.

Friends and relatives came to the funeral, but Tian Tian's grandmother was nowhere to be seen. Everyone was ill at ease, making me nervous. I couldn't tell how much worse things would get. How his flesh would be rendered into unconscious, unfeeling ashes; how his spirit would escape from that macabre pile of death under the ground and fly up through the sky to the heavens. In the highest reaches of the sky there must be a layer of absolute clarity made by God, a different world.

Connie hosted the funeral. Dressed all in black with a fine black veil over her head, she was like something out of a film. She was dignified and proper, but aloof. Her grief just didn't seem to come from deep inside. She had none of the bewildered irrationality of a mother who had lost her son, only the dignity of a middle-aged, attractive woman dressed in black. For a woman, being genuine is essential. Dignity and proper behaviour aren't enough. And so I suddenly wanted to avoid looking at her face, and felt repelled by the tone in which she read her eulogy.

I rushed through a poem dedicated to Tian Tian: 'The last instant/I saw your face/On top of the blackness/On top of the pain/On top of the steam you breathed out on to the glass/In the heart of the night . . . dreaming of the sorrow in a dream/My mouth is sealed/I can no longer say goodbye.'

Then I hid in the crowd. I was at a complete loss. So many people, so many people I didn't know were there, but this wasn't a holiday. It was a nightmare drilling a hole in my heart.

I only wanted to hide, but Tian Tian wasn't there any more and the four walls of the flat had lost their purpose.

# 32

# Who Am I?

'I think, therefore I am.'
Descartes

'I'm just me, a woman, not some "second sex".'
Lacy Stone

'Everything, everything began like this. It all began on this
glamorous and dazzling, yet fatigued and frail visage. That
was the experiment.'

Marguerite Duras

This is how things happen. It makes your head ache, it
makes you scream, and it makes you mad.

I'm not a cold-blooded woman, but I didn't go mad.
*Shriek of the Butterfly* reprinted, and I promoted it at various
universities as arranged by Deng and Godfather, where I
answered questions like, 'Ms Nikki, would you ever "strip"?'
from male students, while female students and I discussed topics
such as 'Whether or not women are the *second sex*' and 'What do
feminists want, after all?'

When I went to Fudan U., I lay on the lawn for a moment,
watching the sky and thinking of him.

Zhu Sha got married for the second time, to the artist eight
years her junior, Ah Dick. The wedding took place three months
and twenty days after Tian Tian's funeral, a fact I was probably
the only one to notice.

The ceremony was at the Lawrence Art Gallery in Fuxing Park, on the same day the groom's exhibition opened. There were a lot of guests, foreign and Chinese, including Madonna. Madonna gave the newly-weds a generous gift – a pair of gold Omega watches – to show her magnanimity. After all, Ah Dick was one of the men she liked most.

I didn't say much to her. I suddenly wasn't so fond of her. Maybe she hadn't said anything to Tian Tian; maybe she didn't deliberately try to control her friends. But I didn't want to be too close to her any more.

There were too many people and the stuffy atmosphere was uncomfortable. I left early.

From Germany came a stream of e-mails from Mark and Shamir. I told them the news of Tian Tian's death, and said I was calmer now because my novel was almost finished and this was the best gift I could give Tian Tian.

Shamir invited me to visit Germany when my novel was finished. 'It will help you get over it. Come and see our sharp-spired churches, the Black Forest and the crowds. And I'm sure Mark longs to see you too.'

Mark's e-mails were long, very long. He told me in detail what he'd been doing lately, where he'd been and how he and his wife had been arguing. I don't know what kind of trust led him to confide in me. Perhaps a woman who writes novels is trustworthy because of her understanding, even if she did steal his blue sapphire wedding ring. I always wear it on my thumb because it's so attractive.

I decided to go to Berlin after Halloween. I like Halloween, with its romantic fantasy, the way it uses the artifice of putting on a mask and pretending to be someone else to chase away the rotten smell of death.

Just before I left, I sorted a few things out. I touched up the manuscript and cleaned up the apartment. I planned to move back in with my parents, so I needed to give Connie the key. Tian Tian's things were still there. I chose one of his self-portraits, a collection of Dylan Thomas poems he'd liked, and a white shirt he used to wear.

The shirt still had his smell. Burying my face in it, it made me realise what it is to lose happiness.

It was a weekend, and I walked for a long time, past the parasol trees on Hengshan Road, and into an alley of memories. There was Connie's Spanish restaurant: brightly lit, with the shadows of flowers dancing about, and in the windows brightly dressed people moving around. As I walked closer, I could hear lovesongs, and polite applause when the singing stopped.

I walked up the steps and asked an employee where Connie was. He led me through a series of doors to where Connie, heavily made-up, stood in the middle of a large group. She was wearing a strapless evening dress, had her hair placed high in a bun. Her lipstick was rich and thick. She looked attractive and smart, like an elegant crane.

A Spanish couple wearing black dancing outfits decorated with pearls were doing a Latin dance to the song. They were young and beautiful. The girl's legs were gracefully held by the hands of the boy, and then they began an eye-dazzling series of twirls. Connie ended her conversation with a white-haired gentleman and saw me as soon as she turned her head. She curtsied to her companions and walked over to me.

'How are you, my dear?' she enquired, hugging me.

I smiled and nodded. 'You look lovely, as always,' I said, and then took out a string of keys from my handbag and handed them to her. I had already told her my plans over the phone.

She looked at the keys, not speaking for a moment, and then

took them. 'Even now I don't understand . . . how things got like this. What did I do wrong? Is this how God treats me . . .

'Okay. Let's forget it. You're a smart girl. Take care of yourself.' We kissed and said our goodbyes, and Juan came over and hugged me.

'Goodbye.' I waved and left. The music and the dancing went on, but they had nothing to do with me.

In the lower courtyard, at the door, I bumped into an old lady. With her head of white hair, glasses and fine white skin, she looked like a professor's wife. I said 'excuse me' several times, but she paid no attention, heading straight for the restaurant.

The doorkeeper rushed to close the iron gate. The old lady tried to push it open, but when that did not work, she began to curse loudly.

'You devil, you evil spirit, ten years ago you murdered my son, but that wasn't enough. Now you've murdered my grandson too. Your heart is black. I curse you: may you be struck dead by a car the moment you leave your hellish restaurant . . .'

Her voice was very hoarse. I stood frozen at her side. I already knew who this uncontrollably angry old woman was, but it was the first time I'd seen her in the flesh.

She hadn't showed up at Tian Tian's funeral, but that must have been because Connie wouldn't let her. Connie had always been afraid of her and avoided her, but Tian Tian's grandmother knew how to find her way to the restaurant.

The doorkeeper tried to calm her in hushed tones. 'Madame, you must have come dozens of times already. It's too hard on you at your age. You'd best go home and rest.'

'Hmmph,' said the old lady with fire in her eyes. 'No one can shut me up! She thinks that everything's all right since she tried to fob me off with a hundred-RMB pension. But I insist on knowing the truth. I want an explanation.'

She began to push the door again, and I hurried towards her and took her by the arm.

'Grandmother,' I called softly. 'I'll take you home. It's about to rain.'

She looked at me suspiciously, and looked at the sky above us covered by a thick blanket of clouds, dark red from the city lights.

'Who are you?' she asked in a low voice.

My heart fluttered. A feeling of tenderness and bitterness engulfed me, and for a moment I didn't know how to answer this tired and helpless old woman.

Who am I, indeed? Who am I?